parchment fall to his ... ds that his father, Jeh... d had the wisdom and ... ears of experience, and ... at wisdom now, to help him. . . . And something in Keridil's soul turned black as he remembered that it was Yandros, Lord of Chaos, who had taken the old man's life. . . .

"Keridil?" He had all but forgotten Sashka's presence in the room, and looked up with a start, as though a ghost had spoken.

"Keridil, what is it? What does she say?"

Jehrek was no longer here to help him ... but Sashka would. And however wrong it might be to confide in anyone outside the Circle, however strongly the Council of Adepts might disapprove, Keridil needed to share this burden with her.

He took hold of her hand and said, quietly, "Sister Ilyaya Kimi has formally asked me to call the Conclave of Three."

Sashka stared at him, stunned. She understood, he knew; but now that the first words were out he had to speak the rest. "She asks me to inform the High Margrave, and to begin the preparations." He paused, then: "Our only hope of defeating Chaos is to sail to the shrine on the White Isle, and open the casket of Aeoris."

THE MASTER

Look for all these TOR Books by Louise Cooper

THE INITIATE
THE OUTCAST
THE MASTER

LOUISE·COOPER
THE MASTER

BOOK III
• IN THE •
TIME MASTER TRILOGY

A TOM DOHERTY ASSOCIATES BOOK

THE MASTER

Copyright © 1987 by Louise Cooper

First printing: May 1987

A TOR BOOK

Published by Tom Doherty Associates, Inc.
49 West 24 Street
New York, N.Y. 10010

Cover art by Robert Gould

ISBN: 0-812-53396-8

PRINTED IN THE UNITED STATES OF AMERICA

0 9 8 7 6 5 4 3 2 1

THE MASTER

UNCHARTED SEA

STAR PENINSULA

FANAAN BAY

NORTHERN MOUNTAINS

WEST HIGH LAND PROVINCE

EMPTY PROVINCE

Sisterhood Cot (Lady Kael Amion)

HANNIK (Margravate)

WESTERN SOUND

MARGRAVATE

FOREST

HAN PROVINCE

CHAUN PROVINCE

MARGRAVATE

PLAINS (ARABLE)

FOREST

SOUTHERN CHAUN

Matriarch's Cot

MARGRAVATE

PROSPECT PROVINCE

PROSPECT ESTUARY

MARGRAVATE

FOREST

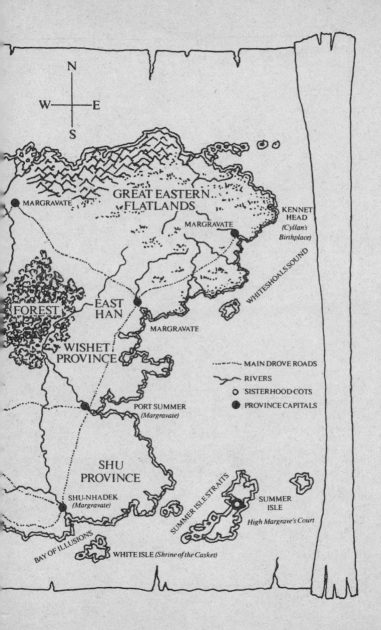

Chapter 1

At this early season, the dense forests that covered most of the western half of Chaun Province provided scant shelter for any traveller. In places the spring buds had burst in isolated explosions of green, and on the forest floor bracken and brambles were tentatively showing new shoots; but, apart from the occasional glowering bulk of a giant pine, most of the woodland trees were as yet leafless.

In a clearing not far from the forest's northerly edge, a tall iron-grey gelding foraged disconsolately in the undergrowth, the broken reins of its bridle trailing behind it and catching on the briars. Its saddle had slipped halfway round its girth, and one loose stirrup banged occasionally on a hind leg, making the animal flatten its ears and snap at the unseen irritant while sweat broke out on its withers. Though otherwise it seemed calm enough, there were telltale flecks of foam around its mouth and ringing the saddle like scum; and every now and again the gelding would pause in its browsing for no apparent reason and jerk its head up suspiciously, alert for some imagined threat.

In the three hours since its extraordinary and terri-

9

fied arrival in the clearing, the horse had ignored the still, slender figure lying sprawled across the protruding roots of a giant oak. Strict training had conditioned it not to leave its rider—whomever that rider might be—and seek freedom; but until the rider showed signs of consciousness, the animal had no interest in her. With the terrors of the last few hours all but forgotten, it was content to stay in the relative safety of the wood and continue grazing until it should be called upon to move.

The girl, clinging frantically to the gelding's saddle as they exploded out of the howling insanity that had snatched them in its grip and hurled them here, had been thrown from the animal's back as it crashed down, screaming, among the undergrowth. She had slammed against the oak's gigantic bole and fallen like a shot bird to lie unmoving among the roots. Her face, half hidden under a tangle of near white hair and the tattered hood of a cloak, was drained and sickly, her lips bloodless; and a bright scarlet stain had spread from her skull across her forehead, mingling with other, older bloodstains that weren't her own. But she breathed . . . and at last, slowly, she began to stir.

As she returned to consciousness Cyllan had no immediate memories of the events that had brought her to the forest. At first, dimly aware that she lay on hard, cold, and damp ground, she thought herself asleep in the hide tent that she'd called home during her four years as an apprentice drover. But there was no claustrophobic sense of enclosure, no stink and bawl of milling cattle, no ill-tempered yelling from her uncle, Kand Brialen.

Her droving days were over. A dream—nothing but a bad dream. Surely, she was still in the Castle . . . ?

It was that thought which brought clarity back to her mind like a hard slap in the face, and involuntarily she jerked upright, her peculiar amber eyes opening and a cry, a name, breaking from her throat before she could stop it.

"*Tarod!*"

The gelding lifted its head and regarded her curiously. Cyllan stared back, bewildered, knowing only that she had never seen this place before. Hammers were beating in her skull; with a gasp of pain she slumped back against the tree trunk, and every muscle protested at the movement, making her feel as though her body were on fire. Her mind struggled frantically to assimilate the impossible evidence of her senses. Where was the Castle? What had happened to Tarod? They'd found her in the stable when she was trying to reach him, dragged her out into the black-walled courtyard where the High Initiate waited; and then, as the Warp had come shrieking overhead, Tarod had appeared—

The Warp. Suddenly Cyllan remembered, and with the memory came a sickness that clutched at her empty stomach and made her retch, violently and uselessly, doubled up against the tree's unyielding bark. She recalled the confrontation in the courtyard, her own escape—she had kicked the High Initiate full in the stomach, bitten the burly man who held her—and her precipitous flight when, trapped and beyond Tarod's reach, she had taken the only chance she had and leaped onto the gelding's back. She'd had some wild idea of riding down anyone who stood in her path, forcing a way through to Tarod; but the horse had panicked, bolted—and careered out through the Castle gates, straight into the path of the monstrous supernatural storm that raged in unleashed chaos outside.

Cyllan shuddered as images of the horrors she had glimpsed in the split second before the storm engulfed her slid past her defenses. The mountains, twisted to impossible shapes and dimensions; the sea seeming to rear in a titanic wall of water, towering thousands of feet to the ravening sky; wild, monstrous faces manifesting from cloud and lightning, serpent tongues darting and voices bellowing with insensate agony—then the black wall had thundered in to meet her and she knew only darkness and madness until she had burst in a howling cacophony of noise and brilliance and buffeting pain onto a scene that almost smashed her sanity with its sheer normality. Then she was hurtling through the air—she heard the gelding shriek as it fell—and the tree, solid, real, uncompromising, obliterated her consciousness.

At last the spasms in her stomach faded, and she pulled herself to a less cramped position. She was alive—and whatever her predicament, that in itself was cause for sobering gratitude. Everyone in the land was brought up from childhood with a paralyzing terror of the Warps; there wasn't a soul alive who hadn't heard the high, thin wailing out of the far north, and seen the bands of sickly color marching across the sky, which presaged the onset of one of the appalling supernatural storms. The Warps were a legacy of Chaos, a last remaining manifestation of the pandemonium that had once ruled unchecked in the world before the rise of Order; when they came, terrifying and unpredictable, every man, woman, and child took shelter. Those who failed to find it had fervent prayers said for their souls by the Sisters of Aeoris, and they left behind friends and relatives who knew that no trace of them would ever be found. Legend had it that the wailing scream that accompanied a Warp as it rode across the land was the massed lamentation of all those lost and damned, borne on the winds of Chaos.

But twice now Cyllan had survived the indescribable horror of the storms; twice she'd found herself carried across the face of the world by the maelstrom and left battered and bruised, but alive, in some distant and unknown place. If the legends were credible—and there was enough gruesome evidence to prove their veracity—then she should be dead, and damned to whatever hell awaited the Warps' victims. Yet she lived . . . and the knowledge of *why* she lived made her shiver as she recalled the calculating and coldly invincible being who had pragmatically chosen to offer her his protection. Yandros, Lord of Chaos, who claimed kinship with Tarod and whose machinations had sparked off the whole ugly chain of events at the Castle of the Star Peninsula, had answered her desperate prayers for help when there was no other hope left to her. She remembered the unhuman smile on his beautiful face when, as she cowered before him, he had revealed his part in preserving her life and bringing her to the Castle when the Warp struck in Shu-Nhadek. As the grey gelding plunged through the Castle gates and into the storm she had screamed his name in a frantic, involuntary cry for aid, and it seemed that again he had answered her. Cyllan had no illusions about Yandros's loyalty or patronage; he protected her because she was useful to him, but should she fail in the task he had set her she could expect no mercy from him. And she knew—as he knew—that, now she had turned her face once from her fealty to the ruling Lords of Order, she would find no forgiveness if she ever came to repent what she'd done. In casting her lot with Chaos, she had irrevocably damned herself in the eyes of her own gods.

Cyllan shivered again and reached to the neck of her grey dress, fumbling at the bodice until she drew out something that lodged between her breasts. She hadn't lost it in the wild flight from the Castle—and she felt an odd mixture of relief and disgust as she looked at the small clear, multifaceted jewel lying in the palm of her hand and winking a cold reflection of the drab daylight. The Chaos stone. A source of power and terror . . . and the vessel that contained the soul of the man she loved.

Reflexively her hand closed over the stone, hiding it from view. Torn between hatred of the jewel's nature and the painful knowledge that without it he was incomplete, Tarod had warned her of its influence; an influence, he'd said, that corrupted and tainted anything it touched, or anyone who possessed it. Bitterly, she reflected how right he was. The stone had already aided her to kill once, firing her with a demonic bloodlust that made her revel in the act of murder. The stigmata of that deed still remained, in the dried, red-brown stains that smeared her hands and clothes, and she knew how easy it was to fall under that dark influence. Only Tarod could exert any control over the stone—and he needed it, for without it he was bereft of all but a fraction of his power. With the Circle, of which he'd once been a high Adept, pledged to destroy him, his life would be in danger until the jewel was in his possession once more.

If, indeed, he was still alive . . .

It wasn't in Cyllan's nature to cry. Her harsh life had taught her the futility of displaying any of the traditional feminine weaknesses, but abruptly she found herself on the verge of tears. *If* Tarod lived . . . The last thing she recalled before the gelding had bolted was seeing Tarod on the steps by the Castle's main door, unarmed and pressed by three or four sword-wielding Initiates bent on cutting him down before he could retaliate. The Warp had been howling overhead and she had seen no more of him—but surely, *surely* even his diminished power was enough to save him? He could have escaped from the Castle—and if he had, he would be looking for her. Though where he would begin, with the entire world to choose from, was beyond imagining.

Cyllan forced herself to look at the stone again,

grimacing as it shone like a malign, disembodied eye
through the lattice of her fingers. Then, carefully, she
tucked it back in the bodice of her dress, feeling it
settle cold and unyielding against her skin. However
ambiguous her feelings towards it, the stone was a
talisman, her one link with Tarod, and if such a
thing were possible it would call him to her. Yandros
might not be able to lend her direct aid, but the
Chaos Lord wanted the gem restored to Tarod, and if
that was her only hope of finding him then she would
do all she could to further Yandros's aim. She closed
her mind to any thoughts of what might happen
beyond that; all that mattered was that she and
Tarod should be reunited.

But a clearing in a forest in the Gods alone knew
what part of the world was hardly the most auspicious starting place for a search. In the short time
since she'd regained consciousness the light had per-
ceptibly faded, telling her that the weather was dete-
riorating. She had no food, water, or shelter, and no
idea how far she might be from the nearest village or
even drove-road. She couldn't judge the time of day;
it might be nearing dusk, and the forest wasn't a safe
place to spend the night—it was high time she put
aside her speculations and looked to the more practi-
cal and immediate problems of survival.

She struggled to her feet, and the gelding raised its
head suspiciously. Brushing debris from her crum-
pled clothes—her skirt was badly ripped at one side,
she noticed—Cyllan put two fingers in her mouth
and gave a peculiar, low whistle. The gelding laid its
ears back; she whistled again, and, reluctantly obey-
ing the summons, the animal approached close enough
for her to take hold of its bridle. As she retightened
the saddle and checked for broken straps, Cyllan was
thankful, perhaps for the first time in her life, for the
four years she'd spent travelling the roads on ponyback
as an apprentice in her uncle's drover band. The

whistle was a trick she'd learned early, and could command the most recalcitrant animal; the gelding would give her no trouble, and she was inured to long hours in the saddle. With Aeoris—she mentally corrected herself, smiling wryly to cover her unease— with *luck* on her side, she should make good enough speed to the nearest habitation.

The harness was secure, and balancing on a tree root to gain height, Cyllan swung herself into the saddle. Peering up through the latticed branches of the trees she tried to discern the lie of the lowering sun, but the tiny patchwork of sky above was overcast. She sat for a moment, considering, then swung the horse's head in what intuition told her was a roughly southerly direction. Most of the forest belts that crossed the western and central parts of the land ran east to west; therefore if she rode south she should reach the edge of the woodland before long, and from there be able to pick up a drove-road without too much difficulty.

She didn't know, and didn't care to speculate, what might await her on her journey. If Tarod had escaped, word would soon be out and the hunt under way for him; possibly for her too, though it was more likely that the Circle would believe her dead. Somehow she must find him before they did. . . .

She touched her heels to the gelding's flanks and urged it forward among the dense, waiting trees.

The singing that drifted faintly from the direction of the main hall in the Castle of the Star Peninsula would have been a delight to hear, had it taken place under less dismal circumstances. The massed women's voices were beautiful, their harmonies rising and falling on the light evening breeze; but Keridil Toln couldn't for a moment forget that the Sisters of Aeoris were singing a requiem for the son of the man who sat opposite him in his study.

Gant Ambaril Rannak, Margrave of Shu Province, listened to the choir with head bowed, one hand unmoving on the stem of his wine cup. Occasionally he looked up at the open window, as though expecting to see something or someone, and Keridil glimpsed the momentary glitter of suppressed rage in his eyes.

At last Gant spoke, quietly, calmly. "The Sisters' singing is very moving. I appreciate the gesture, High Initiate, on their part and yours." He blinked; frowned painfully. "I only regret that their anthems can't bring Drachea back from the dead."

Keridil sighed. He had dreaded having to break the news that the Margrave's son and heir had been murdered while under his protection. Gant had arrived with his wife and entourage only that day, rejoicing to hear that Drachea had single-handedly thwarted the machinations of Chaos and performed a great service for the Circle. His son was a hero— but instead of sharing in his glory, the old man had been greeted instead with the shock of his bloody and ignominious death. Keridil had anticipated ranting, lamentation, accusation; but the Margrave's quiet, bitter grief had proved far harder to withstand. The Lady Margravine had collapsed and now lay in the Castle's best guest suite, tended by Grevard, the physician; but Gant had refused all offers of sedatives or calmatives, and instead, after seeing his son's corpse, had requested a private interview with the High Initiate.

Keridil had now told the full story of Drachea's death; of how he had disturbed Cyllan, after her escape, in the act of stealing the Chaos stone, and of how she had slain him. He had wanted to confess to his own sense of responsibility for the young man's murder, yet apologies seemed grotesquely inadequate; all he could do was wait for Gant to say whatever he wished to say. Knowing the Margrave, Keridil had little doubt that he'd speak his mind.

The singing faded on a final, poignant harmony, and the Margrave nodded his head as though in approval. Then he looked at Keridil again, and this time his eyes were iron hard.

"Well, High Initiate. Only one question remains in my mind. What is to be done to avenge my son's murder?"

Keridil glanced at the notes that he'd made earlier in the day. Though it would bring Gant small comfort, he could at least report that he hadn't been idle.

"I've already set matters in train, Margrave," he said. "You may have heard of the recent experiments carried out in Wishet and Empty Provinces, with message-carrying birds—"

"I've heard of it, High Initiate. In fact, I suggested that the idea might be employed in the search for my son when he first disappeared."

Keridil flushed at the older man's tone. "Indeed . . . well, the early experiments were successful enough for us to put the idea into practice here at the Castle. We have a master falconer visiting us from Empty Province, and his birds have proved reliable and far faster than any relay of horsemen."

Gant's eyes lit feverishly. "Then you can send out—"

"I already have, sir. Three birds were despatched at noon today, to carry word of what's happened here to West High Land, Han, and Chaun. As soon as they land, more birds will leave for the other provinces. The news should reach the farthest outposts tomorrow, and even the High Margrave himself will hear of it within the day."

Gant's eyes narrowed. "And the girl—that murdering little serpent . . . you've conveyed her description to every Margravate? To every militia leader?" His fist clenched involuntarily on the table. "She must be found, High Initiate, and she must be *executed!*"

The Margrave's single-mindedness was understandable in the circumstances, but Keridil had more than

Cyllan's whereabouts on his mind. Of the two people he sought she was by far the less dangerous, and though he was determined to bring her to justice he had more urgent priorities. Nonetheless, he was well aware that Gant must be handled with care; any hint that his son's murder took second place to other considerations would mean more trouble than Keridil could cope with at present.

He said, "Indeed we've circulated her description, Margrave; and I'm confident that she won't be able to escape the search for long—if she's still alive, which we can only surmise. The militia are to be put on full alert, and I've asked for the utmost cooperation from every province. However, I must add that we're dealing with something that could have even greater ramifications than Drachea's murder." He glanced up, saw the older man's expression and continued with caution. "You know now what's happened here at the Castle recently, how it came about, and who perpetrated it. That perpetrator is still at large—and he's a thousand times more dangerous than Cyllan Anassan. Please—" he added quickly as Gant seemed about to protest, "I share your anxiety to find the girl and punish her. But I dare not neglect the search for Tarod. He's far more than just a killer; he's an incarnation of *Chaos*." He leaned forward, intent. "Margrave, you've seen and heard for yourself a little of the havoc he's capable of wreaking. Can you imagine what the fate of all of us would be if such a monstrous power of evil were let loose on the world?"

Gant was silent, and Keridil knew his words had found their mark. "I don't want to cause undue alarm in the land, especially not at this stage," he added quietly. "But I'd be failing in my duty if I didn't spread the warning, and spread it fast. To be brutally honest, our world could be facing a danger the like of which has been unknown since the fall of the

Old Ones. And I'm not ashamed to admit to being afraid."

Had he made a mistake in being so frank? The Margrave's face had taken on a pinched, tight look, and his gaze flickered uneasily to the window and back.

"High Initiate, I find it hard to believe"—he coughed to clear his throat as his voice cracked involuntarily—"to believe that the Circle, in which resides the power and the sanction of Aeoris Himself!—" He made the White God's sign over his own heart but seemed unable to finish the sentence.

Keridil sighed. "I fervently wish that half the tales that are told about the Circle's abilities were true, Margrave, but the bald fact is that, whilst we might have Aeoris's sanction, it would be folly to assume that we have His power, or anything resembling it." His expression hardened. "That's a lesson I've recently learned through bitter experience, and to pretend otherwise would be to court disaster." He clasped his hands together, the knuckles whitening. "Without the jewel I told you of, Tarod's by no means invincible. But if he should find that girl before we do, and recover the stone, he'll regain his full power. And that means the power to summon back the full forces of Chaos and darkness to the world."

"But surely no man can command such sorcery!"

"No *man*, no—but this isn't a man we're contending with. Tarod is kin to Chaos; *born* of Chaos. Don't doubt his capabilities, Margrave. I once made that mistake."

Gant shifted uncomfortably on his chair, chagrined. "This is far more serious than I realized. . . . I understand your concern, Keridil, and I share it." He made a bleak attempt at a smile. "Inasmuch as you have your duty, I also have mine, and I accept that personal considerations must take second place. How can Shu Province aid you?"

Keridil gave silent thanks for the hard edge of innate common sense which characterized the older man, shored up by twenty years of rigid governorship. As well as encompassing the largest and safest seaport in the land, Shu Province also boasted a strong and efficient militia, and the Margravate's resources were among the best to be found anywhere. Gant would make an invaluable ally.

He nodded. "I'm grateful for your support, sir, and your generosity—and I don't mind admitting I'll need all the help I can find, especially in terms of manpower."

"Indeed. But you must realize, of course, that once word of this spreads, although you'll have that help from every quarter you'll also be running the risk of spreading panic throughout the land." He bit his lip. "Fear of Chaos is deeply rooted in all of us, and the thought that it might be summoned back . . ." His shrug, masking a shiver, was eloquent.

"I considered that, but I dare not minimize the peril we're in," Keridil said, recalling the hours of mental torment as he struggled to assess the wisdom of the decision he'd made. "People *must* be told, Margrave. I can't, in all conscience, keep back the truth."

Gant inclined his head. "Yes . . . I see your dilemma, and I think I must agree with you. However, to avoid hysteria it may be necessary to impose certain strictures over and above the laws of our land. In my own province, for example—"

Keridil interrupted him. "I'll sanction anything you consider advisable that falls within my own jurisdiction, sir. And if the High Margrave's consent is needed, I'll do my utmost to secure it."

"Thank you. Speaking of the High Margrave . . . you said that one of your messenger-birds is bound for the Summer Isle?"

"It is, yes." The High Initiate hesitated, wondering

whether it would be advisable to confide fully in Gant; then he decided that there could be no harm in it. "I've also sent word to the Lady Matriarch Ilyaya Kimi, at her Cot." He hesitated. "You may as well know now, sir, that I've asked the views of both on the possibility of calling a Conclave on the White Isle."

Gant stared at him, stunned. "On the . . ." He swallowed. "Surely, Keridil, matters haven't come to that!"

"They haven't, no; but they could. And if they do, we might have no choice but to sanction the opening of the casket."

Gant made the Sign of Aeoris over his heart again. His face had turned the unhealthy color of putty, and he tried not to think about the implications of what the High Initiate had said. Every child was brought up on the legend of the gold casket that had been Aeoris's legacy to His world and His followers after the fall of the old race, when Chaos was defeated and banished. The casket was held in a shrine on the White Isle, a strange, volcanic island off the coast of Shu-Nhadek, and guarded by a hereditary caste of zealots who were the only men allowed to set foot on the Isle's sanctified ground. Only in a time of gravest crisis could the High Initiate, High Margrave, and Lady Matriarch of the Sisterhood of Aeoris sail to the Isle where, in Conclave, they might take the decision to open the sacred relic. And if the casket should be opened, it would summon Aeoris himself back to the world. . . . No, Gant told himself desperately; matters *couldn't* have reached such a pass. . . .

Keridil watched the changing expressions on the older man's face and could sympathize with his obvious distress. The thought of being forced to take a decision that had not been faced for thousands of years was enough to give him nightmares—but if it had to be done, he knew he'd do it.

"Margrave, I believe—and I hope—that the possibility is very remote," he said. "But it must nonetheless be borne in mind." He paused, then added: "At dawn today, I made an oath that I won't rest until Tarod has been found and destroyed, and I promise you now that I'm as determined to see Drachea's killer brought to justice. I mean to keep faith with both pledges, whatever the cost."

For a few moments Gant deliberated, then, slowly and with reluctance, he nodded. "Yes. I understand." He looked up, his eyes bleak. "And I like to think that, were I in your place, I'd have the courage to make the same decision."

Full darkness had fallen by the time Cyllan at last urged the grey gelding through a dense thicket and, to her surprise, found herself clear of the trees on a ridge that overlooked a narrow road. A treacherous but negotiable bank led down to the track, which gleamed the color of old, pale bone under the night sky, and beyond it the brooding mass of the forest stretched away again into utter blackness. This was no main driveway, only a small, neglected tributary that probably carried little or no traffic; but a road was a road, and a blessed relief after the nightmare of fighting her way through endless acres of branches and undergrowth, with the superstitious fear of woods at night all too close to the surface of her mind.

The gelding was uneasy, tired, and becoming rebellious, but Cyllan held it firmly still while she gazed around and tried to get her bearings. A single cold star hung far away to her right, but the familiar constellations were being rapidly obscured by a heavy bank of cloud driving in from what she guessed was the northwest and bringing a chill, dreary wind. The horse snorted and shook its head, smelling rain on the wind. A few moments later the first drops stung Cyllan's face.

Unless she'd judged wrongly the road ran roughly

north to south, and she turned in the saddle to gaze northward, where the pale ribbon vanished among the folds of low hills. Far away in that direction—though how far, she had no way of telling—lay the Star Peninsula, and the grim Castle where she'd had her last sight of Tarod.

Was he there still? She didn't know how much time had passed since the Warp snatched her away; if the Circle had recaptured him he might now be dead. . . . She bit her lip hard, fighting down a powerful urge to turn the gelding's head to the north and ride it to the limits of its endurance until she reached the coast and the Castle. That would be foolhardy—the Circle had marked her as a murderess, and to ride back into their embrace would be to court disaster. All she could do was pray that Tarod was alive, free, and seeking her.

She pressed her heels to the gelding's flanks and set it slithering down the steep bank towards the road. The rain was falling more heavily by now and the animal slipped several times on the wet grass; below, the track had taken on a slick sheen. Reaching the bottom of the slope, Cyllan turned the horse southward, urging it ahead, and as it settled into a steady, ground-covering trot she pulled her cloak more closely about herself in an effort to keep out the worst of the wet. To either side the forest hissed as rain lashed the undergrowth, and the night took on an unreal edge; black silhouettes of trees flanking and looming with only the cold white ribbon of the road ahead to provide a narrow, mesmeric focus. The muffled sound of her mount's hooves seemed to echo her own heartbeats, and she began to feel an uneasy prickling in her scalp, as though a sixth sense warned her that some unseen shadow followed in her wake. She shook the thought off, aware that it was triggered by tiredness and the tricky illusions of the dark. Nonetheless, there were real risks in plenty on

such a road as this, and she couldn't—*daren't*—stop
in this lonely stretch of nowhere, at least until morning broke.

The gelding checked suddenly, breaking the hypnotic rhythm of its hoofbeats and startling her back
to wakefulness. Even as she realized that she had
been on the verge of falling asleep in the saddle,
another sensation assailed her—a sharp stab of instinct that urged her to look back over her shoulder.
And this time it was no product of an overworked
imagination. Her lungs and throat felt stifled and,
aware that she was having to force herself not to
shiver uncontrollably, Cyllan cautiously turned her
head.

There were four of them; black, formless shapes in
the gloom behind her, shadowing her track and slowly
closing. For an instant a terrible image leaped into
Cyllan's mind—tales she had heard of ghouls and
demons, dead things that left their dismal graves to
pursue the unwary traveller—then, faintly on the
wind, she heard a restless metallic jingle as a horse
chafed at its bit, and realized that her followers were
made of flesh and blood.

Brigands. Irrational fear had clouded her mind to
the threat of attack from a physical and all too human quarter—but the mounted men now closing on
her were real enough. A woman riding a good horse
alone at night would be easy prey, and could anticipate nothing beyond a slit throat, if she were lucky. . . .

The gelding was dancing sideways, sensing something amiss. It was possible—just possible—that she
could outrun her pursuers; though the thought that
they probably rode fresh horses, while her own mount
was near-exhausted, chilled her to the bone. But she
couldn't stand and fight them—flight was her only
hope of survival.

She held the gelding back, trying to calm it and
give the brigands the impression that she was, as yet,

unaware of their presence behind her. But they were
moving closer. . . . Now she could hear a faint after-
echo of hoofbeats that weren't those of her own horse.
Carefully, she reached to her throat and with shaking, fumbling fingers unpinned the clasp that held
her cloak. As she did so she felt the Chaos stone dig
sharply against her breast, and the unwonted re-
minder of its presence brought her a flicker of comfort. If Yandros, highest Lord of Chaos, watched over
her, then surely he would aid her if he could. . . . She
gathered up the reins, settled herself more securely
in the wet saddle, pressed her thighs and knees as
hard as she could against the gelding's flanks, then
gripped the unfastened clasp so that the pin protruded from between her fingers—

The gelding sprang forward with a shriek of protest as the clasp-pin jabbed through its hide behind
the saddle cantle. Cyllan crouched over its neck, clinging desperately and precariously and praying that
she wouldn't lose her grip and fall. Behind her, new
sounds cut through the night: men cursing and the
sudden thunder of many more hooves as the brigands spurred their mounts into the chase. Cyllan
lashed the gelding's withers with the looped reins,
screaming at it to gallop faster. It laid its ears back,
eyes rolling, but she felt the powerful muscles beneath her bunch to greater effort. The road ahead
veered crazily, trees seeming to fly past them, and
she tried not to think of what might happen if some
night animal should suddenly skitter across their
path.

Sweat laced the gelding's neck and flanks; sensing
its rider's fear it was racing flat out, but nonetheless
Cyllan could hear the brigands closing on her. Her
mount was exhausted, the last of its stamina draining fast—its utmost efforts wouldn't be enough to
save her. Almost sobbing with terror, she lashed it

again and again, all the while knowing that she had only minutes, at most, before they'd be on her.

"Yandros!" The name broke from her throat in a cracking scream, a last cry of defiance. Ahead, the corpse-white ribbon of the track bent sharply, seeming to plunge back into the forest, and a wild hope surged suddenly in Cyllan. If she could reach the trees she might still elude them—however slight, it was a chance!

The gelding careered round the bend in the track, sliding dangerously—and then it was rearing and skidding on the treacherous ground as the brilliant glare of torches sprang out of the dark and rough voices shouted a warning.

Cyllan felt the animal's hooves sliding from under it; she pitched forward, clutched wildly at a handful of mane and somehow stayed in the saddle. When the gelding regained its feet, she saw a blade flash in the hot light, heard someone swearing. Hands took hold of her as the horse slithered to a halt and all but fell, and she was helped from its back to collapse to her knees on the sodden ground. Through her confusion she was aware of other horses shouldering past her, back onto the road down which she'd come; then at last she was lifted to her feet and found herself looking into the astonished gaze of a middle-aged man.

"Aeoris preserve us, it's a woman!" The words were punctuated by the crackling and spitting of the torch flames as the rain tried, vainly, to extinguish them. More faces loomed, grotesque in the flaring glow, and someone made a great fuss of opening and proffering a small metal flask. Cyllan accepted it gratefully, her throat too dry for speech, and took a good-sized mouthful of the warming, burning spirit.

"There, now." Concern laced the speaker's voice. "You're safe now, lady. Our men'll catch those murdering devils, and they'll hang by morning."

A Chaun Province accent.... Cyllan tried to ex-

press her thanks, but her lungs were straining for air
and still she couldn't speak. Someone took her arm
to steady her, and another asked anxiously, "Are you
harmed, madam? Can you tell us what happened to
you?" The deferential manner of his question made
Cyllan realize that the men had taken her for a woman
of some quality. Her clothes, together with the obvious good breeding of the horse she rode, had created
an impression that was very far from the truth, and
shock made her want to laugh. She took a grip on
herself, aware that she'd be well advised not to disil-
lusion them—to disclose her real identity could be
very dangerous. But it would be a hard deception to
maintain. She'd need to invent a plausible story, and
she felt in no condition for quick or clever thinking
now.

Dissembling, she made a pretense of being about
to faint—as most well-bred women would have done
in such straits—and instantly the men were solici-
tous and apologetic, helping her to the side of the
track and insisting that she sit down. She smiled
wanly at them and whispered, "Thank you . . . you're
very kind."

"It's nothing, lady—but what of your companions?
Surely you weren't riding alone?"

The idea was unthinkable to them, and Cyllan realized that they'd also have seen the bloodstains on
her clothes, and the fact that her horse wore a saddle
designed for a man. She swallowed. "No—I—there
were six of us. My—my brother and I, and—four
servants." And, anticipating the next question, she
added, "One of our packhorses cast a shoe, and we
were forced to make camp for the night in the forest.
We were attacked, and—one of my brother's men
died defending me." She bit her lip, hoping that the
grief and fear she had tried to inject in her voice was
enough to convince them. "In the confusion, my
brother threw me onto his horse and set it galloping

away." She looked up at the questioner, her amber
eyes wide. "I don't know what became of them all. . . ."

They believed her, at least thus far, and one said
with determination, "We'll find them, lady, be assured of it!"

"If they live," another commented under his breath.

"Quiet, Vesey." The first speaker gave him a withering look. "The lady's suffered enough without your
gloomy predictions." He turned back to Cyllan. "We'll
send searchers out immediately, and in the meantime two of us will take you to Wathryn town—it's
but a short ride from here." He rose stiffly to his feet.
"Gordach, Lesk—you'll act as escort for the lady. Take
her to Sheniya Win Mar at the High Tree tavern, and
I'll join you there later." Holding out a hand to Cyllan
he bowed courteously. "We'll have news for you by
morning, madam; I promise."

Cyllan nodded slowly and thanked him, then let
her escort help her on to the gelding, which stood at
the side of the road with its head hanging in exhaustion. She assured them she could ride unaided, but
nonetheless the older of the two men insisted on
taking the reins and walking at her mount's head
while the other rode by her side, short sword drawn
and resting across his lap. The circle of torchlight
fell behind, and Gordach—her younger companion—
assured her that they'd be in no danger without light;
the town was barely a mile away, and besides the
rain was clearing; any time now they'd have one or
both moons to guide them. He was a talkative youth
and kept up a flow of chatter as the horses plodded
on. Cyllan learned that her rescuers were part of a
volunteer militia formed by order of the Province
Margrave in an attempt to stem the rapidly increasing depredations of the brigand bands. Every town of
reasonable size had such a force now, Gordach told
her, and no less than fourteen outlaws had been
brought to justice and executed in their own district

alone. And now with this latest news from the north, there'd doubtless be yet more work for them to do.

Cyllan's skin crawled uneasily and she said, "Latest news . . . ?"

Gordach smiled proudly. "It was brought in by courier only an hour before we left on our patrol, lady. We must be one of the first towns, beyond the province capitals, to have word of it." He paused for emphasis, then leaned towards her and whispered confidentially, *"News from the Star Peninsula!"*

Cyllan's fingers tightened on the gelding's reins and she buried her hands in the animal's mane lest Gordach should see them shaking. Trying to keep her voice even, she said, "I've heard nothing of it."

"No—if truth be told, none of us knows the details as yet. The courier arrived exhausted, and his message won't be broadcast till morning. But I believe" —Gordach smiled at her again, clearly hoping to impress her—"that it concerns a dangerous killer who has escaped the Circle's custody together with his accomplice!"

So the hunt was up. . . . Cyllan licked lips that were suddenly dry, and Gordach talked happily on.

"We'll learn the details at dawn, and hopefully we'll have a description of the two. I've heard that the news was brought from West High Land by messenger bird—if that's true, then it's a wonderful innovation, for the message must have reached our Margrave in hours rather than days." He shifted eagerly in his saddle, gripping the sword across his lap. "I hope the wanted man comes to Chaun Province— we'd earn a great accolade if we could be the ones to apprehend him!"

Cyllan didn't reply, and the man who walked at her horse's head looked back over his shoulder.

"Hush your noise, Gordach. The lady's in no mood for your babbling—begging your pardon, madam, but if he's not told, the boy will rattle on until his tongue drops out!"

Cyllan nodded, but still didn't trust herself to speak. Gordach fell silent, and when she looked up again she saw that they were nearing the town. The hunched silhouettes of buildings showed against the sky ahead, one with a soft halo of light glowing from a window despite the late hour. As they approached, an unseen watcher issued a sharp challenge out of the darkness, and Lesk answered gruffly. Halting Cyllan's horse he hurried forward alone, and she heard a brief exchange of words as her presence was explained before Lesk came back and led the horse on. A man muffled in a heavy cloak touched a finger to his brow politely as they passed, and they rode on into the town.

Though not large by inland standards, Wathryn was clearly a prosperous and busy place. Acres of forest had been cut down as what had begun as a simple timbermen's settlement grew, and Wathryn now boasted several merchants' houses of impressive size, a justice house where courts were held and local business conducted, and a paved market-square. Now though, all was quiet, although Cyllan could hear the sound of a mill-race somewhere nearby where a small river had been tamed.

"Almost there now, lady," Gordach told her, undaunted by Lesk's disapproving scowl. The horses' hooves echoed loudly as they reached the market-square, and now Cyllan could see a long, low building fronting the square, with a stylized painting of a spreading oak tree adorning its facade. A single light glowed in a downstairs window, and Lesk stepped up to the door, hammering on it with a heavy fist.

"Sheniya! Sheniya Win Mar! It's Lesk Barith—I've a guest in need of your hospitality!"

A minute later the door creaked open, and a plump,

middle-aged woman peered out, her eyes widening when she saw Cyllan and her escort.

"Aeoris preserve us, what's this at such an hour? Lesk Barith, have you lost your wits?"

Lesk explained briefly while Cyllan sat mute on her gelding trying to quell a rising sense of dread that threatened to suffocate her. The news of her escape was abroad, and there was a price on her head—by morning, the townsfolk would be able to match her face and all too distinctive hair to the description of the hunted murderess. She desperately wanted to flee, turn her horse about and run while she still could; but both she and the animal were exhausted—to flee would damn her immediately, and she couldn't hope to outrun a pursuit. She had at least a few hours grace—better to keep up her pretense and wait for an opportunity to leave unnoticed . . . if the opportunity was to be found.

Sheniya Win Mar had by now heard the bare bones of Cyllan's story, and her natural instinct took over from indignation at the disturbance. She soundly berated Lesk for keeping the lady waiting while he prated; then, as soon as the girl was helped down from her mount, she bustled forward.

"There now, madam, we'll soon have you warmed and comfortable! What you must have suffered; it doesn't bear thinking about—but you're safe now. Come; come in, and let me find you the best chair. . . ."

Cyllan heard the clatter of the gelding's hooves as Lesk took it away. She resisted the impulse to look back longingly over her shoulder and, taking a deep and nervous breath, allowed the tavern-keeper to lead her inside.

Chapter 2

The hawk was hardly more than a speck against the uneasy sky, a tiny shape arrowing its way eastward on the prevailing wind. It was unlikely that any casual observer on the ground would even have noticed it, but the man who sat in the lee of a rocky outcrop on the slopes of the hills bordering Han and Empty Provinces had seen the bird appear over the horizon, and now watched its rapid progress with narrowed green eyes.

Why the hawk should have aroused both his interest and a measure of disquiet Tarod couldn't tell; but there was something purposeful about its flight, as though it travelled on some mission above and beyond the call of instinct. And the fact that it had come out of the northwest—the direction of the Star Peninsula—could well be significant.

The bird was all but lost to sight now, and Tarod shifted his position, stretching one leg to ease a touch of cramp and leaning back against the outcrop. The morning was chill, but as yet he was in no mood to resume his own journey; he'd walked nearly all night and, as well as being physically fatigued, he needed time to consider his next move.

Tarod had departed the Star Peninsula in a spectacular manner that he had no anxiety to experience again. Before he left, he had sworn to Keridil that he had no quarrel with the Circle; but he believed the High Initiate would take no heed of his word. Keridil wanted revenge for those who had died—and he also wanted the Chaos stone. That gem lay at the hub of this whole ugly affair, and Tarod had to force back the chilly mingling of longing and loathing that always assailed him when he thought of it. Much as he might prefer to deny the fact, he *needed* the stone—it was a vital and integral part of him, for it was the vessel for his own soul. And without it he could only ever hope to be half alive.

But the stone was a curse as well as a lifeline, for it shackled him to an inner self whose essence originated in pure evil—and therein lay the dilemma which had haunted Tarod since he had first discovered the gem's nature. Yandros, Lord of Chaos, had awoken in him memories of a past so ancient that it almost defied imagination, and he couldn't deny that that past had a terrible lure. Yet to acknowledge the stone's true power and realize his full potential would be to turn his back on all that he had ever held sacrosanct. He had been a high Adept of the Circle, a chosen servant of the gods of Order—Chaos was anathema to him. And yet he owed his existence to those same malign powers. . . .

It was a paradox he couldn't resolve, and now it was further complicated by the knowledge that he also owed his life to Yandros. Had it not been for the Chaos Lord's intercession through Cyllan, he would have been consigned to the grisly death ordained by Keridil, and the stone would have fallen into the Circle's hands. That wouldn't accord with Yandros's scheme—Tarod was well aware that the malevolent lord still meant to use him as a vehicle for his plans to challenge the rule of Aeoris and the gods of Order, and Yandros believed that, at the final test, the ancient affinities would defeat any barriers Tarod tried to set against them.

He shivered inwardly at that thought, for he knew that with the stone in his possession again it would be all too easy to succumb to its pervasive influence. And though he wanted to survive, the thought of surviving as a pawn in Yandros's deadly game turned his blood cold.

Yet, he dared not leave matters unresolved, and in the wake of his flight from the Star Peninsula he had realized that there was only one course of action open to him. When the stone's nature had first been revealed to him—and it seemed a long time ago now—he had pledged to take the jewel to the White Isle far in the south and to give it into the safe-keeping of the one entity powerful enough to combat Yandros's power . . . Aeoris Himself. The conflict with the Circle, and all that followed, had made him doubt the wisdom of that decision, but now he saw no other way open to him. He had served Aeoris faithfully, whatever Keridil might say to the contrary— only the White Lord Himself could finally resolve Tarod's terrible dilemma and relieve him of the stone's burden.

But to reach the White Isle would be a fruitless achievement unless he could find Cyllan. . . .

Tarod's eyes narrowed with a sudden, sharp pain. He'd been trying not to think of Cyllan, aware that in spite of what his instincts told him he had no evidence that she was still alive. When the Margrave's horse had bolted into the maelstrom of the Warp with her on its back, his wild despair had found an outlet in rage. But now that his mind had had time to calm and reason, he realized that if Yandros had manipulated events in his own favor once, he could do so again—and Cyllan's well-being was very much in the Chaos Lord's interest. Intuition told him that

Cyllan lived; and he believed that, if she could keep her freedom, she would travel south to Shu-Nhadek, knowing that he too would be making it his goal.

But there would be dangers on the road, not least from the Circle themselves. There must be a price on Cyllan's head as well as on his own, and Keridil would stint nothing in the search for them both. Cyllan had the Chaos stone, but it was of little value to her, while he, without it, was seriously hampered. He had used all the power he could muster to escape from the Star Peninsula, and the exertion of energy had been almost too much for him—he had had to trust to his ancient affinity with the Chaotic origins of the Warp and let it carry him where it would, and while he had survived the experience it had utterly drained him. The Circle might expect him to use his sorcery to discover Cyllan's whereabouts and to transport himself instantly to her side; Tarod knew that, without the soul-stone, his powers weren't up to such a feat. He was little better off than a high-ranking Initiate, and would need all his physical resources to compensate for the loss of his sorcerous potential if he was to find Cyllan before the Circle did.

He smiled wryly to himself, aware that as yet he'd made a poor show of attending to his own physical needs. He'd had no rest since his spectacular departure from the Castle, and carried no food or water, nor any coin to buy them with. Although some game inhabited these sere hills and he was a passing fair shot with a crossbow, he couldn't conjure a crossbow from thin air. His only resources were the clothes he stood up in, an Initiate's gold badge, and whatever small measure of power might be left to him.

He shifted his position again and gazed up at the sky. Behind a pall of restless cloud the sun was marching towards the low meridian of a northern spring. The wind was beginning to bluster as it backed to a more northerly direction, and on the horizon, where the hills rose higher and more barren towards the gloomy mineral mines of Empty Province, the cloud-bank was stained an ugly purple, presaging rain. He judged that it would be several hours before the first squall reached him, and in the meantime the change in the wind meant that his rock alcove was better sheltered. He'd be well advised to rest before continuing his journey; he was close to exhaustion, and sleep was more imperative now than sustenance. Besides, these bleak hills with their old, deserted roads were a safer resting place than any he'd be likely to find once he reached the more populous farmlands.

The rock made a hard and uncomfortable bed, but Tarod settled himself as best he could, wrapping his heavy cloak more tightly round his body. The wind, gusting, moaned like a faraway voice from a half-forgotten dream in his mind, and within minutes he was asleep.

Instinct roused him seconds before the sounds of hooves and heavy breathing impinged on the wind's lonely mourning. His green eyes snapped open—and he found himself staring at a monstrous silhouette that blocked out half the restless sky. A strong, animal smell assaulted his nostrils and he tensed with shock, not knowing whether the apparition was mortal or something out of a chasm of nightmare.

A throaty laugh grated and the monstrosity moved, splitting apart to resolve itself into the shapes of two mounted—and indisputably mortal—men.

"The sleeper wakes." The accent was guttural, and Tarod suspected that it had its origins in the far north of Empty Province. He didn't like its overtones. "Welcome back to the world, friend. And isn't it an honor to have such good companions to greet you?"

Behind Tarod someone sniggered, and he turned his head quickly to see three more horsemen behind

him. The one who had laughed was a pockmarked,
vacuous-faced youth of sixteen or seventeen; the others were older men but no more savory, and Tarod
realized that they were—could only be—a band of
brigands.

He sighed and leaned his head back against the
rock, closing his eyes once more. He had nothing
about him worth looting, so it was likely as not that
these evil-looking ruffians wouldn't give him much
trouble; but their unwonted arrival was an irritation.

The leader, a snake-thin individual festooned with
a bizarre assortment of stolen trinkets over a filthy
fur coat, sniffed loudly. "Our friend doesn't seem to
appreciate our generosity in stopping to pass the
time of day with him." He inched his horse forward
and prodded at Tarod with the toe of one boot. Tarod
opened his eyes. "On your feet, *friend*."

Tarod stared at him. "Are you addressing me?"

The youth sniggered again and the leader made a
mock bow. "Your pardon, sir, if I gave offense! But I
see no one else to address."

The other men laughed uproariously and their leader
grinned at the approbation. His horse inched closer
still and the others followed his example, so that
Tarod was tightly encircled.

"Maybe he's got a legion of demons hidden in his
pocket, Ravakin," one suggested. "Maybe that's who
he thought you were talking to!"

Ravakin smirked, showing a mouthful of decayed
teeth. "Maybe he's got a horse and bags stowed up
his sleeve, more like it. Maybe he'd like to show 'em
to us, as a token of comradeship and goodwill." For
the second time a toe prodded Tarod in the ribs.
"Come on, friend. Where are your belongings?"

Evenly, Tarod said, "You see them with your own
eyes, *friend*."

"The traveller has a sense of humor." Ravakin
leered.

A heavyset man beside him chuckled. "D'you think he'll be as entertaining with a fire lit under him?"

"He'll be a damned sight more talkative. No man in his right mind walks these hills if he wants to stay alive—he's got a mount somewhere. And he'll tell us where it is." He licked his lips. "By the time we've entertained him a while, he'll be *begging* to tell us."

He obviously intended the words to sap Tarod's confidence, and was chagrined when the black-haired man only smiled faintly. Frowning, he gestured to the burliest of his companions. "Search him. See what he's got about him."

"Don't trouble yourself." Tarod rose with a swift, lithe movement that startled them. He threw his cloak back, and his voice was deceptively gentle. "I have no coin, no possessions, nothing that would interest you, gentlemen. If you wish to search for a horse, do so with my blessing. You won't find one, for I don't own one."

The youth piped up in a voice that was only half broken. "He might be speaking the truth, Ravakin. We've seen nothing, and you couldn't hide a worm in these barrens—"

"Shut your clatter!" Ravakin snapped viciously. "He hasn't walked without horse or provisions into the middle of nowhere! Amit, Yil—we'll give our friend here a little lesson in neighborliness to loosen his tongue." As he spoke he urged his horse forward so that its flank, brushing by, knocked Tarod off-balance. At the same moment two of the others closed their mounts in, spinning him back towards Ravakin, their hooves kicking up the dust in a choking cloud.

"Hold, Rav!" The sudden exclamation brought the brigand leader up short. "What's that under his cloak?"

"What?" Ravakin's sly, acquisitive eyes focused on Tarod, but Amit, who had spoken, recognized the distinctive symbol before his leader did.

"Damn us all, Rav, he's an Initiate!"

"Initiate?" The leader gave him a scorching look. "He could be Margrave of the Seven Hells for all I care!" He leaned forward in the saddle, and hot breath laced with the odors of stale food fanned Tarod's face. "Maybe that's what we'll dub him. Our exalted friend, Margrave of the Seven Hells. Come on, Margrave. You're going to dance for us till we tire of you, and then we'll see about relieving you of that pretty trinket if you've nothing better to offer!"

Tarod said nothing, didn't move, and slowly, with relish, Ravakin drew a long knife from his belt. His thumb played on the hilt. "Did you hear me, Margrave of the Seven Hells? We're going to send you to your own domain...." He reached out and, with practiced confidence, touched the point of the knife to Tarod's throat while two of his men started to whistle in crude harmony. "Entertain us, Margrave. Let's see you dance to our tune!"

Tarod had stood impassive throughout the brigands' taunting, but suddenly anger smoldered in him and with it came a resurgence of another, familiar feeling. He'd made no move to challenge his assailants, knowing he was at a disadvantage and unsure of how much power, if any, he could bring to bear against them. But the anger had awoken other emotions, and he realized that, weakened though he might be, he was still far more than a match for such a gaggle of arrogant fools.

"Ravakin." He spoke quietly but the abrupt change in the tone of his voice made the brigand leader frown. The knife blade wavered, and with a contemptuous gesture Tarod reached up to brush it aside. Ravakin's face reddened with rage and he would have struck out, but his horse shifted back, sensing something that, as yet, was beyond its master's comprehension. Green eyes met Ravakin's faded grey ones, and the brigand leader's gaze was held fast.

"I give you one chance," Tarod said softly. "Go about your business—trouble some other traveller, and leave me in peace. You'll have no further warning, Ravakin."

Ravakin continued to stare at him for a few more moments, then he threw his head back and bellowed with laughter.

"A threat! A threat, from the Margrave of the Seven Hells and no less a personage!" Reassured, his followers joined in the laughter. "No knife, no sword, not even a stave about him, and he thinks to frighten *me!*" The laughter died into a hiccup and Ravakin wiped his nose and streaming eyes on his sleeve. Then his broad grin abruptly changed to an ugly scowl and he said with harsh contempt, "Kill him."

In their anxiety to ape their leader's every change of mood, the men were still sniggering, and were slow to react to the command. Before they could make a move, Tarod's left hand shot out and clamped over the nose of Ravakin's horse; and he spoke a single, alien word.

The animal shrieked and reared, and Tarod only just ducked aside in time to avoid its flailing hooves. The brigand leader let out a yell of astonishment that instantly changed to a cry of terror as the panicking beast bucked. He lost his grip and pitched sideways out of the saddle, to land with a bone-cracking thump in the dust. The horse bolted, and Ravakin's cry became a roar of insensate fury as he tried to struggle to his feet, groping for his lost blade. He was halfway up when appallingly powerful fingers took him by the throat and forced his head round at an agonizing angle, until, twisted and racked with pain, he stared into Tarod's ice-hard, green eyes.

The men who survived him could never even guess at the nature of the horrors that Ravakin saw in that moment; the illusions Tarod conjured were for him alone, and they were born of an ancient, malevolent power that delighted in torment. All they saw was the dark and malignant aura that flickered into existence about the man who, until moments ago, had been easy and entertaining prey. Their horses whinnied and reared, and above their noise came the sound of Ravakin's scream, an incoherent plea and protest as his mind toppled over the brink of insanity. His eyes bulged and his face turned purple; his hands clawed desperately at the unnameable phantasms that bore down on him, and among which the cruelly smiling face of the black-haired stranger seemed to burn like fire. He twisted and writhed, gargling as his tongue protruded like a bloated serpent from his mouth—then the transfixed men heard a single, sickening *crack*, as, one-handed, Tarod broke Ravakin's neck.

The brigand band didn't wait to witness their leader's final fate. Even as Tarod swung to face them, incensed still by rage and anticipating attack from behind, they were hauling their mounts' heads around and digging frantic heels into the animals' flanks, spurring them away and not caring where they fled. Their voices, shrill with panic, goaded the animals on, and Tarod was left staring after them as the blindness of fury slowly drained away.

The brigands' voices and the thunder of hooves were lost to the soughing wind, and he reeled back against the rock outcrop, suddenly drained and weak. Not two paces away Ravakin lay, tongue out and round eyes staring stupidly at a boulder a foot from his nose. Tarod looked down at the corpse with a surge of disgust. To do what he had done had been sheer, wanton maleficence. It would have been simple enough to kill the brigand leader, without the need for such savage cruelty; and yet he had been unable to resist the temptation. The power had flowed in him, and he had used it. . . . He looked at his left hand and the ruined base of the ring that he still

wore on his index finger. Even without the Chaos
stone there was evil in him. With the stone restored,
how much harder would it be to fight such a baneful
influence?

On the heels of that thought came a barbed feeling
that he was indulging in self-pity. More important
than his well-being was that of Cyllan, who carried
the Chaos stone and had none of his powers to aid
her. If he was to find her, pragmatism dictated that
he must waste no time and use whatever resources
he had to hand, whatever his conscience might argue.

He straightened, moved to stand over the corpse,
and stirred it with one foot so that it rolled onto its
back. Ignoring the accusing, sightless stare, Tarod
searched Ravakin's body. As well as his short sword,
the brigand leader had carried a sharp and well-
balanced knife in an embroidered sheath, doubtless
the property of some earlier victim; and in a pouch
under his coat were coins—about fifty gravines in
all—and a handful of small but fairly valuable gem-
stones. Enough, at least, to enable Tarod to maintain
an image that would arouse no suspicion in the provincial towns.

He looked up and saw the dead man's horse standing a short distance away, head down and watching
him. It had obviously been trained to stand when
unmounted, and once its fear had receded it obeyed
that training. Tarod raised a hand and snapped his
fingers, uttering a low, guttural sound. The horse
pricked up its ears and approached, uncertainly at
first, then with greater confidence as Tarod added a
silent, mental command to the gesture. It was a good
animal, a big-boned and powerful bay; no brigand in
his right senses would use anything but a strong and
reliable mount, and Ravakin had been an expert in
his own nefarious way. The horse stood passive while
Tarod examined its two saddlebags. In them he found
more coins, a woman's bronze and enamel necklace

and matching bracelet, and a supply of food—dried meat and slabs of a naturally fermented fruit; the rations of a man who travelled light but needed good sustenance. There was also a wine-skin, three-quarters empty but useful for carrying water. Tarod drank the remainder of its contents and ate one of the dried fruit slabs while he checked the animal's harness, buckled the sheathed knife onto his belt, and finally swung himself into the bay's saddle. As the animal raised its head and snorted, eager to be away from the outcrop with its smell of death, Tarod pulled the necklace and bracelet from the saddlebag and dropped them onto Ravakin's body, where they fell with a small, cold *clink*. The brigand's followers wouldn't dare to return here; with luck, the corpse would be found by men from the Empty Province mines and it was possible that these ornaments would eventually be returned to their rightful owner, if she still lived.

He looked over his shoulder. The rain clouds were little more than a mile away now, but he believed the bay could outdistance them. Turning the animal's head south, he urged it into a canter along the rough track.

Cyllan woke to see the ghostly glimmer of false dawn casting the small window of her room at the High Tree tavern into pale relief. She turned over in the soft bed, huddling deeper under the plentiful blankets, and for a few minutes simply stared at the window until her awakening senses had fully returned. Then, alarmed, she sat up.

She hadn't intended to sleep for so long. Although it was still night, the faint shining in the east told her that morning wasn't long away, and she had planned to be far from Wathryn before anyone else was abroad.

She slipped out of bed, wincing as her entire body protested. The fall she'd taken had battered her badly, and the full extent of the bruising was only now starting to make itself felt. To make matters worse, she'd grown unaccustomed to long hours in the saddle during her stay at the Castle of the Star Peninsula, and the ride—especially the flight from the bandits—had given her muscles further punishment. No matter; she must still be away. In the wake of what the youth, Gordach, had unwittingly revealed to her last night, she didn't dare stay in this town a moment past the dawn.

The air was bitterly cold, and Cyllan wrapped one of the blankets around herself before padding to the window and kneeling to peer out. She had been too tired last night to take in anything but the barest details of her surroundings; all she remembered was a market-square and the plump, astonished face of Sheniya Win Mar when Cyllan's escort brought her to the tavern door. The innkeeper had bustled her into a long, low room where brass and pewter gleamed in the light of a banked fire, and had brought her warmed towels and a dry robe, vastly too big, in which she had sat dazed on an inglenook seat while a bowl of hot stew and a cup of wine were set before her. Sheniya had fiercely rebuffed Lesk Barith's attempts to question her guest, and once the man had disconsolately gone the innkeeper lost her initial sense of awe at housing such a lady—Cyllan smiled wryly at the memory—under her roof, and had kept up a stream of comments and reminiscences and opinions, which enabled Cyllan to eat her food and say nothing. Sheniya, it transpired, was a widow whose two sons had long departed the nest, and she had an ample streak of motherliness, which she now lavished on her guest in full measure. At last, having twice almost fallen into the fire from sheer fatigue, Cyllan was bundled up a flight of steep, narrow stairs and helped into bed in the tavern's best room. Sheniya departed with a final, anxious injunction that she should be roused instantly should the lady find herself in need of anything.

Cyllan stared out over the deserted market-square and thought that what she needed was her horse, saddled and provisioned, and a good head start on the pursuit that would ensue when the news from the Star Peninsula permeated through to the High Tree tavern. As yet, so Gordach had said, only a few local dignitaries knew the nature of the message brought by falcon from the Circle's stronghold, but when its full content became common knowledge she would be in danger. Keridil Toln must have given a description of the girl who had escaped the Castle after killing the Margrave of Shu's son, and her distinctive hair and eyes would be enough to damn her at a glance. She couldn't hope to maintain the hastily-concocted story she had told to her rescuers; in the chaotic aftermath of the chase it had served well enough, but it wouldn't stand up to further investigation. If she was to keep her freedom—and, she reminded herself grimly, her *life*—she must flee, while she still had the chance.

She was about to move away from the window when a shadow that moved suddenly at the far side of the square arrested her attention. The stabbing glow of a lantern flared between two buildings, and a man, yawning and wrapped in a heavy cloak, appeared, crossing the wet flagstones towards a monolithic stone slab that stood alone at the square's center.

Cyllan had seen Law Stones in every small town she had passed through during her harsh years as a drover. They were erected in marketplaces, harbors, anywhere, in fact, where people congregated; and on their pitted surfaces were displayed documents of vital importance to the inhabitants. News of the death of any one of the land's three leaders, or of the province's own Margrave, would warrant display on the

Law Stone, as would any new edicts passed by the Court of the High Margrave on Summer Isle . . . any information, in fact, that was intended for the attention of every man, woman, and child in the district, or in the whole world.

She licked lips that were suddenly dry as she watched the man stop by the Law Stone and take from under the folds of his cloak a rolled piece of parchment and a short, blunt-headed hammer. Moments later the dull, staccato sound of the parchment being nailed to the Law Stone cut through the night quiet. The coincidence was too strong—that notice could only concern herself and Tarod. And when dawn broke, a drum would be sounded in the market-square to summon all within hearing to the Stone, where the details of the notice would be read aloud to the townsfolk, so that no one would miss the important news.

Not for the first time, Cyllan cursed her own lack of learning. She could neither read nor write, and so if she wanted to find out what the notice contained she must wait for dawn and the official announcement. But she didn't dare wait. If, as she believed, the parchment contained an edict from the Star Peninsula, the province militia would have been alerted long before the general notice was posted, and by now the hunt must be on. Chances were that the men who had saved her from the brigands had already been given her description, and realized whom they had rescued. The militia might come for her at any moment—she must go, and go now.

The watchman, still yawning, had completed his task and was walking away, his lantern bobbing like a will-o'-the-wisp. Cyllan's eyes were now better adjusted to the dark and she looked round her room. To her immense relief, she saw the clothes in which she had arrived at the tavern laid out neatly over a chair, cleaned and dried. Sheniya Win Mar had been better than her word; she'd promised the dry garments for the morning, but it seemed that her guest's apparent status had been an incentive to complete the task before retiring to bed. As she discarded the blanket and began to dress, shivering, Cyllan reflected wryly that the past few hours had given her an undreamed-of glimpse of what life as a lady of quality must be like. People hanging on her every word, eager to do her bidding and wait on her . . . it was a pity, she thought with some irony, that she hadn't been able to savor such treatment to the full. Now, with the full might of the Circle probably roused to find her, it was unlikely that such an opportunity would ever come her way again.

Carefully, she reached under her pillow and drew out the Chaos stone, trying not to be drawn by its solitary, winking eye. She thrust it into her bodice—it was a pity that the long, full skirt and jerkin were so impractical for a speedy, stealthy exit, but there was no help for it—then dragged her fingers quickly through her pale hair, and tiptoed to the door.

The inn was silent. No telltale sliver of light shone from under any door, and the steep stairwell lay in darkness. Praying that she wouldn't miss her footing, Cyllan crept down the steps, freezing once with heart-stopping terror when a settling joist creaked somewhere in the depths of the old building. After what seemed a small eternity she reached the lower floor, and the heavy door that stood between her and freedom. The door bore a massive bolt, and it was too much to hope that the bolt could be drawn silently. It slid back with a grating rasp, protesting at long need of oiling, and Cyllan's teeth clenched agonizingly together as she listened for an answering stir from upstairs. But no sound came; Sheniya Win Mar, it seemed, slept on. At last, knowing she dared wait no longer, Cyllan eased the door open and slipped out into the early morning.

The cold struck her instantly; the windless, bitter cold of early spring. In the Castle of the Star Peninsula she had had no need of shoes, and the cut-down men's boots she had once worn were long lost to the sea. Now, as the chill of the market-square's stone paving struck up through her soles, she would have given almost anything to have them back, and, too, the cloak that had gone last night during her desperate flight from the brigands. No matter; she must do without—there were more urgent considerations.

Teeth chattering, she moved along the front wall of the tavern, keeping a wary eye on the deserted square, until she reached a side alley. Through an arch she could just discern the outline of low buildings behind the inn, which logic dictated must be the stables. She was halfway to her goal. . . .

Thankfully, it seemed that Sheniya Win Mar kept no stable lad, nor any of the ferocious geese that many farmers used as popular and efficient guardians, and only a continuing silence greeted Cyllan as she unlatched the stable door and glided inside. Dark shapes moved uneasily and she saw the white of a rolling eye; instinctively she made a low, soft noise in her throat, a sound her uncle had taught her to use in calming nervous animals. The horses subsided, and she heard a soft, contented blowing of breath.

There were only three of them in the stables; a swaybacked black mare, a shaggy pony, and the big iron-grey gelding. Harness was ranged on hooks high on the wall; she recognized her own by the mud- and sweat-stains on the leather, and set about saddling the gelding. A swift check told her that the animal had been well fed and watered; giving the saddle-girth a final tug to check its security, she backed the gelding gently out of its stall and turned it towards the door. As they emerged, the animal's hooves rang loudly on cobbles, striking vivid blue sparks, and in consternation Cyllan brought it to a halt, staring up

at the dark bulk of the tavern. For a moment she
thought her luck had held—then a lamp flared in an
upstairs window, and seconds later the curtain was
pulled aside and a pale, indistinct face looked directly down at her.

Cyllan felt bile clogging her throat as she stared,
appalled, at the face. She heard—or thought she heard;
she could never be certain—a voice calling out, and
it snapped her out of the initial shock so that instinct
took over. She reached up, grabbed at the saddle,
and heaved. Her foot, flailing, found a stirrup, and
with a frantic kick she sprawled astride the gelding's
back. It pranced sideways; she gathered up the reins,
still struggling to right herself, then drove her heels
hard into its flanks.

The noise of the big horse careering out of the alley
was enough to rouse half Wathryn town, but it was
too late for any attempt at stealth. Cyllan had been
seen—all she could do was ride for her life. She
crouched over the gelding's neck, shrilly urging it on
and lashing at it with the looped reins; they raced
out across the market-square, missing the Law Stone
by a handsbreadth, and pounded towards the road.
Ahead, a break in the clouds showed a glaring, green-
purple sliver of light where the sun would rise. Cyllan
swung her mount's head to the right, cutting away
from the road and turning southward. She expected
at any moment to hear the sounds of pursuers, but
none came; they reached the trees beyond the town,
and still there were no distant hoofbeats echoing
behind them. At last she allowed the gelding to halt,
and turned in the saddle, looking back.

Wathryn town slept on. Whether Sheniya Win Mar
had recognized her erstwhile guest or whether she
thought herself the victim of a horse-thief, she hadn't
yet roused help—and that was enough to give Cyllan
the start she needed. Ahead lay the great arable plains

of the south and, finally, Shu Province itself, where, if he still lived, Tarod would seek her.

If he still lived . . . Cyllan touched the place where the Chaos stone nestled, and softly murmured a prayer that was not directed to Aeoris. Then she settled herself more comfortably in the saddle, and urged the gelding on into the shelter of the trees.

Chapter 3

"**K**eridil?" The tall, patrician girl had entered the room so quietly that he'd been unaware of her presence until she moved out of the shadows to where the High Initiate stood by the window. He turned, startled, then smiled as she reached up to kiss him.

"You look tired, my love." Her voice was warm with concern. "You should take time to rest for a while—the world won't stop turning while you sleep."

He smiled again and put an arm about her shoulders, hugging her. "In a while. I'll sleep in a while." He nodded towards the window, where the day was brightening. "We're still waiting for the first of the messenger-birds to return. They've taken longer than I'd have liked; I hoped that their news would be disseminated throughout the provinces by now."

Sashka sighed faintly. "Then there's still no word of Tarod's whereabouts?"

"Nothing. We've tried to trace him by magical means, of course; and the Seers of the Sisterhood are using all their skills. But I know Tarod of old—if he doesn't want to be found, it could take more than our Adepts are capable of to locate him."

"You'll find him." She spoke with such venom that

Keridil was momentarily taken aback to hear a hatred that matched his own. "You'll find him, Keridil. And when you do—" The nails of one hand dug into the opposite palm as she clenched her fingers together. When Tarod was recaptured, she would savor his lingering death. Twice now he'd thwarted the Circle; she was determined this time not to be cheated of her pleasure in his final demise. And maybe she would indulge herself by seeing him one last time, to remind him that he had once touched her and known her and loved her. . . . A small, pleasurable shiver ran the length of her spine, and Keridil, noticing, said solicitously, "Cold, love?"

"No . . ." She let one hand stray to his hip and pressed closer against him, aroused by her own thoughts and by memories from the days before Keridil had replaced Tarod in her affections. Then, unbidden, the image of another girl's face focused in her mind: small, plain, angular, framed by unkempt, silver-fair hair. A cold shaft of anger destroyed the burgeoning desire. She moved away abruptly towards the window, her fists clenching again, and said, trying not to betray her feelings, "And what of that peasant girl?"

"Cyllan Anassan?" Keridil watched her, aware of the turmoil in her mind and trying to quell a stab of suspicion as to its cause. "He'll be looking for her; I've no doubt of that—and she has the Chaos stone. It's imperative that we find her before he does."

Sashka hunched her shoulders like some predatory bird. "That wasn't what I meant. I know you'll capture them, Keridil—I *know* it. But when she's brought back to the Castle—what then?"

He didn't answer immediately, and she turned her head to regard him. He returned the look, his doubts still not entirely allayed, and said at last: "There's a price on her head now, not just for abetting Chaos but for Drachea Rannak's murder. In all conscience,

I couldn't decree anything else. But in all conscience, Sashka, neither do I like the idea of executing a woman."

Sashka's eyes narrowed. "Even a woman who killed a Margrave's son and heir in cold blood?"

"Even that." There was a slight edge to Keridil's voice as he added, "Couldn't you kill, Sashka? *Wouldn't* you, for something you truly believed in?"

"If she believes in Chaos, she deserves nothing better than death!"

"I didn't say she believes in Chaos," Keridil replied evenly. "I don't think she does. But she believes in Tarod."

His expression warned Sashka just in time to control her reaction, and she realized that the words were a challenge. If she argued, if she showed emotion or anger, Keridil would suspect the truth—that much of her hatred of Cyllan was rooted in jealousy. She herself had spurned and betrayed Tarod in favor of the High Initiate, but the knowledge that Tarod's feelings had likewise turned to someone else was almost more than she could tolerate. Especially so when that someone was a common peasant-drover with neither beauty nor breeding in her favor. Now, of all times, she mustn't allow Keridil to so much as glimpse the truth. . . .

Her face composed, she paced slowly across the room towards him and laid a hand on his sleeve. Her fingers traced a sensuous pattern on his arm. "You're right, of course," she said softly, conciliating and thankful that she now knew her lover well enough to reveal what she wished to reveal, hide what she wished to hide. "It *is* hard to condemn out of hand. If, for instance, I were defending you—"

He laughed at the idea, but the tension faded. "I hope there'll never be need for that!"

She cast her eyes down and raised his hand to her lips to kiss it, her tongue licking lightly at his skin.

"Still, if such a time were ever to come ..." Her teeth nibbled at his fingers. "If you needed me ..." She let the ambiguous suggestion hang unfinished and was gratified after a moment to feel his arm slip around her waist and pull her towards him.

"If—" Keridil began, then stopped at the sound of a commotion in the courtyard. He swung round towards the window, looked out—

"A bird! One of the messengers has returned!" His hold on her changed its nature and he kissed her quickly, nothing more than a salute, before releasing her altogether. "Love, forgive me—I must see what it brings!" And before she could speak he ran from the room, the door banging behind him.

Sashka stared at the door, then spat out a curse which, from the lips of a girl of gentility and breeding, would have made her mother faint dead away.

The hawk was from southern Chaun. Keridil recognized the distinctive seal of the Matriarch herself— Sister Ilyaya Kimi—as he pushed his way through the gathered onlookers. The Castle's falconer detached the message from the bird's leg and gravely handed it to Keridil, while the bird fluttered its wings and settled on its master's wrist, tired but still ready to lash out at anyone who made an unwary move. Keridil walked a discreet distance away, and as he broke the seal on the tightly-rolled parchment he saw Gant Ambaril Rannak approaching through the small crowd.

"High Initiate." The Margrave had witnessed the hawk's arrival from his window, and his tired eyes were hungry and haunted. "There's news ... ?"

"A letter from the Matriarch of the Sisterhood." Keridil didn't unroll the parchment, despite the other man's obvious eagerness. "I think it unlikely that she'll have tidings of our fugitives. I'm sorry." He tried to soften the words with a sympathetic smile.

"The moment we *do* hear word of Drachea's assassin, I'll send for you."

Gant nodded, swallowing his disappointment and remembering, with an effort, that letters sent between two of the land's three prime rulers were no concern of a mere provincial Margrave. "Of course . . . thank you," he said. "When I saw the bird, I simply wondered . . ." He straightened his shoulders a little. "I'll return to my wife."

Keridil walked with him to the main door, then, as the Margrave climbed the stairs to the upper floors, he hurried back to his study. Sashka rose from her chair as he entered.

"What is it?" There was a keen edge to her tone.

"A message from Sister Ilyaya Kimi."

"The Matriarch?" For a moment Sashka's eyes widened; as a Novice in the Sisterhood she had been taught to revere their supreme head as little less than wisdom incarnate, and, however exalted she might be as the High Initiate's betrothed, the habit died hard. As Keridil sat on the edge of the table and opened the letter, Sashka made no attempt to look over his shoulder as she might otherwise have done, but watched, tense, while he read in silence. And within moments she knew something was amiss.

Keridil read the crabbed, curlicued script with its overelaborate phrasing several times, half hoping that he had failed to interpret the words correctly. But there could be no mistake; the question that he had raised with such trepidation had been answered.

Ilyaya Kimi was now in her eighties and infirm, but her mind—barring her eccentricities and a tendency to fits of petulance—was as sharp as ever. Receiving the High Initiate's message, she had seen immediately the danger inherent in spreading the news of Tarod's escape—although she agreed wholeheartedly with Keridil's belief that the truth couldn't be withheld. Briefly, and with an insight that made him shiver, she outlined her view of the hysteria that could take hold throughout the provinces once the alarm had been raised. Chaos was every man and woman's ancestral nightmare, a legacy from a past that, though long forgotten, refused to die. And there was, she stated, only one course of action that, in her view, the High Initiate must take.

Keridil let the hand holding the parchment fall to his side and rubbed at his eyes with the thumb and forefinger of the other. He wished to all the Gods that his father, Jehrek, were still alive. Jehrek had had the wisdom and judgment that sprang from years of experience, and his son desperately needed that wisdom now, to help him. *If only he hadn't died* . . . And something in Keridil's soul turned black as he remembered that it was Yandros, Lord of Chaos, who had taken the old man's life. . . .

"Keridil?" He had all but forgotten Sashka's presence in the room, and looked up with a start, as though a ghost had spoken. She was watching him, dark eyes wide, one hand reaching tentatively towards him.

"Keridil, what is it? What does she say?"

Jehrek was no longer here to help him . . . but Sashka would. And however wrong it might be to confide in anyone outside the Circle, however strongly the Council of Adepts might disapprove, Keridil needed to share this burden with her.

He took hold of her hand and said, quietly, "Sister Ilyaya Kimi has formally asked me to call the Conclave of Three."

Sashka stared at him, stunned. She understood, he knew; but now that the first words were out he had to speak the rest. "She asks me to inform the High Margrave, and to begin the preparations." He paused, then: "She confirms what I feared most, Sashka . . . that our only hope of defeating Chaos is to sail to the

shrine on the White Isle, and open the casket of
Aeoris."

The townsfolk who had gathered in the small square
fronting the justice house of Vilmado were too intent
on their own business to pay much attention to the
auburn-haired stranger who rode in on a shaggy,
unkempt pony with another trailing resentfully behind her. The afternoon was waning, the sun slanting
in a blood-ruby glow that cast long shadows, and an
irritable wind had risen from the northeast, biting
through clothing and reminding everyone that summer was still a long way off.

Cyllan halted beside a low, shambling row of roofed-
over market stalls and slid from the leading pony's
back, slapping its nose hard as it tried to bite her.
There seemed to be a meeting in progress in the
square; a man in official regalia stood on the steps of
the justice house, flanked by others wearing hastily-
assembled military garb and carrying an assortment
of weapons. The official was speaking to the crowd,
occasionally stretching out both hands in a calming
gesture as his restless listeners began to shout in
reply, but Cyllan was too far away to hear what was
being said. She turned to the first of the covered
market stalls, where a tall, thin woman stood arms
akimbo, frowning at the throng.

"What's to do?"

The stallholder stared down her long nose, her look
unfriendly. "Enough to disrupt my trade and send
me home with an empty pocket, that's what."

She didn't seem anxious to elaborate, so Cyllan
asked, "Is there an inn nearby that might have a
room free?"

"An inn?" The woman stared at her again, making
no secret of the fact that she was assessing the stranger
and contemptuous of what she saw. "Try the Two
Panniers. That's where drovers and their like usually

go." She nodded towards a narrow alley. "At the far end of that street."

Cyllan thanked her and led the surly ponies away. Dank shadows closed round her as she entered the alley, and the smells of the lane gutter mingled with the barely more appetizing odor of soured food. She found the Two Panniers easily enough—not prepossessing, but it fitted the image she now presented— and she tied the animals to a ring in the crumbling wall. Then, on the verge of stepping over the threshold, she paused as fear clutched at her stomach and made her queasy.

What if she were recognized? Two days had passed since her flight from Wathryn; chances were that the Circle's message concerning her escape had by now spread throughout the land, and the crowd at the justice house were even now being told of the servant of Chaos with a price on her head. She'd been safe enough on the road, encountering no one but the occasional band of drovers and one small tithe-caravan, but here in a town she was dangerously exposed. And if she should be suspected—

She checked the train of thought, sternly telling herself she was being foolish. She couldn't hope to avoid every town and hamlet on her journey south-ward; she *needed* to mingle with people if she was to hear any rumor of Tarod or clue to his whereabouts. Besides, she reminded herself, Keridil Toln's search was for a girl with long, pale blond hair, riding a well-bred grey gelding. An auburn-headed drover in charge of two surly ponies would merit no more than a single glance.

The thought gave her courage; but nonetheless her legs felt weak as she pushed open the rickety door of the Two Panniers and stepped inside.

The tavern-room was empty but for a gangling potboy, who looked up as she entered. His eyes took in a plain girl in a man's cut-down trousers, hide coat and riding boots, her red-brown hair twisted into a rough knot at her neck. She smiled tentatively; he grinned back.

"Avnoon."

Cyllan glanced round the room, took in the sluggish fire, the empty tables. There was a smell of food, thankfully more pleasant than the stinks outside. She approached the bar and said, "I'll have a mug of herb beer, and a platter of meats and bread if you have them."

The potboy nodded. "Got plenty. Twill be crowded when that there meeting's done in the square." He was still looking at her and her skin began to crawl—until she realized that his scrutiny was hopeful rather than suspicious. He grinned again. "Got some fresh spiceroots, too; new harvest. I can get you a plate of 'em to go with the meats."

"Yes—thank you."

He hurried round to usher her to a table near the fire; then, remembering his master's constant exhortations, his face clouded. "You got the money?" he asked. "Innkeeper says I can't serve no one without the money. Quarter-gravine."

Cyllan felt in her belt-pouch and pulled out a coin. The lad took it, bit it, then nodded his satisfaction. "I'll fetch your order."

As he loped away, Cyllan leaned her head back against the rough wall and closed her eyes, letting the fire's small but welcome warmth suffuse through her. So far, so good—she was safe to rest awhile and ease her hunger. And, for a time at least, this new disguise would serve her.

The drover-band with whom she'd bartered to exchange the Margrave's gelding for some old clothes, two broken-down ponies, and ten gravines in coin had asked no questions, content to spit and close palms on the deal. Cyllan knew she'd sold the horse for under half its value; the ponies were all but worthless, and the gelding would fetch a good forty or fifty gravines from the right buyer. But the fact that the bargain had been so much to their advantage would ensure the drovers' silence. Her uncle had conducted enough shady business in his time for Cyllan to know the ways of drovers all too well; there'd be no danger there. She'd bought the hide coat and boots from a travelling clothman, and had completed her disguise in the woods the following morning when she stripped the young, copper-brown bark from a bellflower bush, pulped it in the water of a small pool, and, gasping at the cold shock, washed her hair thoroughly with the mixture to stain it auburn. The coloration wasn't permanent; she'd have to hide her hair from the rain and the bark's effects would wear off within a week or so, but until then it would suffice.

She'd made good progress thus far—barring her close brush with disaster in Wathryn—but she knew that as she advanced farther into the well-populated south the journey would become ever more dangerous. She was now, as far as she could tell, in the borderlands between Chaun and Prospect provinces, and the land was becoming kinder; flat, arable country crossed by major drove-roads, but without the dense forests of the north to provide concealment. Last night she'd camped on open ground beside a tributary of one of the great western rivers, only summoning the courage to light a fire when the night became too cold to endure without; during the previous day she'd widely skirted two hamlets, and had forced herself to ride into Vilmado this afternoon simply because to avoid it would have meant a wide and difficult detour. And the farther south she rode, the more towns she encountered, the greater the risk of being captured. She *had* to find Tarod—but she'd heard no word of him, and still had no idea where in all the world he might be.

Last night, warmed by her fire but unable to sleep

through fear of being caught unawares by brigands
or even a local farmer, she'd tried to use her own
simple form of geomancy to make contact with Tarod.
But without her precious bag of stones the attempt
was a failure, and even with the pebbles Cyllan
doubted if she would have fared any better. She
didn't have the skill for such a task, and now even
her hope that Tarod would use his own powers to
find her was waning. If he had tried—if he was *capable*
of trying—then she hadn't the psychic wit to hear
him.

At last she had taken the Chaos stone from its
hiding place and looked at it in the flickering glow,
turning it over and over in her hands and feeling it
pulse as though it had a life of its own. Gazing into
its multifaceted depths, she'd imagined that it became an eye staring back at her, and that beyond the
eye she could glimpse an echo of Yandros's smile
. . . or Tarod's. But the illusion lasted only a moment, and after that the stone was dull again. Later,
as dawn broke, she had roused from an uneasy doze
thinking she heard the faraway high, elemental scream
that heralded the coming of a Warp—but that, too,
was an illusion. Yet, she told herself, if Yandros *was*
trying to aid her in her search, he would surely—

Her thoughts were interrupted by the potboy's return. He placed two plates and a brimming mug on
the table before her, then hovered, shifting from one
foot to the other and clearly hoping to strike up a
conversation. Well, she could lose nothing by talking,
Cyllan thought; taverns like this were the source of a
good deal of well-informed gossip, and potboys renowned for their willingness to repeat what they'd
heard to anyone prepared to listen. But before she
could speak an encouraging word, the sound of feet
tramping down the alley outside drew their attention. There was a rumble of rough voices. A pony—
probably one of her own—squealed, then the door

burst open and a dozen or so men came in, with a few women following behind.

The man who headed the group—short but brawny, and sweating despite the east wind—stopped and glowered at the potboy.

"There's two ponies tethered outside. What did I tell you about letting any dirty ragtag use my hitching ring without so much as a by-your-leave?"

The potboy flushed scarlet and jerked a thumb at Cyllan, though he was too mortified to speak. The innkeeper stared at the girl, whom he hadn't noticed before, then grunted. "Yours, are they?"

"Mine." Cyllan had met too many belligerent tavern-owners in her time to be cowed by the man's manner. She smiled without humor. "And I've paid for my food."

The innkeeper grunted again, a tacit acceptance and as near to an apology as she'd get from him. The potboy said, "Shall I draw you some beer, master?"

"No." The innkeeper glowered at him. "You're to get along to the justice house. They want every able-bodied man or lad who wasn't at the meeting, and they want 'em now. I'd say you count as able-bodied, even if you're not able-brained."

One of the women—around Cyllan's age but black-haired, her mouth painted crimson and her arms festooned with cheap bracelets—laughed shrilly, and the potboy flushed again. "At—at the justice house? Now?"

"Now! You're not deaf as well as stupid, are you? Go on; move those spindle shanks!"

The lad bolted, and the moment he was out of the door one of the men slammed and bolted it behind him, then, to Cyllan's surprise, quickly made a sign against evil. The innkeeper's wife, meanwhile, had hastened behind the counter, but instead of drawing ale for the company she was rummaging in a store-cupboard.

"Here," she said, emerging at last with something in her hands. "Hang this at the door, Cappik."

Her husband stared at her. "Don't be ridiculous, woman!"

"No, no; let her be, Cappik. Can't do any harm, after all, can it?" another of the men argued.

With a shrug the innkeeper gave way, and the woman hung what she carried on the bar of the door. Cyllan recognized it as a charm-necklace—a crudely fashioned string of small beads, with tiny scrolls of paper tied at intervals into the string. Her grandmother in the Eastern Flatlands had had one, though they were rare now; each scroll had written on it a prayer to Aeoris, and the necklace was intended as a powerful amulet against demonic forces.

As the woman looped the necklace over the door-bar, the atmosphere in the tavern-room underwent a change, as though her small gesture had brought into focus something which no one had previously been willing to admit or face. Tension flowered from nowhere and became palpable; the men stared silently at the slowly swinging necklace, and Cyllan's psychic senses instantly picked up the cold taint of fear. She said nothing, merely continued eating, while the landlord's wife poured ale for the men with a good deal of unnecessary noise and bustle. The sounds were intrusive against the quiet backdrop; even the brash girl had fallen silent. Finally mugs were passed around, and the beer seemed to revive flagging spirits, for talk broke out again though it was low-pitched and desultory. Cyllan tried to concentrate on what was being said, but could only catch the occasional word—until a footfall by her table made her look up, and she saw the innkeeper standing over her.

He grunted by way of preamble, then said, "Just came in today, did you?"

Cyllan nodded. "No more than an hour ago." Her

pulse quickened, but she gave no outward sign of her unease.

"It'll be dark in a couple of hours. Where do you mean to go tonight?"

She couldn't fathom the reason for such searching questions, and his manner was making her nervous. She shrugged. "I was planning to ask if you had a room unoccupied."

To her surprise, a look of relief spread across the landlord's face, and he hitched his stomach up over his stressed breeches. "We have, and if you can pay you're welcome." Without waiting for an invitation, he sat down opposite her. "I wouldn't advise anyone to take to the roads after dark, not now." He paused, his shrewd grey eyes assessing her. "You're a drover?"

Cyllan had carefully prepared her story before she rode into the town, and she nodded again. "I'm heading to Southern Chaun to meet up with my cousin's band."

"Easterner, aren't you?"

"Yes. From the flatlands." There could be no harm in admitting the truth; half the drovers in the world came from that province or its northern neighbor.

"Thought so. Knew the accent; we get a lot of 'em through here. Where've you been trading?"

"Wishet," Cyllan lied. "I had a dozen good blood mares to deliver in Port Summer." She grinned. "I could have done with one of them left over to take me westward, instead of those two spavined nags outside."

The innkeeper guffawed, and she knew that that small embellishment had allayed any lingering suspicions he might have had. It was disconcerting to realize how easily she could slip back into the mannerisms of her old way of life, and she reflected wryly that, despite Tarod's influence, she was still a peasant-drover at heart; the role fitted her like a well-worn glove.

The innkeeper's laughter faded abruptly and he wiped his mouth with the back of his hand. "Wherever you're bound, you'll be travelling by day and keeping to the main drove-roads if you've got a half-gravine of sense."

Cyllan was suddenly alert. "Will I? Why?"

"You haven't heard what's afoot?"

She shook her head, and the man grunted, beginning to sweat again. He was clearly embarrassed at admitting to caring a whit for a stranger's welfare, but the fear that lurked poorly hidden behind his eyes drove him to be more forthcoming than his nature dictated.

"No," he said. "Maybe if you've ridden from Wishet the story hasn't reached there yet. . . ." He leaned forward across the table, pitching his voice low, and abruptly the fear in his look blossomed into a real and immediate emotion. "Word's come from the far north—from the High Initiate of the Circle himself." He made the Sign of Aeoris over his heart, and Cyllan had the wit to do the same. "Two people—if you can call 'em human—have escaped from the Circle's justice, and the whole land's going to be in a ferment till they're found."

"Why?" Cyllan asked. "What have they done?"

The landlord licked his lips uneasily. "Murder, sorcery, demonology—but that's only the beginning. It isn't so much what they've done as what they *are*." He glanced towards the door with the charm-necklace hanging bizarrely on it, then added, making the Sign of Aeoris again, *"Servants of Chaos."*

The words were spoken from the corner of his mouth, as though he was terrified of being overheard by some supernatural agency. Cyllan opened her eyes wide and hoped that her expression of shock was convincing. *"Chaos?"* she repeated in a whisper. "But surely it doesn't exist any more?"

"So we all thought. But the word comes from the

High Initiate himself. And while these evil-doers are at large, we're all in danger." He shuddered, leaning back and giving her a stern, appraising look. "I wouldn't be a drover travelling the roads with those fiends loose in the land. Not for all the wine in Southern Chaun!"

"Hey, Cappik! What're you doing, keeping your guest to yourself and away from decent company?" A tall, swarthy man loomed at the table and shouldered the landlord aside to sit down, giving Cyllan a gap-toothed grin as he did so. He raised his mug to gesture at her. "I reckon that's what we all need tonight. Decent company."

One by one the others were gathering round, gravitating towards the fire. The landlord's wife added new logs; they arranged themselves at nearby tables, the women finding room where they could, and Cyllan was soon the center of a good deal of attention. There was no danger in their interest; it was merely the natural, idle curiosity felt towards any stranger and a chance to divert their minds from less pleasant thoughts. Tongues loosened as darkness fell and more beer was drunk, and the men began to speculate on the news from the north and what it might mean. Cyllan listened whilst saying little, and although the talk became wilder and more exaggerated as the ale took effect, she knew that much of her companions' carelessly professed courage was pure bravado; the fear engendered in them, and in the whole town, by the news from the north was real and deep-rooted.

It was late when she finally climbed the rickety ladder of steps that led to the inn's upper floor. Downstairs, a few of the bolder drinkers had defied their terrors to stumble home through the dark, but most had made themselves as comfortable as they could around the fire, and the Two Panniers was bolted and barred for the night.

Her bed was narrow, hard, and not particularly

clean; but after two nights in the open she was thankful for it. Blowing out the candle and pulling the thin blanket up around herself, she thought over what she had heard tonight.

Tarod was alive. The message from the Star Peninsula had banished her doubts, and she held the knowledge to her like a precious secret. While he lived and was free, she had hope ... but the High Initiate's decree left her in no doubt that the entire land would be in a furor searching for him, and for her. And the word that the two fugitives were servants of Chaos added a deadly element. Fear had been a tangible companion in the tavern-room tonight; once word spread, that fear would grow like a brush fire in high summer.

But, for a short while at least, she was safe from discovery. Tomorrow she would move on southward, and with luck and the gods—she refused to consider *which* gods—on her side, she might learn more on her journey that would help her to find Tarod.

Cyllan settled herself more comfortably in the narrow bed. The soul-stone lay hard but warm against her skin; she slipped one hand into her shirt and let her fingers close round the stone's hard contours as she fell asleep.

Chapter 4

Tarod's horse pranced restlessly beside the last of the five timber wagons that rolled slowly along the main drove-road from Han towards Wishet Province. At his side the unfamiliar weight of a heavy sword slapped irritatingly against his leg, and he wished he could be rid of the thing, and rid of the toiling caravan, which for two days now had kept him to a snail's pace. Alone, he could travel light and fast— but he had given his word to the elders of Hannik town, and to break it now would attract suspicion that he could well do without.

Two nights ago he had slept in Hannik at an inn almost in the shadow of the Province Margrave's residence, drawn there by a drover's story that the "Chaos Lord's accomplice" had been apprehended in the town. Arriving, he had found Hannik in an uproar that centered around a fair-haired girl caught trying to ply her meager talents as a fortune-teller, and the small tricks Tarod had used to disguise himself had unwittingly led him into the furor. The gold Initiate's badge—taken from the body of a man he had killed in the Castle—and an ability to shift, subtly, the image he presented, gave him the perfect identity at a time when no one would think twice about encountering a Circle Adept on an urgent journey. The town elders had seen the arrival of an Initiate in their midst as a gift from the gods, and had asked Tarod to preside over the girl's trial.

The bitter disappointment he had felt when he finally set eyes on the terrified horse-breeder's daughter from Empty Province was still like a knife driving between his ribs when he recalled it. Her cell—a room in the justice house—was hung about with charms and amulets and hex symbols, while the girl crouched sobbing and protesting her innocence in a corner. The appearance of an Adept of the Circle had sent her into a paroxysm of terror, and she flung herself at Tarod's feet, begging for salvation and absolution. Savagely, Tarod turned on the elders and berated them for fools in thinking that such a near-simpleton could possibly be the Circle's fugitive. They apologized profusely whilst at the same time trying to justify their caution, and at last, remembering his assumed role, Tarod acknowledged that they had been right to follow the High Initiate's exhortation and take no chances. The girl was released, and the elders begged Tarod to accompany the five wagons that were due to set out in the morning, insisting that an Initiate's presence in their midst would be a guarantee of safety as well as boosting the morale of the hastily-assembled militiamen who were to guard the train on its journey.

"After all, sir," said the senior elder, an unctuous man to whom Tarod had taken an immediate dislike, "no minion of evil"—he carefully avoided using the word *Chaos*—"would dare to make any move against a caravan in which an Adept rode."

Tarod smiled thinly. "What makes you think these fugitives would think of such an act? Their purpose is to avoid capture, not court it."

The elder bristled. "Even demon-worshippers must

eat, sir! Wealthy men travel with this convoy; merchants, ship-owners. With such an evil loose in the land, we can take no risks, as I'm sure your High Initiate would agree."

Keridil doubtless would. . . . Aware that he'd only arouse the old man's suspicions by arguing further, Tarod made a careless gesture. "Very well. I'll ride with the caravan until our paths diverge."

And so for two days he had accompanied the lumbering wagons and their escort, struggling to check both his mount's impatience and his own. They had encountered few other people save for a group of militiamen from another town, but nonetheless tension among the travellers was rife, and increasing with every mile they covered. By now the messenger-birds from the Castle had completed their work, and there wasn't a settlement of any size in the remotest province that hadn't heard the news of the fugitives' escape. In Hannik, Tarod had seen a copy of Keridil's proclamation, and its content had surprised and disturbed him. The High Initiate warned that the minions of Chaos were abroad and must be apprehended at all costs, before they could achieve their evil and deadly aim—to unleash the forces of pandemonium throughout the land.

He hadn't believed Keridil could be so implacable in his hatred, or so blind. The High Initiate knew—indeed, had known even before his first betrayal of their old friendship—that Tarod owed no fealty to Chaos; yet he was prepared to twist the truth in any way that suited the purpose of recapturing his enemy. And already Tarod was seeing for himself the results of Keridil's action. His warning had struck home to the countryfolk, stirring every deep-rooted superstition, every ancestral memory, every formless fear in their minds; and, like dry tinder, that fear was catching fire so fast that Tarod doubted the ability of any power in the world to stem it. Hannik had been just a beginning—how many more innocents like the horse-breeder's daughter would fall victim to the terror-inspired persecution of their own kind?

A sharp, atavistic shiver ran along his spine at that thought, as, involuntarily, his mind dredged up an old memory. That particular wound had healed during his years at the Star Peninsula, but now he could recall the macabre event as clearly as if it were happening all over again. Himself as a twelve-year-old child, standing bewildered and horrified in the midst of a screaming mob, while the shattered body of his cousin lay at his feet, killed by a monstrous power which he hadn't dreamed any human being could possess.

It was only a game. . . . He could almost hear his own childish voice protesting in terror as the mob closed in. Council elders, sober merchants and tradesmen, other boys' mothers, all wielding stones and baying for his death . . . yes; he knew how the horse-breeder's daughter must have felt. Keridil, wittingly or not, had opened the floodgates to a deadly tide.

A commotion near the head of the caravan drew him suddenly back to the real world. The second timber wagon was stopping, forcing those behind it to a grinding, protesting halt, and over the creak and squeal of the carts and the neighing of horses he could hear men shouting. A young and inexperienced militia guard cast Tarod a look of helpless appeal whilst struggling to control his own unreliable mount. Tarod sighed. In every matter, from the largest to the smallest, the caravan's escort turned to him for authority and guidance, and their ineptitude was beginning to wear on his patience. He signaled to the young guard to fall in behind him, and spurred his horse towards the head of the convoy.

". . . and I saw it as plain as the nose on your face! You were—"

"Take back that insinuation, or by Aerois, I'll—"

The wind flung snatches of the furious altercation past his ears as he approached, and he saw that the driver of the second wagon was quarreling with a merchant who rode beside his cart, both deaf to the hesitant entreaties of the escort leader as he attempted to intervene. Tarod's voice cut icily through the conflict.

"What's the meaning of this?"

The wagon driver swung round in his seat, one arm gesturing wildly at the merchant, and as he did so Tarod noticed the intricate charm-necklace he wore. "Treachery!" The driver's voice was shrill with hysteria. "This man, claiming to be a merchant—he's one of *them!*"

The merchant opened his mouth to make a furious rebuttal, but before he could utter a sound Tarod snapped, "Be silent!" The man's jaw worked apoplectically and Tarod added, "I can't pay attention to both of you at once! You'll have your chance to speak—for now, I'll hear the wagoner."

Gaining confidence, the driver began again. "We've a spy in our midst, Adept, I'm sure of it—a *Chaos* spy!" He made the Sign of Aeoris hastily before his own face. "Not two minutes since, I saw him take something from his pouch—he held it up to his face, and he murmured to it, and then he *kissed* it. It was a stone, a jewel—the High Initiate himself says that the Chaos fiend carries his soul in a jewel, and that it's a deadly gem. Sir, there's something evil about this—I sense it; I *smell* it! If these escaped demons can assume disguises, then surely—"

His voice tailed off as Tarod treated him to a searing look. The merchant was beginning to protest again, and Tarod touched light heels to his horse's flanks, guiding it closer to the man. "Your friend seems to believe he has a genuine reason for suspicion. What do you have to say?"

The merchant snorted. "The fool's drunk too much ale! He's been swigging from that skin beside him since we set out—"

"Then what he claims to have seen was pure imagination?" Tarod's tone was a challenge.

The man's face reddened. "Well . . ."

"I'll ask a simple question, and I anticipate a clear answer. Did he or did he not imagine that he saw you making some ritual obeisance to a jewel?"

In his heart, Tarod cared not one whit for the rights and wrongs of the argument; he'd have been content to allow the two to resolve their squabble as best they could. But he had to remind himself that he was posing as a genuine Adept of the Circle; with Keridil's exhortations fresh in everyone's minds, not to show a lively interest was unthinkable.

The merchant turned redder still and mumbled something that was muffled by his cloak collar. Tarod's eyes grew dangerous.

"I'm waiting for your answer, merchant."

Slowly, and with great reluctance, the man reached into his belt-pouch and drew out something that he seemed loath to display. But at last his clenched fingers opened, and Tarod saw a small and irregularly shaped piece of quartz lying in his palm. He reached out, took it without a word, and held it up to examine it.

Someone had, at some time, taken a crude stone-cutting chisel to the quartz's uneven surface. Carved into it, ragged but just recognizable, was a familiar symbol—a circle, or what passed for one, bisected by a jagged line; and an attempt had been made to mark the symbol's outlines with some form of dye which was now all but worn away. It was nothing more than a good-luck charm, no doubt purchased at a usurer's price from some scrofulous charlatan at a Quarter-Day fair.

Tarod let his fingers close round the quartz, and smiled humorlessly at the merchant, whose cheeks were by now afire with guilty embarrassment. "I don't believe," he said evenly, "that we have a servant of Chaos in our midst. More likely, we have a gullible and superstitious fool who has spent too much time listening to the blandishments of itinerant tricksters!" He opened his hand again. "What did the seller of this bauble tell you? That it was imbued with the energies of the gods themselves, that it would protect you against every ghoul and demon a man's imagination can conjure?" Turning in his saddle he held the quartz out towards the wagon driver. "There's your Chaos stone—as crude a piece of trumpery as it's ever been my misfortune to see!" His gaze rested pointedly on the charm-necklace dangling on the driver's jerkin, and the man had the good grace to blush almost as deeply as the merchant. Tarod waited until he was sure the wagoner had understood the significance of the symbol cut into the crystal's surface, then he raised his arm and flung the stone as far from the road as he could.

"The Circle doesn't look kindly on charlatans who profane the sacred for their own profit," he said crisply. "And it has little more time for fools who are duped by such tricks." The merchant was watching him, half abashed and half resentful; Tarod stared him down and he dropped his gaze. "Under the circumstances I've some sympathy for you—these aren't easy times. But I'll warn you now, both of you—I want to hear no more wild accusations, and I want to see no more acts of childish superstition!" He turned to the wagoner, who was slowly removing his own charm-necklace. "This pathetic affray has already delayed us. I'd strongly suggest that no more is said on the matter!"

Without waiting for either man to reply he turned his horse and rode back to the rear of the caravan, followed by the young militiaman, who throughout the exchange had said nothing but who now watched him in mute admiration. Slowly, the lead wagon began to move and the others followed; as the creaking convoy got under way once more Tarod settled his horse to a slow, long-striding walk, and lapsed into uncomfortable thought.

He might well have been wrong to pour scorn on the two protagonists and their superstitions. After all, if their amulets gave them comfort what harm could they do? But he had sensed something far darker underlying the altercation; something that echoed the unhappy affair in Hannik. Fear had seeded suspicion, and that suspicion was flowering rapidly into hysteria. If a simple and pitiable belief in good-luck charms could lead to accusations of being in league with Chaos, how long would it be before any act, any word, any gesture would be interpreted as a sign of evil intent?

Perhaps, he told himself, his thoughts ran too fast and too far. But the hope was quickly followed by a realization that his instincts were right. In all his years as an Initiate he had rarely travelled beyond the Star Peninsula; he had grown used to living in a community that understood the nature of superstition and had largely risen above it. But in the outside world matters were very different. To these people Adepts were hardly lower than gods in their own right, and the Castle a place to be revered and dreaded. Little wonder that they were responding to the High Initiate's message like children frightened by a fireside tale. . . .

Did Keridil realize, he wondered, that with his talk of demons he was in danger of releasing a far greater evil than anything Yandros had thus far manifested? Or did he consider the price worth paying, for the sake of exacting revenge? That thought was chilling, for it hinted at aspects to the High Initiate's character which, even prejudiced as he was, Tarod wouldn't have attributed to him.

He glanced speculatively at the sky, which once again was threatening rain. The weather, though dismal, had been oddly calm thus far on his journey—almost *too* calm. No storms, no Warps; nothing that suggested the untoward influence that Yandros might be capable of asserting should he choose to. It was as though some other agency were at work, blocking anything the Chaos Lord might do to disrupt the world, and he wondered what other, more arcane wheels the Circle might have set in motion in their search for him. Doubtless they'd use all their occult skills to call on the power of Aeoris to aid them—but could they truly claim the gods' sanction for the soul-eating fear that was spreading like a disease as a result of their work?

Except for a few dark moments, Tarod had never questioned his loyalty to the Lords of Order; but now a worm of doubt was moving within him. The truth had yet to be put to the test—but if Aeoris and His brethren meant to leave the world to the mercies of their self-appointed servants whilst doing nothing to stem this growing peril, then, somewhere, Yandros must be laughing.

He recalled the tear-blotched face of the terrified girl in Hannik. She had been one of the first victims, but there'd be many more to follow in her wake. The nightmare, every instinct told him, was only just beginning. . . .

The heavy rains of recent days had largely avoided Southern Chaun Province in the far southwest, and so the timber and thatch of the farmhouse was dry enough to make a spectacular blaze. Dense, oily smoke roiled up from the roof; the old vine that rambled over the walls shrivelled and crackled and writhed into twisting, dying snakes; and already the brilliant glare of fire was leaping in every window.

Beyond the house the two barns were also beginning to catch, and in the distance, on the well-tended fields, men moved like phantoms in rising clouds of smoke as they set torches to the young crops.

With a roar and a sudden towering eruption of flame the roof of the farmhouse caved in, and against the noise of the inferno a woman screamed in desperate but helpless protest. The smallholder's wife knelt in the yard, trying to gather her three young children into her arms whilst an older woman in the white, now smoke-grimed robe of a Sister of Aeoris wrestled her back. A few paces away her husband sprawled in the dust. He had tried to prevent this insanity, but a blazing brand across the face had put a stop to his protests, blinded him in one eye, and left him with a scar he'd carry for the rest of his life.

And, at a safe distance from the injured farmer and his hysterical family, a group of sober smallholders and minor local dignitaries watched the destruction with gloomy satisfaction. A very regrettable necessity, they agreed, but a necessity nonetheless. The herder lad who had reported the strange ritual he'd seen his master performing at sunset last night had acted well; loyalty, however commendable, had to take second place to the necessity of exposing a servant of Chaos in their midst. . . .

The house, and the lifetime's possessions it contained, burned; and at last the spectacle was over and the farmer's wife's cries had subsided to deep, racking sobs. The self-appointed head of the deputation walked slowly across to where the white-robed Sister stood, and looked down at the landswoman with a mixture of pity and disgust.

"We shall, of course, have to make some provision for the children," he said.

The Sister's eyes were hard. "My main fear, Elder, is that they may have been tainted with their father's sin. I think it would be for the best if they were housed at my Cot for the forseeable future. That way, we can ensure that any sign of corruption is eradicated before it can take hold."

"Indeed . . . indeed." The elder sighed. "Such an unfortunate occurrence . . . do you know, Sister, the man still protests his innocence? He claims that he was mixing a potion—something handed down by his grandmother, a devout woman, he insists—with which he meant to protect his family *against* evil."

She smiled, but there was no amusement in it. "With due respect, Elder, if you know your catechisms you'll also know that lies and trickery are the hallmark of Chaos. Of course it's possible that the man was speaking the truth—but would you have been prepared to take that risk?"

"No . . ." the elder looked across the yard at the smoldering skeleton of the house. "No. I would not."

The Sister turned and leaned down to grasp the sobbing woman's cloak-collar. "Come; get up!" Over her shoulder she called to another, younger Sister who hovered in the background. "Sister Mavan, kindly get the children into the cart. The girl seems attached to that toy weaving-loom she's clutching—she may keep it, if it will ensure her good behavior."

The farmer's wife stared at the Sister with mute and bitter hatred, but she was too emotionally exhausted to protest as the children were shepherded away.

"You should consider yourself fortunate," the Sister told her coldly. "In many other provinces, your children would have been turned out with you, to fend for themselves. You should give thanks to Aeoris that here we live under the kindly grace of the Matriarch herself, and that she is the soul of clemency!"

The woman didn't answer, and the Sister gazed

down at her with a sudden rush of contempt and suspicion. "What, aren't you repentant even now? You have your life—what would your thrice-damned gods of Chaos have given you in return for your service?"

"We have never—" the woman began savagely; then, seeing the Sister's steel-cold eyes, she fell silent once more.

"You'll learn a lesson from this day," the Sister told her relentlessly. "You'll learn the foolishness and the futility of *daring* to turn against the laws of the gods! And as you and your husband wander the roads, destitute as you deserve to be, perhaps you'll reflect on Aeoris's mercy, and pray to Him for forgiveness—if you value your souls!"

She shivered at the thought of the disaster that might have resulted had not this serpent in their midst been uncovered in time. The High Initiate's message had warned of the deadly power loose in the land; warned of their enemies' cunning, and exhorted the Sisters to be vigilant for any signs of Chaos's insidious influence. And if the dark powers could infiltrate one of their own kind to pose for years as an Initiate of the Circle, Aeoris alone knew what deviltry they might wreak on the malleable minds of countryfolk such as these. She remembered that black-haired demon they sought; she had seen him at the Castle when she went as part of the Matriarch's deposition to Keridil Toln's inauguration ceremony, and the thought that even the Circle had been duped by him was chilling. For that reason alone she was determined not to relax her vigilance for a single moment in pursuit of evildoers. One bad fruit could corrupt an entire harvest. It was her holy duty to see to it that such bad fruits had no chance to infect others with their rot, and she was satisfied that, thus far, she had acquitted herself well.

*   *   *

In Wishet Province, five women awaited trial on charges of witchcraft. They had been attempting to sell charms at the Port Summer market; and whereas in previous seasons they would either have been driven out of the town or, more likely, tolerantly ignored, now they languished in the justice house with the chilling knowledge that their fate would be far less pleasant.

In West High Land, bad weather in the Western Sound kept the fishing fleet confined to the perilous cliff-harbors of Fanaan Bay. Lady Kael Amion, Senior of the largest Sisterhood Cot in the province, received word that the fishermen blamed their misfortune on the machinations of Chaos, and wasn't inclined to disagree with them. And when scapegoats were sought, and found, she did nothing to intervene. Aeoris chose to punish transgressors in His own way—if one or two innocents suffered along with the guilty, then perhaps the lesson would be learned all the better. Hearing that seven people had been put naked into a wicker cage, their bodies daubed with hex signs, and the cage dropped into the deep sea beyond the bay's shelter, she made no comment but simply retired to her chambers and prayed for their souls.

In Empty Province, a miner gave shelter to a merchant whose horse had cast a shoe on the southwestern road, offering him a bed for the night and an adequate if crude meal. He was later accused of harboring a servant of Chaos, and when the merchant—whose hair happened to be black, as several witnesses testified—couldn't be traced, the charge was considered proven. There had been no executions in the area for a generation, but there was no shortage of suitably sized rocks among the waste heaps of the mineral-mines, when the hastily convicted man was stoned to death.

And in the Great Eastern Flatlands, which felt the

sting of having spawned the Chaos-demon's accomplice, no man dared speak a careless word to his neighbor lest that word be enough to damn him. The few stone-readers who still kept up the ancient tradition closed their doors overnight—though one or two were still found and dealt summary justice, with their town elders none the wiser. The fleet refused to venture out into Whiteshoals Sound until every sail on every boat had been painted with charms, and complex symbols were daubed on doors and shutters throughout the province. Hysteria mounted; every fair-haired girl and black-haired man went in constant fear of arrest, and the Margrave, his resources stretched to breaking point, proclaimed a curfew.

Somewhere, Tarod thought, *Yandros must be laughing.* . . .

Four days after departing Vilmado, Cyllan had picked up the main drove-road that ran southeast from Prospect into Shu Province. Thankfully, the journey had thus far been uneventful; one of her ponies had cast a shoe, but a farrier at a hamlet a couple of miles off the road had replaced it, and had also been ready to spread the latest gossip concerning the fugitives.

Rumor, it seemed, was piling upon rumor. Tarod had been reported captured in two different provinces, herself in three, and there were numerous reports of their having been seen together. There were also tales of a disastrous spring crop failure in Han, flooding in Wishet and a monstrous Warp that had swept down through West High Land, Chaun, and Southern Chaun, claiming fifty lives—all signs, the farrier insisted, that the dark powers were using their servants to wreak havoc among the godly followers of Aeoris.

Cyllan gazed about the forge's interior, where every nook and cranny was festooned with amulets and daubed with holy symbols, and she shivered despite the heat of the fire. Everyone she had passed on the road, or encountered in towns and hamlets, had displayed some charm against evil, and encounters with any strangers had been rife with tension and suspicion. Even the loquacious farrier had been unwilling to take her commission at first, and only a good deal of persuasion on Cyllan's part had convinced him that she was harmless. Matters, she realized, were rapidly getting out of hand—people were being arrested as sympathizers with Chaos on the flimsiest of hearsay; old spites were finding outlets in wild accusations of witchcraft and demonology; no one could trust his neighbor or even his own family not to turn against him. In every settlement men were forming into hasty militia forces and taking the law into their own hands, and it was only thanks to good luck and an occasional measure of guile that Cyllan had avoided the zealous search for supposed evildoers.

She'd taken the precaution of buying a charm-necklace which she wore around her throat to avoid drawing attention to herself, but it did little to allay the creeping unease that was now a constant companion. The sickness of fear that was tainting the world had taken its toll on her, too, and hand in hand with it went her rapidly diminishing hope of ever finding Tarod before the Circle found her. She couldn't, she knew, evade them forever, and even if the Circle might eventually be ready to abandon the hunt for Tarod's paramour, they would never cease to search for Drachea Rannak's murderer.

Cyllan shuddered and tried to put the disquieting thoughts out of her mind and concentrate on the road. A little way ahead she could see a small cairn of stones, newly built, at the side of the track, and around this makeshift shrine travellers had piled offerings—small treasures, items of food, trinkets and colored scarves—as a plea to Aeoris for protection on the road. She had seen several such shrines during the past few days, and as she drew level with the cairn she wondered if she too might leave something, a coin perhaps, just as a token. . . .

The wind strengthened unexpectedly, a sharp, soughing gust from the north that bit through her coat and brought gooseflesh to her arms, and in its cold whine she imagined she heard an unhuman laugh. The Chaos stone, hidden beneath her shirt, pulsed suddenly hot against her skin as though in warning, and her pony shied at the cairn.

Sweat broke out on Cyllan's face and neck as she calmed the animal and edged it past the shrine. The gusting wind *might* have been coincidence—but it had followed so instantaneously on the heels of her thought that she doubted it. And that laugh—real or imagined, it had chilled her to the marrow, for it seemed to mock her for daring to think that she might appeal to Aeoris for protection.

She looked up at the dull, pewter-grey sky, then over her shoulder at the road behind her. An image was in her mind, called back from that day in Shu-Nhadek when the Warp had struck. She had seen a figure, a phantasm, beckoning to her from the far end of a noisome alley as the storm screamed in from the north; she remembered the brazen hair, the graceful but deadly hand summoning her, the star that burned at the phantom's heart . . . and she half expected to relive that nightmare now as she turned her head.

But the road was deserted. . . .

The ponies had quieted as the cairn with its offerings fell behind. Cyllan pulled the collar of her coat more closely around her cold cheeks, and dug her heels into her unwilling mount's flanks to urge it onward.

Chapter 5

The sun had just passed meridian on the following day when Cyllan saw the outlines of a large town ahead. She halted her ponies, staring at the distant rooftops and wondering whether or not to attempt to skirt the place. This part of Prospect Province was vaguely familiar to her—she had travelled this way several times with her uncle's drovers—and, if memory served her correctly, there was little alternative to riding through the town. Farmland stretched away to either side, and with newly-planted crops growing in their fields the holders hereabouts wouldn't take kindly to a stranger trampling across their lands when there was a good road to be followed. Fortune had accompanied her so far; she must trust to it again and face the town.

She heard the tolling of the bell when she was still a half mile out, carried on a light breeze which had backed into the southeast overnight, and the sound of it made her apprehensive. Every town worthy of the name boasted at least one great bell, usually sited in a tower atop the justice house, but it was only rung to signify an event of considerable importance. Something was afoot here, and Cyllan had no wish to become embroiled in it.

Carefully she surveyed the land to either side of the road, but there was no sign of a track through the fields. Very well; it seemed she had no option but to continue. At least the townsfolk would be less inclined to trouble a stranger if they had matters of their own to concern them. . . .

The town boundaries were marked by a humpbacked stone bridge spanning a small but busily chuckling river tributary, and the two men who guarded the bridge turned their heads at the sound of approaching hooves. They had been craning towards the town, clearly anxious to find out what was to do, and Cyllan reined in as she drew level with them.

"State your name, and your business," one of the guards demanded.

"Themila Avray, drover, from West High Land." Cyllan had used the alias before, inventing the clan name and adopting the given name of a woman who, Tarod had told her, had once been his dearest friend and mentor at the Castle. "I'm bound for Shu-Nhadek, to meet my cousin at the Quarter-Day fair."

The guard's narrow eyes took in her auburn hair, her clothing, the charm-necklace on her breast, and his expression relaxed slightly. "You'll be lucky if you can get through the town before the day's out," he told her.

The bell was still ringing, an urgent summons. "Why?" Cyllan asked.

"There's a trial to be held in the market-square." The guard grinned lopsidedly. "Rumor is, they've caught the Chaos-demon's accomplice."

"Caught—" Cyllan checked herself and swallowed, realizing that luck was, indeed, with her. She made a sign over her breast, knowing the man expected it. "*Aeoris . . .*"

The guard stood back and waved her on. "Best

hurry, if you want to see the fun." He grinned again. "I'm just hoping my relief'll turn up before it's all over!"

Cyllan thanked him, and urged her ponies on over the bridge.

Even before she reached the market-square, Cyllan's progress was hampered by the press of people who were converging from every direction, and any hopes she might have had of being able to ride through the town and leave it behind were quickly dampened. It seemed that the entire populace was turning out, summoned by the tolling bell, and by the time the square came in sight it was clear that, like it or not, she must stay until the trial was over.

The square was packed and the crowd spilling over into the neighboring streets, and only the fact that she was on horseback enabled Cyllan to reach an open space from where, provided she stayed in the saddle, she had a good view of the proceedings. The trial was to be conducted on the steps of the justice house, as the building's interior had proved inadequate to the event, and the officiators had already emerged and taken their places as she reined in, halted by the press of people.

An elderly man in black seated himself stiffly in a chair, flanked by a knot of town dignitaries and a uniformed militiaman whose task, apparently, was to read the charges brought against the prisoner. Searching among the group on the steps Cyllan saw, amid an armed guard, a blond-haired girl, her face drawn with terror, and the spectacle made her feel suddenly sick. The girl was even younger than she was and, whatever evidence might be trumped up against her, Cyllan knew she was innocent. But what defense could she possibly have against the superstitious dread of her peers?

Two years ago she had witnessed a trial, in a Wishet

Province town where she was trading with her uncle's drovers, and memory of that event gave Cyllan a small measure of hope for the girl. An Initiate had presided then, and the evidence of both sides had been heard with a reassuringly sober impartiality, the final verdict fair if not entirely popular. There was no Initiate to conduct matters today, but perhaps that was just as well—the Circle's anxiety to find the Chaos Lord's accomplice could prejudice the judgment of any Adept, however high his principles. Cyllan looked at the miserable girl again, and her lips moved in a silent prayer to any powers, Order or Chaos, who might be prevailed on to prevent a miscarriage of justice.

Her hopes, however, were short-lived. From the farthest edge of the square it was impossible to hear every word of the speeches, the accusations and the depositions, but it soon became clear that the assembled officials were determined to appease a crowd that hungered for blood. Every now and then a speaker was drowned out by a roar of outrage, and the prisoner's attempts to protest her innocence were met with the howls of a mob in full cry.

Cyllan felt sweat breaking out on her skin and trickling uncomfortably down her back, accompanied by an ugly sickness in the pit of her stomach. In the name of the Lords of Order, these good and pious people were condemning an innocent without any hope of redress. Witness after witness stepped up to give evidence, and though the girl shook her head frantically, and wept, and pleaded with her judges, the weight of opinion was in full spate against her. Quite what she had purportedly done Cyllan couldn't discern; and besides, the exact nature of her alleged crime hardly seemed to matter. She was young, her hair was blond and she was a stranger to the district— those three factors alone were sufficient to condemn her.

Although to Cyllan the proceedings seemed to take an eternity, in reality the trial was obscenely brief. Abruptly the bell in the justice house tower boomed out its sonorous message, and the crowd in the square fell silent as the senior elder rose from his chair to speak.

"The evidence brought against the prisoner has been carefully analyzed and considered." His voice, reedy with age, nonetheless cut clearly across the heads of the throng, and Cyllan's stomach turned at the hypocrisy of his words. "And it is with the deepest regret that we, the faithful custodians of the holy laws of Aeoris"—here he paused to make the Sign, ostentatiously, in the air before him—"find all charges against this unfortunate puppet of darkness to be proven."

A muttering in the square swelled to a full-throated yell of approval, which only died down as the old man made a pacifying gesture towards the crowd.

"These are troubled times," the elder continued when the tumult finally subsided. "But we all share a duty which, however onerous a burden, must be fulfilled if we are to truly serve the gods who grant us succour." He paused. "Like any other devout citizen, I have no taste for vengeance. But can I—can *we*—truly call ourselves disciples of those very Lords who grant their spark of godhood to our souls and our lives, if we neglect our clear duty when that burden falls upon us?"

The old man was a master of rhetoric, Cyllan thought bitterly. He praised the mob for their piety, and they hung on his every word. All about her folk were nodding, murmuring, congratulating the elder and themselves. . . .

"We have no hatred in our hearts!" the elder continued, raising his voice. "Indeed, we are moved to *pity* for this unfortunate slave of evil, for hers is a soul which cannot know the blessing of the true gods!"

Another, longer pause. "But we cannot allow such pity to sway us from righteousness. And I believe that if our great lord Aeoris Himself were to sit in judgment upon the verdict of this court, He would not find that verdict wanting." He raised his head with a beatific smile, and a thousand throats roared their approval.

Cyllan's ponies snorted and stamped, frightened by the uproar, yet too hemmed in to escape. She leaned over her own mount's neck, whispering soothingly to calm it whilst drawing the other pony as close to her side as she could. Hot fury welled in her. She could do *nothing*—this mockery of a trial had been decided even before it began; the townsfolk wanted a scapegoat for their terrors, and the elders, like marketplace players, courted their favor by providing such a one. For a single, wild moment something deep within her urged her to force her ponies through the crowd to the justice house steps, there to bring out the Chaos stone and scream to these pitiful dupes that the true object of their fear stood among them undaunted.... But even as the insane idea glanced through her mind she felt the hot, warning pulse of the gem at her breast and knew that, whatever savage injustice might be perpetrated here today, she could play no part in rectifying it.

The elder was speaking again. "My friends, good citizens—though it grieves my heart to pronounce sentence upon this poor creature here before us, justice must take its course." He turned to face the now silent girl, his profile outlined hawkishly by the glow of the waning sun. "For one who has consorted with the powers of Chaos, there can be but one end. I hope you will join me in praying to Aeoris for this unfortunate, that in His wisdom and mercy He may forgive her transgressions and release her soul from its servitude to evil."

Silence greeted his words, but Cyllan saw several

people make the Sign of Aeoris in the air before them. The girl was staring at her judges, unable to believe the fate that awaited her; then she turned her head away as though withdrawing, detaching herself from the madness around her.

Cyllan wanted to escape from the square before events took their inexorable course, but there was no room to turn and nowhere to go. The crush was increasing, swelled by new arrivals from the farther reaches of the town and also by the fact that a section of the crowd was drawing back to form an aisle between the justice house and the square's center, where a Law Stone stood gaunt and bare. The prisoner was hustled down the steps towards the stone, and she seemed suddenly to realize what awaited her, for she began to scream and struggle, fighting her captors with all the strength she possessed. The guards shook her violently to quiet her, but Cyllan could hear her deep-throated sobs as, finally manhandling her to the stone, they bound her to the rough granite and drew back.

Only a stubborn and terrible sense of reality convinced Cyllan that she wasn't asleep and dreaming as she watched the appalling progress of events from then on. A low, susurrant murmur vibrated through the square, setting her ponies fidgeting and dancing again, and she could only stare helplessly as the crowd shuffled menacingly towards the Law Stone. There was movement at the front of the throng circling her—then the voice of the elder, who still stood on the steps of the justice house, rang across the square.

"Let the unhappy task be done."

The sound of the first stone as it struck the girl was shocking and sickening against the background of silence. Her body jerked violently and she cried out, but the press of thrusting, jostling people, those at the back craning their necks to see, all but hid her from view. A second stone missed its mark, then a third struck her on the temple, and suddenly, like a pack of hounds loosed on a hunted animal, the mob closed in with a bloodlusting yell.

"No . . ." Cyllan's own whisper was harsh in her ears, but the crowd were too intent on their victim to notice. "Yandros, *no* . . ."

They had been waiting for this moment, she realized, knowing what the outcome of the trial would be, and prepared for it. Those stones hadn't materialized from nowhere . . . the mob had known that this ancient and barbaric method of execution would be invoked, and every man and woman among them had come well prepared.

She stared with a hideous fascination as stones, pebbles, even spars of wood, rained down on the girl's unprotected body. Blood made a grisly pattern on her face and now she was screaming, unable to maintain her futile courage any longer and writhing against the ropes that held her. Cyllan didn't know how long it was before her slight figure finally slumped into unconsciousness, but even when her senses had fled, the sea of arms continued to rise and fall, and the sounds as rock met unresistant flesh made Cyllan feel sick with shock and disgust.

At long last it was over. An eerie silence descended on the square, and gradually, like an ebbing tide, the townsfolk began to move away, withdrawing from the ruined and bloody shell of humanity that hung like a grotesque doll from the Law Stone. The elders, their own part in the charade complete, had made a dignified exit, and finally Cyllan realized that her path was no longer blocked by the milling throng.

Her pony sidestepped, flattening its ears, its nostrils flaring at the alarming scent of blood. Cyllan turned it away from the Law Stone, knowing that she couldn't continue her journey, couldn't cross the square while the girl's corpse hung there. She slid from the saddle, almost falling as her legs threatened to give way under her, and hid her face in the pony's mane, wishing that she could be sick, faint—anything to banish the hideous afterimages of what she had witnessed.

A wine-seller began to ring a handbell behind her, shrilly proclaiming that her wares were the best to be found in the province, and the ponies reared and whinnied in fright at the noise. Cyllan swung round and saw a makeshift stall laden with skins, jars, and cups. For a moment she could only stare, numbed, at the brisk business the seller was already doing; then an impulse urged her to stumble forward. Wine might help her to forget what she had seen. . . . She dug into her belt-pouch and pulled out the first coin she found: a half-gravine.

"Give me a full skin." Her voice was harsh.

The woman grinned broadly. "Gladly, lass! And you'll drink to the health of our good elders, eh?"

The wine-skin was pressed into Cyllan's hand. She received no change and knew the woman was robbing her, but she was past caring. The ponies followed her uneasily as she stumbled towards the edge of the square, where she would be out of the crush. Tears were starting to flow as she slumped down against a whitewashed wall and, with shaking hands, uncorked the brimming skin and raised it to her lips.

". . . Is she merely asleep, d'you think? Or taken ill?"

"I don't know . . . wait, and I'll see."

The female voices impinged on Cyllan's hazed mind as though through a heavy fog, and although she knew that she was the object of their scrutiny, she didn't seem able to unlock her tongue and tell them that she was well enough, and to leave her be. She heard a footfall, then sensed a figure stooping over her.

"No, she's not ill." There was faint amusement in the voice. "She's drunk!"

"I am *not* . . . ohh!" Cyllan found her voice at last and attempted to protest, but an injudicious movement sent pain throbbing through her head, and her back was so stiff that every muscle resisted violently. She opened her eyes, wincing at what seemed to be intolerantly brilliant light, and finally focused on the two women who were bent over her.

One was middle-aged, the other younger, and both were dressed in travel-stained white robes, with riding boots beneath and short but heavy cloaks about their shoulders. The square was dark and the women carried lanterns; it was their light which had seared her eyes. Sisters of Aeoris . . . Cyllan shut her eyes again and tried to struggle upright. She had been lying against a rough wall and her clothes were soaked through with damp, exacerbating the stiffness in her body. There was a vile taste in her mouth and she wiped an unsteady hand across her lips, resisting the temptation to spit.

"Here, now; let us help you." A hand took her arm, gently but firmly, and she was raised to her feet. "Can you stand unaided? Do you feel well enough to walk?"

Cyllan forced herself to nod. "I'm all right . . . thank you, I don't need—" She stopped as a retching spasm set her stomach lurching. "Oh *Gods* . . ."

The two women tactfully and sympathetically guided her into an alley where, painfully, she lost the contents of the wine-skin that she'd drunk before collapsing. Unpleasant though the experience was, it helped to clear her head, and she felt considerably better when she turned to face them once more.

"Thank you," she said indistinctly. "You're—very kind."

"Nonsense, child. Succouring those in trouble is part of our calling, and it's clear that you're in need of comfort." The older woman, who had spoken, smiled at her. "I am Sister Liss Kaya Trevire, and this is Sister Farial Mordyn. We are travelling through Prospect on our way south, so we're strangers here. I suspect that gives us something in common."

"Yes . . ." Despite her deep suspicion of the Sisterhood, Cyllan was warming to Sister Liss. "I am—" She checked herself, realizing with a sobering shock that she had been on the verge of giving her real name. "I am Themila Avray, drover, from West High Land."

"And what of your band?" Sister Liss pursued. "Are you housed at one of the town inns?"

Cyllan shook her head. "I'm alone. That is—I'm on my way to meet my cousin in Shu-Nhadek."

The Sisters were shocked. "Surely you haven't been travelling this road unaccompanied, now of all times?" Farial asked. "It's unthinkable—there are so many dangers!"

"Indeed," Liss agreed. "Not least of which, it seems, is the danger of falling into temptation." She glanced with grim humor at the empty wine-skin, which lay discarded in the gutter. "Even in a respectable town there are too many rogues for comfort. Have you checked your belt-pouch, child?"

Cyllan's eyes widened, and involuntarily she put her hand to her breast. To her relief, the Chaos stone still lay hard and cold beneath her jerkin, and she hastily felt in her pouch, hoping that the women hadn't taken heed of her first gesture. The pouch's contents were complete. . . . She smiled sheepishly. "All's well."

"No thanks to your lack of vigilance," Liss admonished her. "You've been fortunate, Themila. You are very young, and I know how easy it is to give way to temptation when you have only the rashness of youth and inexperience to guide you. But to indulge in this kind of behavior . . ." She indicated the empty skin. "It can only lead you on a downhill road."

The homily was well-intentioned, but Cyllan felt bitterness well within her. Perhaps these good Sisters had only arrived in the town after the grisly spectacle of the trial and its outcome; but either way, they must know what had taken place here. How could they condemn anyone for reacting as she had done?

Without realizing it she had glanced towards the Law Stone in the center of the now empty square. The girl's broken body had been removed, but the torches in their high brackets, which burned around the square, showed dark smears on the stone's surface that didn't look like shadow. Sister Farial saw Cyllan's expression, and touched her colleague's arm lightly.

"I think I understand," she said, and nodded towards the stone. "In the light of today's events . . ."

Sister Liss's look softened. "Ah, yes. Of course." She touched her tongue to her lips. "Thankfully, our party was spared from witnessing the execution, as we only arrived in the town when it was all over. It must have been a very distressing spectacle."

Cyllan shrugged, angry that she'd shown weakness and yet mollified by the Sisters' obvious sympathy. "She was younger than I am," she said harshly.

"So I heard. And doubtless you couldn't help thinking that, but for the grace of Aeoris, you might have stood in her place." Sister Liss sighed. "These are sorry times. All we can do is pray that they'll soon be over."

Cyllan couldn't stop herself from protesting at the woman's fatalism. "But she was *innocent!*" she said; then, realizing that she'd made a dangerous slip, added, "That is—there was no evidence against her, nothing that any rational thought could have supported! Yet they—it was as if—" She made a helpless, frustrated gesture, angered by her inability to articulate what she felt. "They wanted a victim, and they didn't care whether that victim was guilty or not."

Liss smiled sadly. "I understand your feelings. But you must remember that more dangers attend us all now than the simple apprehension of the two fugitives. Chaos is a deadly enemy, and possessed of great guile. Its servants will lose no opportunity to seek out the weak and the dissolute, and corrupt them to its service." The smile faded. "Harsh as it may seem at times, we are charged to uphold Aeoris's laws, and we can't take the risk of allowing evil to take root among us. It's not a pleasant fact to face, but it's better that innocents suffer than that the guilty go free."

Fortunately, before Cyllan could speak, they were interrupted by the arrival of four more women, who formed the remainder of the Sisterhood party. Liss told Cyllan's story, and the other Sisters immediately pressed her to travel with them.

"You can't possibly continue on the road alone," she was urged. "And the more of us who ride together, the safer we'll all be."

Cyllan tried to argue, but the women were adamant, and Liss had the final word.

"My conscience could never be easy if I allowed you to go," she insisted. "If anything were to befall you, I couldn't live with myself. Would you wish that fate on me?"

It seemed to Cyllan that, unless she were prepared to face another hasty flight during the dark hours, she was effectively trapped; she had no defense against their arguments. But then it occurred to her that the situation could have advantages. Who, after all, would dream of casting suspicion on a girl in the company of six Sisters of Aeoris? Provided she kept a constant guard on her tongue, what better protection could she ask?

She smiled, slowly but with returning confidence.
"If my presence won't be a burden to you . . ."

"The very idea!" Liss was relieved and pleased.
"We rest for tonight at the Minstrels Tavern, and I'm
sure there'll be room to house you with us. Then in
the morning, an hour after sunrise, we'll be on our
way."

The Sisterhood party left for the south as the sun
was beginning its climb into a blood-red sky streaked
with only a few purple-edged smears of cloud. Sister
Liss pronounced the weather a good omen, and once
the town was left behind they made steady if slow
progress.

Cyllan rode towards the rear of the group, just
ahead of the Sisters' four baggage ponies. She was
privately thankful to have company; last night her
sleep had been racked with nightmares that re-
volved round the executed girl, and with the dreams
still fresh in her mind she had no desire to be alone
with her thoughts. Her fellow travellers were content
to enjoy the ride and the landscape, and what little
conversation there was was idle and therefore safe.
The only unsettling factor was the presence of the
dark-haired, thin-faced woman who rode a little way
ahead of her.

She had exchanged no more than a few words with
Sister-Seer Jennat Brynd since their first meeting,
but on several occasions she had noticed the woman
watching her with more than idle interest. Cyllan
hadn't bargained on encountering a seer among her
new companions, and she wondered how far Jennat's
talents extended—the thought that her own mind
might be an open book to a truly skilled psychic was
chilling. She had had little contact with the seer, and
thus far all was well, but she was anxious not to
encourage Jennat's society, for her own safety's sake.
The journey to Shu-Nhadek should take about four

days if there were no untoward delays; she wouldn't need to maintain her deception for much longer.

The rest of the day passed without incident, and they spent the next night at a cramped but clean roadside inn. Pleading tiredness, Cyllan went to bed as soon as they had eaten, leaving the Sisters to talk and share a jar of wine, and trying to forget the speculative glance that Jennat Brynd had cast in her direction before she retired. In the morning they left early, Sister Liss giving thanks to Aeoris for another fine if chilly day, and by midafternoon they had reached a wide river spanned by a wooden pack-bridge. One of the baggage ponies had begun to limp, and they reined in while Cyllan offered to examine the animal and see what was amiss with it.

Liss slid thankfully from her saddle and pressed the knuckles of both hands into the small of her back. "I don't mind admitting that I'm glad of the rest," she said, looking at the lowering sun and allowing its warmth to bathe her face. "And thankful, too, that we're moving farther south. The days are longer down here, the sun's rays stronger ... it's a blessed relief after the northern lands!"

Farial, who had also dismounted, was searching through a pack strapped to one of the baggage ponies, and drew out a wrapped package and a skin of fruit juice. "This would be a pleasant enough place to stop under any circumstances," she said. "Perhaps we can sit on the grass for a while and relax—that is, if Themila thinks her task will take a little time?"

It took Cyllan a few moments to remember that she was the one being addressed, and she looked up quickly, allowing the baggage pony to rest its troublesome leg on the ground. "I don't think it's anything more than a stone in his hoof," she told the Sister, then smiled. "But it could take an hour to put right, if you'd like."

Farial laughed. "Very well—then let's make ourselves comfortable." She spread her cloak among the lusher grass where the land started to slope towards the river, and sat down. "I've fresh drinks for us all here, and the cakes I bought from the town bakery this morning."

Within a few minutes all six of the women had settled themselves on the grass, and Cyllan, having prized the stone from the pony's hoof with the point of her knife, joined them. Farial handed her a slab of cake, and she squatted at the edge of the group, reaching behind her to fix her bunched hair more securely.

Her fingers came away from her hair smeared with red-brown stains. . . .

Cyllan had completely forgotten that the effects of the bellflower dye must be wearing off by now. Drovers' inns didn't furnish their rooms with looking glasses, and it hadn't occurred to her to worry about the color of her hair. By now, the copper-brown could be streaked halfway back to its natural white-blond and that could be enough to damn her.

Quickly she glanced at the Sisters, but they were occupied with their food and drink—all, that is, save for Jennat Brynd, who was watching Cyllan and, as their gazes met, smiled a slow, pleasant smile. With a tremendous effort Cyllan made her lips quirk nervously in response, then she pointedly turned her attention to the cake in her hand.

For a time there were no sounds but the ripple of the river and the contented munching of the horses as they cropped at the grass nearby. Sister Liss's head had drooped forward and she seemed to be asleep; Farial was fussily tidying the litter of their small feast, and Jennat, propped on one elbow, was engrossed in examining the contents of her belt-pouch. At length she drew out something that caught the sunlight with a brilliant flare, and those nearest to her looked up in surprise.

"Scrying, Sister?" Farial inquired amiably.

Jennat smiled. "Yes. It was the river that gave me the notion. So smooth and quiet, and the way the current catches the sunlight and reflects it is quite hypnotic."

Farial turned to Cyllan. "You must pay no attention to Sister Jennat, Themila. She chooses the unlikeliest moments to practice her art—though in truth we're all very proud and envious of her skills."

Cyllan nodded uneasily, and Jennat's dark eyes met hers.

"Oh, but I don't want to distress our new friend," she said solicitously. "It's easy for us to overlook the fact that, to outsiders, our way can sometimes seem disconcerting. One forgets that the magical skills aren't widely practiced beyond the Sisterhood."

Despite the softness of her voice, the words were a clear challenge. Cyllan regarded her through narrowed lashes. "Please, don't let me deter you, Sister. I'm not afraid."

Jennat turned the small scrying-glass over and over in her hands. "Perhaps you've seen something of this nature before?"

"I saw a stone-reader once, at a fair," Cyllan said. "But I believe he must have been a charlatan."

"Most self-professed diviners are. To develop a true talent takes both dedication and years of study."

Cyllan didn't reply, and with another of her slow smiles Jennat turned her attention back to the scrying-glass. After a prudent pause Cyllan got to her feet and, hoping that her actions seemed casual, walked slowly down the gentle slope to the edge of the river. By the bank the water was crystal clear, and she fancied she saw fish moving sleekly among the dappled shadows. She tried to concentrate on watching them, but it was impossible; Sister Jennat's subtle insinuations had breached the mental wall behind which she'd hidden her deepest fears, and she felt sick with trepidation. The sensation, coupled with an irrational hope that by physically distancing herself from the seer she could evade her scrutiny, had driven her to get as far away from the Sisters as she could, while she collected her wits.

Surely, she told herself, Sister Jennat presented no real threat? It was possible—no, *likely*—that her imagination was seeing shadows where none existed. Only a few more days to Shu-Nhadek, and then she could forget that she'd ever encountered these women. . . .

"Themila?" A voice behind her made her start, and she turned to see that Jennat had left the others and walked silently down the bank to join her. "Are you feeling unwell?"

"No—no." Cyllan shook her head, not meeting the other woman's gaze. "I just thought to—to look at the river."

"Ah." Jennat, too, gazed out across the smoothly flowing water. "It is a peaceful sight, isn't it? Still, it would be all too easy to slip into the temptation of tarrying. I came to tell you that Sister Liss has woken and says that we must be on our way if we're to reach habitation before nightfall."

So her errand was innocent enough. . . . Cyllan clenched her teeth against an involuntary sigh of relief, and turned to go. Jennat made to follow—then abruptly paused.

"Oh, Themila—I hope you'll pardon my curiosity, but . . . do tell me, why do you dye your hair? Its natural color is such a pretty shade."

Cyllan stared at the sloe-dark eyes in the smiling, guileless face as her stomach turned ice-cold. Jennat's question had caught her completely unawares, and she had no answer.

"Jennat! Themila! Come; we've wasted enough time!" Sister Liss's impatient cry broke the terrible hiatus, and gratefully Cyllan turned, raising one arm in acknowledgment. Without waiting for Jennat, and without giving her a chance to put her question again, she ran up the bank to where the horses were tethered.

Pulling the animals away from the juicy grass took time and effort, but finally Cyllan had her own ponies back on the road and checked their harness whilst she waited for the other women to mount up. She was about to swing herself into the saddle when a voice spoke, quite clearly but also quite casually, from a short distance away.

"Cyllan . . ."

"Yes?" She turned without thinking at the sound of her name—her *real* name—and only when she found herself face to face with Jennat did she realize the terrible mistake she'd made.

Jennat smiled. "Will you show us the jewel which you keep so carefully next to your skin?"

Sister Liss paused at her horse's head. "Jewel? What jewel is this, Jennat?"

Cyllan held her breath striving to appear a good deal calmer than she felt. Jennat, sure of herself now, continued to stare at her. "Sister Liss, I think it's perhaps more important to establish the small matter of our friend's identity."

Liss realized suddenly what the seer was implying. "You called her *Cyllan*. . . ."

"And she answered me. I believe that, if my scrying-glass doesn't deceive me, her full name is Cyllan Anassan."

Farial gave a little cry of shock, and Liss's eyes widened. "Jennat, you don't mean—"

"Look at her hair!" Jennat interrupted, pointing. "It's no more that color than mine is! She's fair—so fair that her hair's all but white! And my glass showed me a gemstone which she keeps hidden, a clear jewel. Search her, Sisters, and I believe you'll find the very stone that the Circle are seeking!"

Shock had kept Cyllan rooted where she stood, but abruptly she realized that she was lost. She couldn't bluff her way around Jennat's accusations; her only hope was flight.

She made a frantic leap for her pony, but even as she slithered astride its back Jennat rushed at her, grabbing her arm. Cyllan lashed out, the pony plunged, and, off-balance, she felt herself slipping, falling from the saddle. She landed with a thump, the pony's hooves only just missing her skull as it reared in fright, and the fall knocked all the breath out of her. Before she could struggle up again, three of the Sisters were kneeling beside her and holding her down.

"Keep her still!" Jennat cried breathlessly, ducking Cyllan's flailing arm. "We'll soon find out the truth—"

"Jennat!" Sister Liss shouted, dismayed. "Jennat, this is unseemly! You are a Sister of Aeoris, not a brawling tavern wench! Get up at once!"

Jennat paid no attention. She had thrust a hand into Cyllan's shirt, tearing the fabric, and her fingers closed round the soul-stone. Cyllan struggled like a feral cat but couldn't free herself, and Jennat sprang to her feet, triumphant.

"Sister Liss, *look!*"

Cold, white radiance spilled across Jennat's palm as she opened her hand to display the jewel. The older woman flinched and hastily made the Sign of Aeoris. "*Gods preserve us . . .*"

Those Sisters who weren't engaged in pinning Cyllan to the ground gathered round, exclaiming. One reached out as if to touch the stone, then swiftly withdrew her hand. Liss turned to look down at the girl who lay on the grass, and the mute defiance she saw in Cyllan's eyes banished any last doubts.

"So all this time we've been harboring a serpent in our midst," she said unsteadily. "Gods help us, I can hardly believe it. . . ." Then her mouth set into a hard line. "Hide that jewel away, Jennat. It's an evil thing, and I won't risk our being tainted by it. Wrap it in a cloth. It mustn't see the light of day again until it can be given into the hands of the High Initiate."

Jennat gazed at the stone and licked her lips uneasily. "And what of the girl? What are we to do with her?"

"Poor child." Liss continued to regard Cyllan gravely. "How one so young could be so corrupt. . . ."

"Should we take her to the next town for trial?" Farial asked.

"No—this is beyond the jurisdiction of the local elders, or even the Province Margrave. She must be delivered to the Castle of the Star Peninsula, to face the judgment of the Circle itself." Her gaze lingered a moment longer, then she shook her head and turned away. "To think that she could have deceived us so . . ."

"Even the High Initiate was deceived by these fiends," Farial reminded her solemnly. "We shouldn't reproach ourselves, Sister."

"No. No, perhaps you're right. Though when I think that, if it hadn't been for Sister Jennat—ah, never mind. We must turn our attention to the practicalities. We will need an armed escort to conduct us to the Star Peninsula, and if there are any Adepts visiting the province who might be called upon to aid us, I'll feel a good deal easier about the journey." She gathered up the cumbersome skirts of her robe. "Bind the girl, Sisters, and secure her in her pony's saddle. We'll rest at the next town tonight, then tomorrow we'll turn northward."

Chapter 6

Keridil Toln watched the departing hawk until it was no more than a tiny dot in the sky, indistinguishable among the flecks of cloud stippling the blue. If he could trust falconer Faramor's calculations—and past experience had taught him that he could—the vital message would reach its first destination in less than two days, and be relayed to its second the day after that.

He expressed his thanks to Faramor, but didn't encourage any further conversation; there was too much on his mind now to allow time for pleasantries. Quickly he climbed the steps to the Castle doorway and went through, giving an involuntary shiver at the sharp contrast between the interior's warmth and the cold of the morning; then he turned towards his own apartments.

His study was empty, but he could hear someone moving about in the private suite beyond. Keridil paused briefly to warm his hands at the fire, then pushed open the door to his inner chambers, expecting to find Sashka awaiting him. But instead he saw Gyneth Linto, the elderly steward who had been his father's servant before him. Gyneth was stooping

over a large ottoman that stood in the room's far
corner; as Keridil entered, he straightened and bowed
formally.

"Is the bird away safely, sir?"

"Yes." Keridil crossed the room and looked with a
degree of distaste at the items that the old man was
bringing out of the ottoman. A long cloak, heavily
embroidered with gold thread ... a clasp, bearing
his own seal and made of solid gold ... a gold circlet
... the High Initiate's staff of office ...

"There's a touch of tarnishing on the circlet, sir,"
Gyneth said, holding it out for him to inspect. "But
nothing that a little polishing can't put right."

"Good." Keridil waved the circlet away, not wanting to think about the regalia until circumstances
forced it. "I want to travel light, Gyneth," he added.
"No baggage train, no large entourage—time is of
the essence on this journey."

The words came out more sharply than he'd intended, and the old man regarded him for a few
moments before replying placidly, "Of course, sir."
He replaced the circlet carefully on top of the folded
gold cloak, then, with a tactful touch of diffidence,
added: "Is anything amiss, sir? If I might venture to
say, you seem troubled."

Shrewdness and experience had given Gyneth more
accurate perceptions than any seer, and Keridil sighed.
"It's nothing of any consequence. Just watching that
bird leave, and knowing that I've committed myself
to this beyond the point of no return ... it makes me
doubt my own judgment. I wish to the Gods my
father were still alive."

Gyneth pursed his lips. He rarely ventured an opinion on Circle matters, but it saddened him to see his
master so distressed. "The old High Initiate was a
very wise man, sir. In all the years I served him, I
never knew him to make a rash decision, or an un-
sound one." His gaze met Keridil's. "I believe that,

in your place, he would have acted exactly as you have done."

Keridil smiled thinly. "Thank you, Gyneth—I appreciate your loyalty, whether or not you're right." He rubbed his still cold hands together and forced a briskness he didn't feel into his voice. "Doubtless we could debate the matter all day, but I can't afford that indulgence. What's done's done, and we have to look to the future." He glanced round the room. "You seem to have completed most of the preparations."

"Yes, sir. There are one or two minor questions to clarify, but they'll keep until later."

"Good. And where is the Lady Sashka?"

Gyneth gave him an odd look that, he thought, carried a faint hint of disapproval. "She retired to her suite, sir. She said to tell you that she is packing for the journey."

"Packing?" Keridil was nonplussed. "But it was understood that she isn't to accompany me!"

"Quite, sir. However, I thought it wasn't my place to point that out."

"No . . ." The relationship between Sashka and Gyneth was uneasy at the best of times; Sashka made no secret of her dislike for the old man and her mistrust of his influence on Keridil, and though nothing would ever induce Gyneth to admit as much, Keridil suspected that the feeling was mutual. But Gyneth was too well bred a servant to make his feelings public, and the knowledge that Sashka would soon be the High Initiate's consort made him doubly punctilious in his manner towards her—he wouldn't have dared argue. Nonetheless, Sashka had agreed with Keridil's insistence that the long journey was too arduous and possibly too dangerous for her to undertake. Whilst he might take chances with his own safety, nothing in the world would induce him to risk hers, and he had thought the matter settled.

"Shall I send word to the lady that you wish to see her, sir?" Gyneth's voice impinged on his thoughts.

"What? Oh—no, Gyneth; let it be for now. I'll speak with her later and see what's to be done."

"Very well, High Initiate. Then, with your permission, I'll go and see Fin Tivan Bruall about your horses."

Keridil nodded thanks and dismissal, and when the old man had left the room he sat down on the bed, pushing aside the neatly folded garments that littered it. Tomorrow, he was to start on a journey upon which might hinge the future of the entire land . . . and right at this moment he'd have given almost anything to turn time back and revoke the decision he had made as the sun rose this morning.

Last night he had spent all the dark hours kneeling in vigil before the votive flame that burned perpetually in his study, and he had prayed fervently for guidance. Dawn had found him hollow-eyed and exhausted, but with the leaden certainty in his heart of what he must do. Stiff with weariness, he had sat at his great table and picked up the two letters that lay there, rereading them both for the hundredth time, though he already knew their contents by heart: the Lady Matriarch Ilyaya Kimi's formal request that he should call a Conclave of Three—and the stiff scroll that had arrived the following day, bearing the seal of the Summer Isle Court and inscribed personally by the High Margraye Fenar Alecar with an identical plea.

It should, Keridil knew, have been easy to bow to the majority verdict and order the Conclave without any further thought. But he felt his responsibility keenly as the custodian of the world's spiritual laws and the prime vehicle for the gods' word and the gods' will. In all their long history since the fall of the Old Ones a Conclave had never been called; and it was strictly written that it might be invoked only in the event of a dire peril that no other power could avert.

Was this such an occasion? Or had the rousing of ancient, dormant fears taken too strong a hold on them all, and distorted the truth out of proportion? Keridil knew he could never be certain of the answer; he must trust to his own judgment. The Conclave would be little more than a formality, its outcome a foregone conclusion—and then he, as High Initiate, must climb to the shrine on the White Isle, unlock the clasp which would open the sacred casket, and prepare to meet Aeoris face to face.

To call the great god back to the world . . . It was a responsibility that chilled him to the marrow. If the judgment of the Conclave was ill-founded, what wrath would he incur? What punishments would be unleashed on them all? To trifle with a god was the ultimate insanity. . . . *What if the decision to open the casket should prove to be wrong?*

Keridil looked at the two letters again, then at the growing sheaf of reports and depositions that had been flooding in, by messenger-bird and by despatch rider, from almost all the provinces. Trials, accusations, executions—flooding and crop failure—inarticulate terrors and pleas for the Circle's help or advice—the fear of Chaos was running riot through the land, and nothing save the destruction of those evil forces could stop it. The Adepts had tried everything they knew to track down the fugitives and with them the Chaos stone; but their rituals and conjurations proved fruitless, and that in itself had convinced Keridil of the true extent of the peril they faced.

He had, once, looked on the face of Chaos, and the memory was burned forever on his brain. Yandros, the quintessence of evil, with his golden hair and ever-changing eyes and beautiful, malignant smile . . . Yandros, who had mocked the Circle and chal-

lenged them, if they dared, to stand against him
when his forces rose to conquer . . . Yandros, who
had called Tarod *brother* . . .

No, Keridil thought, he wouldn't trifle with a god—
but neither would he trifle with Chaos. And if the
soul-stone wasn't found and destroyed, the gates that
had been closed against the dark powers so many
centuries ago would be breached, and the world would
be engulfed in madness.

And so, with a hand that wasn't quite steady, he
had taken up pen and parchment and written the
vital words that would commit him finally to his
decision. Only the High Initiate had the sanction to
order the Conclave, and as he at last set his seal to
the paper the unsteadiness in his hand had become a
palsied shaking, so that the hot wax splattered across
the parchment's surface.

It was done. And within minutes the message could
be on its way, carried by hawk to speed to its destination. He could send for the falconer . . . or he could
tear the parchment into shreds, burn the fragments,
forget he had ever considered such a deed. . . .

Keridil licked dry lips, then rang a small handbell
that stood on the table. When Gyneth answered the
summons, he looked up and said, "Gyneth—will you
send for falconer Faramor, and ask him to meet me
in the courtyard immediately."

There could be no going back now. As soon as his
message reached the Matriarch's Cot in Southern
Chaun, Ilyaya Kimi would begin her preparations for
the journey to Shu-Nhadek. And a day or so later, a
ship would set sail from the Summer Isle, bearing
the young High Margrave and his entourage. Keridil's
own journey would begin in the morning, as he and a
few chosen companions rode hard for the south to
meet his peers.

He stared bleakly at the clothes that Gyneth had

laid out, and realized how tired he was. A night without sleep had taken its toll, and even on previous nights when he'd sought his bed he had been racked by nightmares. He'd be in no fit condition to face an eight-day journey unless he could rest for a while, and until Gyneth returned later he should be free from interruption.

He pushed the folded garments aside, making space for himself on the bed, and stretched out. For a few minutes uneasy thoughts continued to assail him; then, mercifully, he drifted away into a sound sleep.

Keridil was woken two hours later by the light touch of a hand on his brow. He stirred, then opened his eyes to see Sashka sitting beside him, a gentle smile on her face.

"You've been asleep, love." She pushed a strand of hair away from his mouth.

Keridil blinked and struggled to sit up. "What's the hour?"

"Past noon. I'd have come to you earlier, but I've been with Father and Mother in our rooms." She paused, then added: "Packing."

He remembered what Gyneth had told him, and reached out to take hold of her hand, squeezing it. "Sashka, you're not thinking to come with me? After all that we said—"

"I know what we said, Keridil. But did you really believe I'd let you go without me by your side? I want to be with you—and I feel that you'll need me."

She was more right than she knew, Keridil thought; but he still couldn't agree to it.

"No, love," he told her. "It's too long a journey, and too dangerous. The entire world's in a ferment, and the Gods alone know what we're going to encounter on the way south. Should the powers of Chaos realize what's afoot there could be attempts to stop us reaching our destination, and if any harm should come to you because of me—I couldn't bear that!"

Her eyes flashed angrily. "D'you think I lack the courage to face danger?"

"No—no, of course not! But—"

"And d'you think I could wait behind, not knowing where you were or how you fared? What would I do whilst you were away?"

"Your father is returning to Han. Go with him, love; you'll be safe at your home."

"The Castle is my home now—if I went to Han, I'd go mad with waiting and fretting!" Sashka argued. She locked her fingers with his, aware that he was beginning to weaken. He *wanted* her with him, she could tell; and she was determined to wear down his protests. Keridil was about to embark on the most momentous course that any High Initiate had ever taken, and when it was over he would be famed throughout history as the savior of his people; the man who had saved the world from the threat of Chaos. No power on earth was going to stop her from being at his side when that history was made.

"Listen to me, Keridil," she said, softly but persuasively, "I couldn't bear to be parted from you, not now, not while you have this burden to bear." Her fingers traced a gentle line around his jaw and she saw with satisfaction his answering, hesitant smile. "Once, when I was so distressed after—well, after the events that began this whole unhappy affair—you gave me your strength and your love, when I thought that life was no longer worth living. I've never been able to repay the debt I owe you, until now."

Keridil shook his head, though he was still smiling, "You gave me yourself, love. You could do me no greater honor than that."

"But it isn't enough; not for me." Sashka was pleased with her stratagem, and it was clearly working. "I want to show you now that, as you helped me when I so desperately needed help, I can be a pillar of strength for you in return. Please, Keridil—I'm not afraid of what's to come. I'm only afraid of any ill befalling you, and I want to be by your side to prevent it."

Keridil remembered the day when Tarod had been brought back, captive and drugged insensible, to the Castle. Sashka had been pledged to marry him, and she had, he thought, shown tremendous courage in overcoming her grief and despair at the revelations about him. She had been bereft, and he had tried to offer her comfort as she faced up to the grim truth. He had made her laugh—a small beginning, but an auspicious one—and slowly she had forgotten her misery as their love took root and flourished. . . .

He wanted her with him. Her presence would give him strength, as she had said, and keep doubt and fear at bay. And if she was so determined to come, he had no more arguments to counter her.

He said, "Sashka . . . if you're sure . . ."

Her expression broke into a sparkling smile, and she flung her arms around his neck. "I'm sure! Of course I'm sure!" Relief and triumph flooded through her as she released him, and her smile changed to one of fond concern. "You should rest for a while longer," she said solicitously. "If we're to leave at dawn tomorrow, you'll need all your strength."

"There isn't the time. Gyneth will be back soon, and—"

"Never mind Gyneth! If he finds your door locked, he can't trouble you." She rose, moving gracefully across the room, and he heard the sound of a bolt being pushed home. "There," Sashka said, "now there'll be no one to disturb us." She came back to the bed and sank down on it, her arms winding warmly, possessively around him. "We're together, and we'll stay together from now on." Her voice was soft and persuasive. "That's all that matters."

*   *   *

The big bay horse cantered at an easy, ground-eating pace on the track, hooves kicking up eddies of dust in its wake. Since leaving the timber-caravan as it lumbered along the edge of the forest that straddled the border between Han and Wishet, Tarod had made good speed southward, and was now crossing the arable plains of Prospect. The weather was little short of perfect—high, brilliant skies with a brisk and drying east wind—but the fresh optimism of the elements was in obscene contrast to the sights he had witnessed on the road.

Tarod's fears that the superstition sweeping the land in the wake of the Circle's warning would explode beyond all proportion had proved well-founded. A madness was gripping the countryside, turning just and sober citizens into panic-stricken avengers of imaginary wrongs. Three men had been hanged in the last town he passed through, for what crime Tarod didn't know; he had stopped to stare, appalled, at the corpses left dangling stiff and grotesque from the gibbet as a warning to others, and had seen the hex signs chalked on the ground in their shadows. Farther on the road he had heard of a group of merchants ambushed and massacred at the edge of the forest; there was talk of winged demons that materialized from thin air and carried off screaming victims, whilst ghouls crept out of the trees to feast on the dead. Crops said to harbor unearthly things that crawled from the fields at night were burned by their terrified owners, without thought for the starvation to which they condemned their families; three times now he had seen a distant pall of smoke that told of another farmer's livelihood charred to ashes. And not an hour ago he had passed the burned-out skeleton of a market cart, the horse lying in the shafts with its throat cut and other blackened shapes, mercifully indistinguishable, half-hidden beneath the broken wheels. Here, too, there were hex marks on the track, daubed, by the look of it, in the horse's blood. . . . He hadn't investigated closer.

Madness. And all in the name of Order. . . . Tarod was assailed by an ugly thought which had haunted him all too often of late, and which questioned the justice of a god who allowed such grisly deeds to be done in his name. This sickness was more like the work of Chaos, and it played directly into Yandros's hands. How could Aeoris watch such wanton anarchy and do nothing to intervene? How could the Circle, His emissaries, allow the death and destruction to continue unchecked?

He forced the thought back with an effort. With the horror of all he had seen fresh in his mind, it would be easy to succumb to doubts, and such doubts would suit Yandros's purpose. But for the Chaos Lord's machinations, the world would still be at peace with itself—he had to hold fast to his trust in the gods of Order, hold fast to his own resolution, and not allow uncertainty to prey on him. Once he found Cyllan, and regained the soul-stone, he could try to end this insanity. . . .

Goaded by that thought he spurred his mount on faster, glad to feel the willing response of the animal's powerful muscles under him. The road was quiet—no one travelled now unless forced to do so—and so when he saw, ahead of him, a telltale dust cloud that moved against the fields' backdrop, he reined in to a jog, shielding his eyes against the sun to see what was afoot.

The dust cloud was drawing nearer, and at last Tarod made out the silhouettes of several horsemen. Light glinted on metal, and he guessed that the newcomers were militiamen from a nearby town. Doubtless they'd stop him and that would mean a delay; but the Initiate's badge should stand him in good stead, as it had done before.

His guess proved accurate, and within minutes he was waved to a halt by the group's leader. They surrounded him; eight nervous, suspicious and inexperienced men, some barely out of adolescence.

"State your name, sir, and your business on this road." The leader—doubtless elected solely on the grounds of seniority—snapped out the challenge but without real conviction. Tarod met the man's eyes, exerted a little of his will, and the leader saw a brown-haired, grey-eyed but otherwise unremarkable stranger before him; a face he wouldn't later recall. Tarod smiled thinly and drew the folds of his cloak aside so that the distinctive golden badge winked in the sunlight.

"Circle business," he said crisply. "I trust that doesn't place me under suspicion, Captain?"

Flattered by the title yet chagrined by his error, the man flustered. "No sir—of course not! I'm sorry sir—it's just that we're under orders, from the Margrave himself you understand, to stop all strangers on this road and . . . well, check that they're what they seem to be, sir, if you take my meaning."

"Your Margrave's a wise man to take such precautions," Tarod said. "Tell me, what news is there in Prospect? I've ridden from the north and I've heard no reliable reports for the last three days."

One of the younger men edged his horse forward and whispered in the leader's ear. The man nodded emphatically, then looked at Tarod and cleared his throat.

"Well, sir, there's a rumor . . . that is to say, it was confirmed this morning, to the best of my knowledge . . . the girl—the Chaos-fiend's accomplice—she's been captured!"

Tarod thrust back an irrational surge of hope, telling himself that it was just another false trail like so many before. "Indeed," he said. "You'll forgive my scepticism, Captain, but others have made such claims before, and they've proved unfounded.''

"They have, yes—but our Margrave has sent word that this is no idle boast.'' The militiaman looked proud. "It's said that the girl has in her possession a jewel. A colorless jewel.''

Surely it wasn't possible . . . Aloud, Tarod said, "I see . . . and has she been brought to trial?''

"No, sir; not so far as I know. In fact—'' The militiaman looked a little sheepish. "What I heard is that this isn't a matter for our local justices. The girl's to be taken north, to the Castle of the Star Peninsula; but it's a long journey, and a hazardous one. If it were possible for someone in authority to take charge of the matter . . .'' He coughed. "If you see what I mean, sir.''

Tarod did. He'd been led astray by false reports before, but this time it seemed there could be real evidence against the girl, whoever she was. Time-wasting or not, he had to be sure.

He nodded. "Very well. In the light of what you've told me, I'll postpone my own business. Where's the girl being held?''

The militia leader looked relieved. "At Prospect town itself, sir. It's about ten miles distant, no more.''

"Then I'd suggest we set out without further delay.''

"Thank you, sir!'' He barked out unnecessary orders to his men, who were already turning their horses about, and the cavalcade set off. As they rode, Tarod tried not to think about what he might or might not find at their destination. If the captured girl wasn't Cyllan, he'd suffer nothing beyond yet another disappointment. But if she was . . . he hadn't considered how he might free her if she was taken; his pretended role wouldn't stand him in good enough stead to simply overrule any other authority and take her away. If he could gain possession of the soul-stone, he could use the powers that at present were beyond his reach—but he didn't want to dwell on that possibility.

In a little under an hour the rooftops of Prospect were visible ahead, rising above the pale stone of the six concentric walls that surrounded the town. The walls had been built to protect the fruit orchards— for which the province was renowned—from early frosts, and allowed Prospect town to boast the earliest summer crops anywhere in the world. The party rode through one of the wide arches set into the outermost wall, and followed a paved path through ranks of trees heavy with white blossom. Their heady scent hung heavy on the air; one of the militiamen started to sneeze violently and the fit only subsided when at last they clattered beyond the boundary of the sixth wall and into the town itself.

Prospect was one of the oldest towns in the land and, as Tarod had to admit despite his preoccupation, one of the most beautiful. Mellow stone towers rose at intervals, dominating the jumble of sloping, red-tiled roofs. The paved streets were wide and airy, overlooked by houses adorned with stone porticoes and balconies; the architecture lent itself to an atmosphere of pleasant and prosperous well-being.

That atmosphere, however, wasn't present in the air, nor in the faces of the people they passed as they rode towards the justice house. The terrors souring the world had affected Prospect as much as anywhere else, and its normal bustle was sharply subdued. Townsfolk went about essential business with closed, tight expressions, and a newcomer without even the smallest psychic talent could have felt the palpable tension pervading the place.

The militia leader reined in where the streets opened suddenly and unexpectedly into a broad, tree-lined avenue, and he turned in his saddle to address Tarod. "The justice house is directly ahead of us, sir. Shall I ride on and inform the town elders of your arrival?"

Tarod shook his head. He was aware of his pulse beating too fast, and tried to quell it. "No. There's no need for formality."

"Whatever you say, sir." The man spurred his horse forward, and they clattered along the avenue to the tall, bland-faced building that rose at the far end. A motley of people had gathered outside as though waiting for something; they drew apart to make passage for the riders, and many stared openly as they recognized the Initiate's badge at Tarod's shoulder. He closed his ears to the muted rustling of whispers at his back and slid down from the saddle, handing his horse's reins to one of the younger militiamen.

As they ascended the steps, the doors of the justice house opened and four men emerged. Tarod immediately recognized the aging, greying individual who led them; he had met the Margrave of Prospect at Keridil Toln's inaugural celebration and they had had an uneasy discussion about the rise of lawlessness in the land. The meeting seemed a lifetime ago, but the Margrave was a shrewd man and likely to remember the face of the renegade Adept. Tarod concentrated, allowing a small measure of power to flow through him—he saw the Margrave blink as though momentarily disconcerted, then the old man's face cleared and he held out a hand in greeting.

"Adept—I'm at a loss for words. I hadn't dreamed the Circle could respond so quickly to my message!"

Tarod frowned. "Message, sir?"

"Then you're not an emissary from the High Initiate?" The Margrave seemed perplexed.

"We encountered him on the road, sir," the militia leader explained hastily. "It was sheer chance that he was riding this way, and—in the circumstances—we thought he might aid us."

The Margrave looked relieved and clasped Tarod's hands again in a welcome more fervent than the first. "Then it was a very fortunate accident!" he said with obvious relief. "Have my men explained to you, Adept, the nature of our problem?"

"They tell me you've apprehended a girl who you believe is the Chaos creature's accomplice," Tarod replied. "You'll forgive my being blunt, but this is the fifth or sixth such claim I've had to investigate since I began my journey, and not one so far has had any foundation."

The Margrave shook his head emphatically. "Believe me, this is no false alarm. I understand your scepticism—we've had our share of hysteria here in Prospect, and there have been any number of accusations without evidence to back them." He looked up at Tarod as though challenging him to argue with his next words. "I'm not a fool, or at least I don't believe I am. And neither is Sister-Seer Jennat Brynd."

"A Sister of Aeoris? I'm sorry, I don't quite follow."

"It was a party of Sisters who discovered the girl's real identity," the Margrave told him. "Apparently she had been travelling with them for some days, and Sister Jennat's suspicions were aroused. She used her talents to investigate the girl, and learned the truth." His mouth pursed into an expression that might have been distaste or unease. "The girl had been calling herself Themila something—I can't recall the clan name—but when the Sisters discovered a jewel she was carrying hidden about her, they were certain they had found the fugitive."

Tarod's skin crawled. *Themila*—the coincidence was too great to be dismissed. He had told Cyllan of Themila Gan Lin, his one-time mentor; it was a name she would remember. . . .

Forcing his voice to remain even, he asked, "And what of the girl herself? Has she confessed?"

The Margrave shook his head. "No. She has refused to speak since she was apprehended. She simply sits and glares at all who approach her." He shuddered delicately. "It's not a look I wish to see too often. If half the stories surrounding her are true, I don't like to speculate on what she might be capable of." He paused. "But I ramble—there's time enough to explain the rest later, and I've already neglected the most basic of courtesies. You must be parched after your ride, especially in this dusty weather. Allow me at least to offer you a cup of wine."

The offer was difficult to decline; if he showed himself overeager to see the prisoner, the old man might suspect his motives. Tarod forced himself to smile. "I'd appreciate it, Margrave; thank you."

Followed at a polite distance by his small entourage, the Margrave led Tarod through the cool corridors of the justice house to an anteroom set aside for receiving important guests. Tarod had to quell his uneasy impatience when the old man ordered a servant to bring not only wine but also food, and made the best effort he could to eat delicacies that his stomach didn't want while the Margrave elaborated on the circumstances of their prisoner's arrest. The Sisters, he said, had intended to turn north and take their captive back to the Star Peninsula, but as soon as the news reached his ears he had insisted that the undertaking was too dangerous. It would be safer to send word to the Circle so that they might arrange a secure escort, but the message had only been despatched via one of the new courier birds that very morning, hence the Margrave's astonishment at the prompt arrival of an Adept in the town. Tarod listened courteously to the flow of words, occasionally nodding or murmuring agreement, but inwardly he felt close to breaking point. If the captured girl *was* Cyllan—and, he reminded himself, that had yet to be seen—then time was running short; a messenger-bird would deliver the Margrave's letter to the Castle tomorrow at the latest, and Keridil wouldn't waste a moment in acting on it. He had to cut across the

Margrave's vociferousness without making the ploy too obvious.

He realized suddenly that the old man had asked him a question which, lost in his own thoughts, he hadn't comprehended. He looked up quickly. "I'm sorry; what did you say?"

"I asked, sir, if you have ever seen this girl for yourself? I gather she was held for some time at the Castle of the Star Peninsula."

"Yes . . . I saw her once or twice."

"Then you'd recognize her again?"

"Certainly." Tarod took the opportunity which the Margrave had unwittingly offered him. "In fact, sir, I think it would be as well if I were to see her without any further delay."

The Margrave looked dubious. "I don't wish to impose on you, Adept. You must be tired—"

"I'm greatly refreshed, thanks to your hospitality."

"Well . . . it's as you wish, of course." The Margrave rose stiffly and led him out of the anteroom and along farther corridors towards the rear of the building. As they walked, Tarod asked suddenly, "Margrave, what has become of the jewel the girl carried? I trust it's in safekeeping?"

"Indeed, yes. Sister Liss Kaya Trevire has it in her possession, and I understand she has taken precautions against its influence."

"Very wise of her. And where is Sister Liss now?"

"She and her companions are lodged here at the justice house." The Margrave looked unhappy. "It's hardly fit accommodation for the Sisters of Aeoris, but they insisted on staying close to the prisoner."

Tarod nodded and made no further comment. They had by now reached a barred door under which bright daylight showed. A man stood on guard, and at a gesture from the Margrave he hastened to lift the bar and pull the door open.

They emerged into a small, walled courtyard flooded

with sunlight. A flowering tree in one corner had
shed a carpet of white petals over the flagstones and
over the roughly-constructed wooden cage that stood
nearby. In the cage something moved, but Tarod's
view was blocked by two white-robed figures who
stood before the cage and seemed to be pushing something through the bars. At the sound of the door
grating the two Sisters of Aeoris looked round, then,
recognizing the Margrave, straightened and turned
to face him.

"Sisters . . ." The Margrave hurried forward but
Tarod hung back, unable to bring himself to look
more closely at the cage. The old man was explain-
ing the circumstances of the Adept's arrival, and at
last he turned to Tarod and said, "Adept—may I
present Sister Liss Kaya Trevire, and Sister-Seer
Jennat Brynd."

Both women bowed in the formal manner adopted
between Sisterhood and Circle, and Tarod looked
first at the fair-haired, middle-aged Liss, then at the
younger, darker Jennat. He knew instantly that the
seer was skilled; unlike many of her kind, whom the
Sisterhood promoted for political rather than spiritual reasons, she had a true talent. He'd have to be
careful. . . .

"Sisters." He nodded to them both in turn. "The
Margrave tells me that you've apprehended one of
our fugitives. If it's true, the Circle will be very much
in your debt."

Jennat was watching him carefully, and he de-
tected a challenge in her eyes; but it was Sister Liss
who spoke.

"I believe there can be little doubt of the girl's
identity, Adept."

He couldn't put off the moment any longer. Turning, Tarod looked directly at the wooden cage, and a
hand seemed to close tightly round his heart and
lungs and squeeze them, so that he couldn't breathe.

She was bedraggled and dirty, her hair a bizarre skewbald of blond and copper-brown; but the small, pinched face and wide amber eyes were so painfully familiar to him that recognition was like a physical blow. Their gazes met, locked, and her hand flew to her mouth in disbelieving shock—then she covered her face and he heard her gasping, indrawn breath.

She looked almost exactly as she had done when she had broken through the temporal barrier to arrive wet and exhausted at the Castle, and poignant memories crowded Tarod's mind. With them came the first surge of anger at her predicament, and he knew that unless he took unremitting control of it, the rage might overwhelm him. Fighting it down, he became aware that the Margrave and the two Sisters were watching him.

"Well, Adept?" The Margrave licked his lips uncertainly. "*Is* this the girl the Circle are seeking?"

He couldn't deny it. The Sisters had proved Cyllan's identity beyond all shadow of doubt, and they were waiting only for his confirmation. Slowly, Tarod approached the cage, and as he did so Cyllan let her hands fall from her face. He allowed his left hand, hidden from sight of the Margrave and Sisters, to make a small, warning gesture, and he hoped she understood.

"Yes," he said, his voice even. "This is the girl."

As the small group moved away from her prison, Cyllan's gaze followed Tarod with a hunger and longing that made her shiver uncontrollably. Since the nightmare of her capture had begun she'd thought of nothing but him, tormenting herself with visions of a short-lived future in which all hope of seeing him again was gone. Before their arrival at Prospect town she'd made two attempts to escape from the Sisters, but both had failed; and though it wasn't in Cyllan's nature to admit defeat, she had realized that any further attempt at flight was pointless. Even if she could escape—and that in itself was unlikely—she couldn't hope to retrieve the Chaos stone, and without it Tarod's cause was lost. She had no power of her own; all she had was the ability to silently defy and curse her captors, while she waited to be taken to her death.

But now . . . She rubbed fiercely at her eyes, still partly convinced that she must be asleep and dreaming, but Tarod's tall figure didn't waver and vanish. He looked gaunt, tired, unkempt; but he was alive, and he had come to her. Somehow he had deceived the Sisters and the Margrave, and for the first time since her own deception had been discovered Cyllan felt hope renewing itself. If he could just find a way to—

Sister Jennat, on the edge of the small group, suddenly looked over her shoulder directly at the cage, and Cyllan felt a sharp *frisson* of discomfort, as though her thoughts were being spied upon. She'd forgotten Jennat's talent, in the shock of seeing Tarod, and quickly turned her face aside, trying to cloud her mind and block the seer's attempt to probe. After a few moments Jennat looked away, and she allowed herself to breathe again. With luck on her side—and she desperately needed luck now—the dark Sister had had no chance to find anything suspicious in what she saw. Drawing air into her lungs, and striving to quell the pounding of her heart, Cyllan sat back to wait. It was all she could do.

"There's no question as to the girl's identity," Tarod told his companions. "As I explained to the Margrave, I saw her during her captivity at the Castle, and despite her disguise I'm not in any doubt. However, there is still the matter of the jewel. I'd like to see it for myself."

He became aware instantly of Sister Jennat's sharp

scrutiny, and warning bells rang deep in his mind. Something—he couldn't judge what, though it hardly mattered—had alerted the seer, and he could sense a sly, subtle attempt to probe his thoughts. Quickly he blocked them, saw her flinch momentarily, and realized that, although she couldn't tell what he was thinking, his retaliation had made her all the more suspicious. An unpleasant sense of urgency began to worry at him. Intimidated though Sister Liss might be by the authority of a high-ranking Adept, Jennat was another matter. He had to get Cyllan away, before the Sister's doubts could take root and grow.

Liss bowed her head, acquiescing. "Of course, Adept, if you wish to see the gem I have it here in my pouch. Though—forgive me—I wonder if it might be unwise to expose it? We took certain precautions, you understand, and—"

Tarod's uneasy impatience redoubled, but he tried to keep it from his voice. "I appreciate your concern, Sister Liss, but I need to be sure of its authenticity."

"Sister—" Jennat hissed the word involuntarily, then blanched as Tarod turned a swift, angry glance on her. Liss was fumbling in her belt-pouch, her movements infuriatingly slow, and it was all Tarod could do to stop himself from physically shaking her into greater haste. He didn't dare look towards the cage at Cyllan, and prayed silently that Jennat wouldn't turn her attentions to her and see what was in her mind. He felt a disturbing mixture of impatience and dread as he watched Liss's clumsy efforts—he needed the stone, wanted to touch its familiar contours and know that once again he controlled its power; and yet the fear that he might succumb to the jewel's ancient influence, that the servant might become the master, was all too strong.

"Here it is." Liss finally drew out a tightly-folded piece of white cloth, and Tarod saw the lightning-

flash sigil of the White Gods embroidered on it. He
kept the relief he felt from his voice as he spoke.

"Thank you, Sister. If I might see the stone . . . ?"

Jennat was biting her lip, glancing nervously from
Tarod to Liss and back to Tarod. The older woman
began to unwrap the cloth; through its folds something glittered coldly, and Tarod felt a surge of raw
emotion, of power; a sensation he had all but forgotten and which struck him so unexpectedly that he
didn't think to control it—

"Sister, *no!*" Jennat's frantic cry cut the still air
like a sword-blade, and at the same moment the final
folds of the cloth fell away to expose the Chaos stone
in Liss's hand. Tarod swung round, and his gaze
locked with the dark girl's—her face was a frozen
mask of horror, and in her eyes he saw stunned
recognition of his true self.

Sister Liss was turning, alarmed by Jennat's warning but not yet comprehending what her seer had
understood. Without pausing to think, Tarod snatched
the jewel from Liss's palm—and a massive physical
shock jolted through him, as though he'd been struck
by a thunderbolt. His left hand clenched round the
gem, and an atavistic, titanic sense of power flooded
his mind, wiping out all reason and setting fire to an
instinctive fury. He couldn't think as a logical, mortal man—Jennat's face was a blur, the Margrave's
querulous cry like a distant, meaningless bird-call—
he flung his left arm out towards Jennat and the
power surged within him.

The flowering tree in the corner erupted in a
column of white flame, and light blasted across the
courtyard. Burning branches whirled down on to the
cage, and the wooden bars blazed up like torches.
Tarod saw Cyllan reel back, and he screamed her
name, summoning her to his side. She staggered,
regained her balance—then he saw her fling herself
through the roaring arch of fire that consumed the

cage, her figure lit grotesquely and her face distorted
with a wild triumph. She reached him and his right
hand locked on hers—the clutch of her fingers was
ferocious—then through the mayhem he heard Sister Jennat shrieking.

"No! No! Sister, help me! Stop them!"

Men were bursting from the doors to the justice
house, the Margrave was trying to block Tarod's path,
and he saw Jennat, a blur of white robes and flying
dark hair, hurling herself towards him. He didn't
think—he *couldn't* think; the instinctive fury was too
great. A gesture, and Jennat screamed like a tortured
beast, her body twisting about in a gruesome dance
before she crashed to the ground, her bones smashed
and all traces of life obliterated from her eyes.

Through a red daze Tarod saw Sister Liss backing
away on all fours and heard her wailing on a high,
insensate note. He dragged Cyllan to his side, swung
round, and came face to face with the Margrave. The
old man's features were distorted by terror but he
was trying to block their path, his militia behind
him. Tarod raised his hand again and the old man
reeled sideways, buffeted by a force that punched
him across the courtyard. The militiamen fell back
in horrified confusion and Tarod clove through their
midst, only dimly aware of Cyllan at his side. The
door split, burst apart by the insane force erupting
from within him, and they were running through
corridors that warped and fragmented before them.
Faces loomed and fell away crying out in fear, the
double doors at the main entrance were before them—

The crowd outside in the avenue parted like leaves
before a gale as the dark, demonic figure ran from
the justice house. To Tarod's twisted consciousness
the scene was a nightmare of crazed shapes and
howling sound; the Chaos force had control of him
and the milling bodies and screaming voices had no
meaning. Black light flickered about him, lighting

his stark face and possessed eyes. At the edge of the
crowd something moved, and he sent out an implacable mental summons; the big bay horse reared and
danced, but his will held it and he was dimly aware
of lifting Cyllan, flinging her astride the animal and
springing into the saddle behind her. The sensation
of the powerful, bunching muscles beneath him
brought back a measure of sanity—he screamed a
command and the horse spun about, launching into
a standing gallop as it raced towards the town walls
and freedom.

Chapter 7

Sweating, shaking, the bay horse stumbled to a halt under the shelter of a vast pine tree that marked the edge of Prospect Province's southern forest. The last bloodied streaks of sunset were still just visible in the west, but dusk had drained all color from the woods, merging shadow with night and casting a charcoal-dark pall over the humping landscape.

Tarod slid from the saddle, his spine jarring as his feet struck the uneven ground, and for a moment he pressed his face against the animal's flank, feeling drained and exhausted. Then he reached up and his hands caught Cyllan about the waist to lift her down. Her face stared back at him, a pale, indistinct oval in which only her eyes looked smudged and dark in the deepening twilight. He felt her fingers clutch his arms to steady herself, then she slithered to the ground and suddenly was clinging to him with the desperate hunger of a frightened child.

"*Tarod . . .*" She said his name over and over again as though it were a talisman, and he drew her to where a tangle of briars formed a natural shelter, fallen pine needles making a soft carpet on the turf.

131

Together they sank down on the makeshift couch, and at last she raised her head and gazed at him.

"I thought I'd never see you again." Her fingers touched his face tentatively, as though she didn't trust the evidence of her eyes. "I'd been searching for you, listening to every rumor, hoping . . . I believed you must be alive, but—"

"Hush." He kissed her, moved by the aching familiarity of her skin beneath his lips. "Don't say anything." Her hair brushed against his face and he pushed it aside, his fingers tracing the contours of her face. She felt so small, so vulnerable. . . . When he kissed her again she turned her head so that his mouth found hers, and he pulled her closer, the cloak he wore enveloping them both. Tired though he was, feelings were awakening that he couldn't and didn't wish to stem; driven by an understanding that he dared not acknowledge, he needed her and wanted her in a way he'd never known before.

She made to speak but his lips quieted her, and he felt her responding to him, uncertainly at first but then with increasing fervor as recent terrors gave way to the emotions of the moment. By the tree the bay horse snorted and Cyllan started nervously. Tarod smiled and drew her closer against him.

"It's all right, love," he told her softly. "Nothing can harm you. Not now . . ."

Much later, she woke from a restless sleep and saw him standing at the edge of the forest, silhouetted against a sky steeped in thin, silver-grey light. Both moons were high, but barely more than crescents; an insidious wind had risen and rustled in the burgeoning trees, lifting Tarod's black hair back from his face and casting his profile into sharp relief. Beside him the bay stood head down and dozing. From the set of his shoulders Cyllan knew that Tarod hadn't slept; his restlessness was a palpable aura.

She got quietly to her feet, gathering up his cloak with which he'd covered her, and walked slowly towards him. Hearing her approach he turned, and she saw that he held something in one hand—something that glittered coldly. His smile was touched with sadness.

"You should be sleeping."

"I'm not tired, not anymore." She touched his hand; it was chilled and she cast the cloak around him. "And you . . . ?"

"I don't think I could sleep, even if I wanted to." His fingers moved restively, and the Chaos stone caught and reflected a sharp sliver of light. For near on two hours Tarod had stood gazing out at the landscape with its moon-distorted perspectives, searching his own mind for the answers to a dilemma he knew he couldn't resolve, and he felt incapable of expressing to Cyllan the feelings that stirred in him. He had thought himself immune to the Chaos stone's influence, but he'd been wrong—yesterday's ugly events had proved that beyond all doubt. The old power had returned to him, and he'd used it without considering the consequences. . . . Now, he was torn between loathing of the stone and the heady knowledge that he was whole again. However evil the jewel might be, whatever its Chaotic legacy, it contained his soul—it was an integral part of him, and without it he'd been little better than an empty husk.

Last night when he'd made love to Cyllan he had been stunned by the intensity of his own emotions. The long, lonely days when he had existed soulless and empty had left their mark, and he'd all but forgotten how great the strength of human passions, good or ill, could be. It was as though his existence had taken on another dimension; one where every sense, every feeling, every thought, was brighter and clearer and sharper. He had once told Cyllan that until his soul was restored to him he could never love or give in the way that he really desired to, and now he realized how true his words had been. Yet the stone, without which he was only half alive, had imbued him with an evil to which he'd already succumbed once, and would doubtless succumb again. That was the nature of the dilemma, and Tarod was finding it hard to live with himself.

He was turning the stone over and over in his hand, and suddenly he felt Cyllan's fingers tangle with his, arresting his movement. "Your thoughts aren't happy, Tarod," she said quietly. "Were you thinking about what happened in Prospect?"

He looked down at her, then sighed. "Yes. And I was wondering what I'd see in your eyes when you woke, and asking myself if I could face it."

"Why should you not be able to? Do you think I've changed so much?"

Tarod shook his head. He made a tentative attempt to release his hand, but she would not let go. "Yesterday, for the first time, you saw the force that truly moves me, Cyllan," he said. "You saw my soul, and that soul isn't human. You saw *Chaos.*"

"I saw *Tarod*, as I see Tarod now—and as I touched and felt Tarod earlier tonight."

"Then maybe you don't yet understand what I really am."

Her face was partly obscured by the curtain of her hair, but even in the dimness he could see an odd, burning intensity in her eyes. "Oh yes, I think I do," she told him stubbornly. "I know that you love me enough to have saved my life, no matter what the cost to you. As to whether that motive is born out of Order or Chaos—it doesn't *matter*, Tarod! It's a *human* feeling, a *mortal* emotion." Her fingers squeezed his, hard. "Doesn't that prove where the real truth lies? Yes; you killed someone. But you killed them to save me. And I'd be a hypocrite, wouldn't I, if I condemned you for doing no more than I've done myself?"

He realized what she was saying, and at last something that he'd heard but doubted was confirmed. He was a little disconcerted to find that the confirmation came as no surprise.

"Then you *did* kill Drachea Rannak . . ." he said.

Cyllan turned away from him. "Yes. I killed him, and I can't regret it. I've tried to make myself feel remorse, but I'm not capable; not after what he tried to do to us." She released his hand at last and walked away to the edge of the trees, staring out at the Prospect hills but taking in nothing of the vista. "I used the stone to kill him, and I'd use it again—I'd use it now, if I had to. Does that make me evil?"

"No. But—"

"Tarod, if you find it hard to reconcile your conscience, then I can only pray you'll understand and forgive me for what I've done. . . ."

He stepped towards her. "You know there's nothing to forgive. If—"

She interrupted again, her voice unexpectedly harsh. "I don't just mean Drachea. There's more."

"More?" Tarod hesitated, then laid his hands on her shoulders, drawing her towards him though she still wouldn't face him. "Tell me."

He felt Cyllan shiver, and this time it seemed she had to exert a great effort of will to speak. "You rejected your own soul because you wanted no part of an evil legacy," she said. "Yet I couldn't follow your principle, and I think that makes me far more evil than you. You see . . . I made a pact with Chaos to secure your freedom."

Tarod's fingers tightened reflexively on her shoulder muscles, but it was the only outward sign of the shock he felt. Slowly Cyllan raised her left arm and turned her hand palm up so that her coat sleeve fell back. Even in the gloom he could see the dark scar, like a burn, that marred her skin.

"Yandros made that mark," Cyllan told him quietly. "He kissed my wrist to seal our bargain."

Stunned, Tarod took her arm, but his touch was gentle. Her skin was puckered and as he touched the scar he could sense its origin; a stigma that time wouldn't erode. With terrible clarity he remembered Yandros's face; the proud, smiling mouth, the ever-changing eyes, the power that defied mortal concepts. . . . He'd challenged Yandros once, and defeated him; but he understood Chaos in a way no other sorcerer could, and knew how to use the dark Lord's own weapons against him. The thought that Cyllan, unskilled and unprotected, had faced such a power, chilled him to the marrow.

He said, not knowing how to put his feelings into words, "How did he—how *could* he break through? He was banished. . . ."

Cyllan hugged herself. "I called him—prayed, I suppose you might say—and he answered. That's all I know. He appeared in my room, and—and he agreed to aid me." She shut her eyes, trying to squeeze out the memory of that sense of appalling power and the paralyzing fear that it could still engender.

Tarod let out a long, sharp breath, fighting back an impulse to curse the world and everything in it. "Cyllan . . . Cyllan, what you did was *insane! Why* did you act so recklessly?"

She turned round at last, her eyes glittering. "What else was left to me? You were about to die, and Yandros was the only one, apart from me, who wanted you to live!" A strange, bitter smile distorted her face. "Do you think Aeoris would have intervened to save your life?"

She'd called on the quintessence of evil, opened herself to damnation, and all for his sake. . . . Tarod was moved to black rage at the thought of what she must have suffered, and painfully touched by her courage. True, he would have done as much for her,

and more, without a second thought; but he was too
well acquainted with Chaos to fear it in any form.
Cyllan was another matter.

Misinterpreting his silence, Cyllan pulled away from
him in sudden distress. Her challenging bravado had
been short-lived; now she hung her head.

"I'm sorry," she whispered. "I know what he's done
to you, what he is—but I had no choice! I *had* to save
you, and his was the only power I could turn to.
Tarod, please—don't hate me."

"*Hate* you?" He paused, then caught hold of her
and, when she tried to resist, pulled her forcibly into
his arms and held her tightly. "Cyllan, don't you
know me better than that?" His tone was fierce. "All
that matters, all I care about, is the risk you ran! I
know Yandros, and he gives nothing without taking
more in payment." The grim thought that he'd tried
not to voice suddenly wouldn't be held at bay any
longer. "What did you promise him in return for his
aid?"

Cyllan looked up, blinked. "My loyalty."

"Loyalty . . ."

"It was all he asked." She laughed in an odd,
broken tone. "He said I'd already damned myself in
the eyes of my own gods by calling on him; so what
had I to lose?"

Such generosity wasn't in Yandros's nature. He *must*
have had some ulterior motive, and that motive boded
ill. . . .

"He wants you to live, Tarod," Cyllan said. "He
told me as much. And it seems that he wants me to
survive, too . . . at least for the time being." She
smiled, though it was a wan effort. "I asked him to
kill me, to release you from the bargain you made
with the High Initiate, but he refused. He said . . . he
said that I might be of use to him. And so the pact
was made."

He touched her face gently, emotion clouding his

green eyes. "I don't know what to say; words are inadequate. So much love; so much courage . . ."

She shook her head. "I wasn't brave. I was afraid of him—and I'm afraid of him still." She looked up into his face. "I'm so afraid of what might happen if I fail him!"

His mind touched hers and he sensed the depth of her fear. His green eyes narrowed, and a look flickered in them that for an unnerving moment reminded Cyllan all too sharply of the Chaos Lord.

"Yandros won't harm you," Tarod told her softly. "Whatever he might claim, his power in this world is limited. I've defeated him once; I can do so again." His tone hardened. "If he threatens you, I'll destroy him. Believe that, Cyllan."

He couldn't tell whether she was convinced by his words—and he didn't care to question his own belief in them—but after a few moments a little of the resistance he'd sensed in her muscles receded, though her body was still painfully tense.

"What are we to do now?" she asked simply.

The decision hadn't been easy . . . but Cyllan's bravery, and the fear she now felt as a result of what she had done, had served to cement Tarod's resolution. He pressed his face against the crown of her hair and said, "We'll go on to Shu-Nhadek, as we always meant to do. We'll find passage, somehow, to the White Isle—"

"But—"

"No; hear me out, love. We'll find passage to the White Isle, and there we'll appeal directly to the only power in the world that can help us."

Cyllan stared at him in terrible dismay, but said nothing.

"Only Aeoris Himself can counter the evil of the Chaos stone," Tarod went on. "Yandros gained a foothold in this world through me, and only I can make the decision to turn that tide. I'm not strong

enough to fight him alone. I *must* surrender the stone
to the White Lords . . . it's the only way."

"But it's more than just a jewel, Tarod; it's your
own *soul.*"

"I know. But you've seen the insanity that's been
turned loose on the land. Directly or indirectly, it's
Yandros's doing; it's like a disease eating at everyone
and everything, and if it isn't stopped there'll soon
be no cure. It *has* to be done, Cyllan. And at least, at
Aeoris's hands, we'll find the justice that the Circle
denied us."

She couldn't argue with his reasoning; but neither
could she silence the still, small voice that whispered
a warning deep in her mind. She was tired—too tired
for coherent thought, despite what she'd said to Tarod,
and she could see the need for sleep in his eyes even
if it eluded him. She stepped back, disengaging herself from his arms but keeping a hold on his hand,
and looked over her shoulder at the dark, misty hills.

"Come back to the shelter with me." Her voice was
gentle. "The moons are sinking; it'll be dawn before
long. We should rest while we can."

He followed her as she moved towards their hiding
place. Sleep would be a blessing, if he could find it,
and when they lay down he drew her close to him,
covering them both with his cloak. She nestled her
head in the crook of his arm, and he thought she'd
drifted away when her voice, low-pitched, surprised
him.

"Tarod . . . When this is over—*if* it's over—"

"When, love. Think of it only as when."

A slight movement told him that she was nodding
acquiescence. "When it's over . . . I hope I can see
Sister Erminet again. She was so good, so kind—
without her I'd have lost you, and I don't think I can
ever repay that debt."

"I know what she did." Unbidden, memory of the

old Sister's face came sharp and clear to Tarod's mind, and his voice caught on the last word.

Cyllan turned in his arms. "Tarod? What is it?"

He might have spared her the truth, at least for tonight, but to do so seemed an insult to Erminet, for whom honesty had been a watchword. "Erminet is dead," he said simply.

"Dead . . . ?"

"The Circle discovered what she'd done to aid us, and she was arrested. She took her own life whilst under guard in the Castle." Tarod realized that his own voice sounded remote, detached; it was far from what he felt. "She was a skilled herbalist," he went on, touched by the disquieting sensation that he was speaking into a void. "She would have felt no pain, no suffering—though the Gods know that's little comfort!" His tone had become savage, and he controlled it with difficulty. "She didn't deserve that fate. And hers is yet another death to place at my door."

"No. At Keridil's," Cyllan said in a small voice.

He sighed. "Keridil would have had no quarrel with Erminet had it not been for me, and I won't try to escape that truth."

"No, Tarod." Cyllan squeezed her eyes tightly shut against the tears that welled in them. "Sister Erminet would have argued that with you. I can almost hear what she'd say."

I make my own decisions for my own reasons, and if you think your opinions would sway me you can think again, Chaos-fiend or no! It was a fair paraphrase of what Erminet might have acidly retorted to any attempt to influence her. She'd made her own decisions, as much so in the manner of her death as in anything else. Perhaps, despite his self-recrimination, Cyllan was right.

"Aeoris keep her soul," Cyllan whispered.

Tarod's fingers touched her hair. She was almost

asleep, unlikely to comprehend what he said. "Or Yandros . . ." he replied softly.

Rain had moved in during the night to sweep across the western reaches of Southern Chaun. The sight of the grey, drizzling curtain soaking the fields beyond the Cot's elegant windows irritated Ilyaya Kimi as she sat impatiently waiting for her chamberwomen to arrive. Everything was ready, the journey planned down to the last detail—and now this. She could anticipate a thorough wetting even on the few short steps between the main door and her litter, and she was far too old to run for shelter, even if the idea alone weren't an affront to her dignity. So, she would sit cramped and jolting in that damned palanquin while the damp seeped through to her bones, with nothing better to do than listen to the rain pattering on the canopied roof. And before her lay all the tedium of rough tracks and Prospect Estuary to cross before her party even reached a decent drove-road. . . .

She slapped a hand petulantly down on the arm of her chair and, with difficulty, eased herself to her feet. The chamberwomen were late—she had told them to attend her promptly one hour after the tocsin had rung for morning prayers, and the sandglass on her table told her that the hour was well past. Pursing her lips in anger Ilyaya reached for the little handbell that stood beside the glass, and shook it vigorously. She was gratified moments later to hear footsteps running along the passage outside, then the door burst open and her two servants appeared.

"Your pardon, Matriarch; we were so busy with the preparation of the litter—"

"Knock." The old woman interrupted their apology. "How many times must I tell you? *Knock* before you enter my room! Go out and do it again."

The chamberwomen exchanged wry glances before doing as they were bidden, and when they entered for the second time Ilyaya gave a curt nod of satisfaction.

"Better. You're both late, but we'll overlook the matter this time. How do the preparations progress?"

"Well, Madam. The palanquin is harnessed, pack-horses loaded, and Sister Antasone reports that the escort has been sighted approaching the Cot. They should be here within ten minutes, and then we can leave just as soon as you wish it."

"Good." There was little point prolonging the departure, however reluctant she might feel to face the journey. Better to get it begun and therefore over with the sooner. "And the arrangements at Shu-Nhadek?" she demanded.

"The messenger left two days ago, Matriarch, to take word to the Margrave. He'll be sensible of the honor you do him, and will house you in the greatest comfort."

"If he's yet returned from the north, he will," Ilyaya observed sourly. "If not, Aeoris alone knows what manner of shambles we'll find awaiting us." She eased herself stiffly back into the chair, sighing with relief as she sat down. "Very well. You may bring me my travelling cloak, and my personal valise. And I want to see the Mistress of Novices before we leave."

"Yes, Madam." The women departed on their errands, leaving Ilyaya drumming gnarled, impatient fingers on the arm of her chair.

Sister-Senior Fayalana Impridor was alone in the Hall of Prayer when the Matriarch's servant found her. The Novice-Mistress looked up from the pile of books of Aeoris's Law that she was tidying in the wake of the morning dedications, and smiled her slow smile.

"Good morning, Missak. Is the Matriarch ready to depart?"

"She is, Sister, and she asks that you attend her before she leaves."

"Certainly—I'll come at once." Fayalana put down the books, brushed at her robe, and followed Missak towards the door. Just as they reached the passage she raised a quirkish eyebrow and asked, "And how is the Matriarch today?"

The question had clear implications, though only the senior Sisters ever had the temerity to voice them. Missak smiled thinly.

"Between ourselves, Sister, she was a little pettish and we thought she might go into one of her moods, but it seems to have passed off."

"Providence be thanked for that," Fayalana said fervently. "We all have enough to cope with as it is . . . not, of course, that the Matriarch can help her small foibles. It's an affliction that will come to all of us as our years advance."

Missak nodded. "Sometimes, Sister, I've woken in the night and asked myself whether she should be making such a journey at all. She's over eighty, after all, and not strong."

Fayalana's eyes softened kindly. "I know how you feel—it worries us all. But this is something that can't possibly be delegated, Missak. Aeoris's own law forbids that anyone save the true triumvirate of rulers may sit in Conclave—there can be no proxies; no substitutions, you understand."

"I understand, yes. But . . . she should *retire*, Sister. At her age, she shouldn't have to carry such responsibilities."

Fayalana's dark eyes seemed to turn inward for a few moments, as though she saw some hidden meaning in the other woman's words. Then her face cleared and she said dryly, "I agree, Missak. But I wouldn't care to be the one delegated to suggest it to her!"

At about the time the Matriarch's party began its cumbersome journey southeast towards Prospect Estuary, a ship rocked on the light swell of the dock on

Summer Isle. Both on deck and at the shoreward end
of its gangplank there was a good deal of activity;
men hurried back and forth with provisions, furnish-
ings, trunks; a seemingly endless stream of goods
making the perilous crossing from shore to ship. On
the afterdeck, under the shadow of the great mast, a
youngish man wearing the distinctive blue 'sash of a
ship's master watched proceedings with a relaxed
but practiced eye while the crew sat about on or near
the rail, talking desultorily or playing Quarters or
Strike Anchor. Occasionally a burst of laughter rose
above the general hubbub as someone made a profit-
able win.

At the back of the dock, well away from the confusion, two caparisoned horses stamped restlessly in
the harness of an open carriage until a sharp word
from their driver quieted them. Behind them, one of
the carriage's two occupants watched the distant activity with intense interest. He was a thin, brown-
haired youth of some seventeen years, his good looks
marred by a prominent nose that dominated his face.
He was attempting to grow a moustache, both to
counter the effect of the nose and to make himself
look a little older; but thus far it was only poorly
developed. His elaborate clothes—wide-sleeved embroidered jacket over silk trousers, heavily embossed
belt with a short and purely decorative sword hanging from a scabbard—were creased with sitting. The
carriage springs creaked as he stretched a cramped
leg and sighed, and his companion, a much older
man, glanced sidelong at him.

"Are you tired, High Margrave?"

Fenar Alacar rubbed at his eyes. "Not really, Isyn.
Just tired of waiting."

"It was your own idea to come and see the preparations for yourself." The older man hesitated, then
smiled a little sheepishly. "With all due respect, sir."

"Don't call me that, Isyn—you know it makes me

uncomfortable! You were 'sir' to me for so many years while my father was alive, and I can't get used to the idea of everything being reversed now!" Fenar was trying to hide his boredom and frustration, but the effort was too great. "This"—he indicated the bustling dock with an imperious sweep of one hand, which reminded Isyn sharply of the old High Margrave— "all seems such an unnecessary fuss and waste! Damn it, it's less than a day's sailing to the mainland, and once we put in at Shu-Nhadek I'll be housed as well as if I were still at my own court! Yet look at it— enough food for a whole troop of militia, my own dishes, cups, knives; even my own chair to sit on! It's ridiculous!"

Isyn shook his head. Twelve years of tutoring, and still the boy didn't seem to fully understand what he was, and why he must be so treated. "It's a necessary precaution, High Margrave, especially with things as they are. We daren't take the smallest risk of any harm befalling you."

Fenar snorted. "And so I have to have an army of cooks, food-tasters, bed-makers, chair-dusters—and I have to suffer the frustration of waiting and waiting while the damned ship's loaded with a vast quantity of superfluous nonsense!" He looked sidelong and resentfully at his tutor-turned-adviser. "If the powers of Chaos mean to prevent the Conclave by luring me to my death, I imagine they'll find a subtler method than poisoning!"

Isyn refused to rise to the bait. Seventeen or no, the boy *was* High Margrave, and his elevation was still recent enough for him to want to test his authority on occasion. It was a way of covering for his insecurity, and the older man could understand it.

"It's worth remembering, sir," he said gently, and using the term Fenar hated quite deliberately, "that the High Initiate's party won't arrive for at least another three days; more if they're held up by bad weather. And speaking personally, I don't relish the prospect of spending the intervening time in Shu-Nhadek with only the Lady Matriarch for company."

There was a pause, then Fenar snorted again, but this time with suppressed laughter. "Gods, the very idea of it! D'you know, Isyn, I can hardly believe that the old woman's still alive. She was older than old when I last saw her, and I was a child then. She must be a hundred if she's a day by now!"

His words were disrespectful and he was exaggerating, but Isyn felt privately relieved by the display of childishness—it suited the lad far better than his earlier attempt at arrogance. The next few days, he thought, would be a trial in more ways than the obvious; Fenar Alacar feared the impending Conclave, though nothing would make him admit it; and when he was afraid he would, like all young and untried creatures, react in one of two ways—either by retreating into sulkiness, or by trying to flaunt his position as absolute ruler, at least in theory, of all the land. Isyn had glimpsed the beginnings of such a reaction last year when the new High Initiate had visited the Summer Isle court; awed by Keridil Toln, Fenar had at the same time resented his confidence and the aura of the highly occult Circle that he carried with him. Then, he hadn't had the self-possession to challenge Keridil; now, if they found themselves in disagreement, it might be different—and the High Initiate would be too formidable an opponent for Fenar to cut his teeth on.

The boy was fidgeting again. He'd seen the sense in Isyn's words, but they did nothing to assuage his impatience.

"I don't see why we have to go to Shu-Nhadek at all," he said irritably. "There's no need for so much pomp and ceremony. Why can't we simply sail from here directly to the White Isle?"

Isyn didn't reply, but his brows knitted together in a sharp frown, and Fenar made an angry gesture.

"Oh, I know. Thus it is written, thus it must be. Just because some musty old manuscripts moldering away in the far north say that we have to follow this ridiculous procedure—don't frown at me like that, Isyn; I don't appreciate your disapproval."

Isyn's normally placid temper was starting to fray, and he interrupted. "You may not appreciate it, High Margrave, but you have it, whether either of us wills or no. And you'd have more than disapproval from the Guardians if you tried to set one foot on the White Isle from the deck of the *Summer Sister*."

Fenar shrugged. "Would I? They're nothing more than gatekeepers, however they like to cloak themselves. I could command them to—"

"I'd defy any mortal man, living or dead, to command the Guardians." Isyn spoke so quietly and yet with such conviction that the young man was surprised. "No High Margrave, or High Initiate or Matriarch for that matter, has set eyes on the Guardians for generations, save from a distance, and none would dare—yes, sir, I said *dare*—to go against their will."

Fenar licked his lips uneasily, and Isyn pressed home the point. "You've heard the stories—I taught them to you myself when you were barely fledged. I'm only surprised you could have forgotten them."

Some of the older tales hinted that the Guardians, the hereditary caste who for thousands of years had inhabited the White Isle, weren't even truly human, but were descended from angelic beings in whose charge Aeoris had placed His casket. Wild stories, doubtless, but it was said there could be no smoke without fire. . . . Every now and then the Guardians sailed their strange barque to the mainland and took a handful of chosen women back to their stronghold to bear them children and so ensure the continuance of the caste. The women returned after a year or so, and never spoke of what they had seen; most were taken into the Sisterhood, or made convenient marriages later. The male children born on the Isle grew up to become the next generation of Guardians. No one ever speculated on what happened to the female children.

The bright sun was obscured suddenly by a stray wisp of cloud drifting from the west, and a wing of shadow passed over the dock and the carriage. Fenar glanced up, shivering as though the momentary gloom were an omen, and when he looked at Isyn again the anger had faded from his eyes.

"I'm sorry, Isyn," he said awkwardly With the need to apologize to anyone lessening as he grew more accustomed to his status, humility was becoming unfamiliar, and Isyn appreciated the effort this took. "I forgot myself, and I was wrong. We must, of course, do as protocol dictates." He forced a smile. "I don't want to make a fool of myself, do I, on what must surely be the most momentous task I'll ever undertake? I can just imagine what my father would have said—called me an arrogant little tyke and given me a whipping, I should think."

Isyn inclined his head in amused acknowledgment, and Fenar hunched his shoulders. In the wake of his apology and confession he was trying to salve his dignity and appear adult. The comment about his father had been a conciliatory gesture; now he wanted to erase it and move on. Isyn considered himself too old to remember the impatience and frustration of being seventeen, but nonetheless he could appreciate the boy's feelings.

He said, nodding towards the dock, "It seems the activity's slowing down. I would imagine the ship will be ready to sail on the next turn of the tide."

"Yes . . . though perhaps after all I'll take your advice, Isyn—bearing in mind the prospect of the Matriarch's company." Fenar studied his nails, self-conscious. "Doubtless there are a hundred and one small tasks I've overlooked and should attend to before embarking."

"Doubtless. And you must bid farewell to your lady mother, the Dowager Margravine."

The High Margrave looked up quickly, then the lids came half down over his grey eyes, masking their expression. "That I've already done. At least, I sent a message to her yesterday, and had her reply this morning. She sends her love, but begs to be excused from a meeting."

Isyn sighed inwardly. Since the death of her husband the Margravine had retired completely into herself, living out her days in an isolated dower house some way from the court, tended only by three serving-women, and grieving ceaselessly. She saw no outsider, not even her own son, and the consensus of opinion was that she was simply wanting to die.

"She asked to be remembered to you," Fenar added.

"Did she?" Isyn was surprised, and touched. "How kind of her."

A slightly strained silence fell between the two for a while then, until Isyn, alerted by footsteps, looked up to see the dock overseer approaching the carriage. On the *Summer Sister*'s deck the crew were suddenly active, the ship's master calling out orders in clipped but carrying tones.

He touched Fenar's shoulder, and the boy blinked.

"I think," Isyn said, smiling, "that if you have tasks to complete, sir, we might as well return to the palace and attend to them. If I read the signs right, the *Summer Sister* is ready to sail when the High Margrave commands it."

Chapter 8

Tarod's keen eyes saw the small cavalcade approaching from the west against the glare of the setting sun, and he reached out to touch the bridle of Cyllan's horse, bringing it to a well-trained halt. She shifted in her saddle, squinting as she tried to follow where he was pointing, then looked at him and saw the unease in his expression.

"What is it, Tarod?"

"I don't know." He couldn't explain the intuitive foreboding stirring within him; this was by no means the first party they had encountered on the road, but a sixth sense told him that it was no ordinary convoy, and he was wary.

Cyllan looked again. The sun was sinking into a bank of cloud and the glare was suddenly lessened, so that she could make out individual shapes among the cavalcade.

"They're moving quite slowly," she said. "There's something in their midst; something large. . . ."

"It's a palanquin." Tarod frowned. "And most of the riders seem to be dressed in white."

She glanced uncertainly at him, beginning to share his unease. "Do you know who they are?"

150

"I know who they *should* be—but it makes no logical sense, unless—" He hesitated, then shook his head as though dismissing whatever unspoken thought had been in his mind, and instead turned his attention to the south. Three miles ahead, across a stretch of pleasant moorland, it was just possible to make out the contours of Shu-Nhadek in the evening haze, while beyond its blurred outlines the sea glittered like a knife on the horizon. Almost their final goal . . . they'd planned on reaching it by nightfall, and it seemed they weren't alone; at its present speed, he judged, the distant company would cross their path a mile outside the town.

His horse stamped and snorted, not understanding the delay, and Tarod turned to Cyllan. "Best play the lady for a while again, love. We may have to exchange a social grace or two before we reach Shu-Nhadek."

She smiled wryly and swung her right leg back across her mount's withers, hooking her knee over the elaborately-designed pommel of her saddle. She found the sidesaddle posture awkward and uncomfortable, but no woman of quality would dream of riding any other way—and a woman of quality was precisely what Cyllan was pretending to be.

With more than enough coin in his pouch to see them to their journey's end, Tarod had reasoned that ostentation was their best form of disguise. The populace was alerted to hunt down two fugitives, and no one was likely to consider that fugitives might hide by drawing attention to themselves—the concept wasn't logical. And so he had stopped at the next sizable town and, while Cyllan waited outside the walls, had bought new clothes for them both and two well-bred horses to replace the big bay: a chestnut gelding for himself, and a mettlesome but good-tempered grey mare for Cyllan. From then on, while he blurred their appearance and the memory of their faces in the minds of those they encountered, they had travelled under the guise of a prosperous vintner and his wife, and Tarod had noted with irony the ease with which they had passed through towns and villages. Rumor was still rife everywhere, but they heard little of it; ordinary folk would not dream of approaching wealthy strangers to share the latest gossip, and so, although they had made good speed to Shu-Nhadek, they'd heard nothing of the latest news.

And in every town and village there was still sickening testimony to the terror rife in the land. Accusations, trials, executions, vengeance—the tide showed no sign of turning, and the sights they saw on the road served both to strengthen Tarod's resolve, and to increase his anxiety to reach Shu-Nhadek, and beyond it his ultimate goal, as quickly as possible.

He touched his heels to the chestnut's flanks and it moved on, Cyllan's mare keeping pace. The light was failing rapidly as the cloud-bank swallowed the sun; ahead the first lamps were beginning to twinkle in the harbor town, mirroring the fainter glitter of stars in the easterly sky.

They heard the first sounds of the cavalcade as they reached the point where the western and southern roads merged for the final run into Shu-Nhadek. In the twilight the approaching figures—who were, as Tarod had said, mostly dressed in white—might have been ethereal ghosts, but the clatter and thump of several dozen hooves, the jingle of harness, proved they were solid enough. At the meeting of the roads Tarod and Cyllan reined in, and Cyllan's eyes widened as at last she recognized the riders for what they were.

"Sisters . . ." Her voice was almost inaudible.

The grey mare sidestepped, disturbed by her rider's sudden disquiet, and Tarod spoke a word that settled her. "I thought so. . . ." He watched the approaching group with eyes that were suddenly narrowed to slits. "And if I'm not mistaken, they're from Southern Chaun."

"Southern Chaun?"

"The Matriarch's Cot." He had counted eight women on horseback and five heavily-built male escorts, while in the midst of the convoy an elaborately-decked litter swayed, borne by four more horses and swathed in richly-embroidered curtains. Its occupant wasn't visible.

"You see that?" He nodded towards the litter. "That's the palanquin of the Matriarch herself, Lady Ilyaya Kimi."

He realized that Cyllan didn't understand, and added, "Lady Ilyaya is over eighty, and she hasn't left her Cot for ten years. She was too infirm to attend Keridil's inauguration—and if she's riding in that palanquin now, there's only one circumstance that could have brought her here." His hand, light on the reins, tightened its grip suddenly. "It means that Keridil has summoned a Conclave."

The leader of the Matriarch's escort called a sharp warning as he saw the two indistinct figures motionless by the meeting of the roads, and metal rattled as the five men drew their swords. The two figures didn't move, and after a moment the men relaxed as they realized the strangers presented no threat—merely a merchant, or some such, and his wife; doubtless awed by the cavalcade and wisely reining back to allow them to pass.

The convoy trotted by in stately grandeur; near its head, one of the older Sisters spared a glance for the two riders, whom she saw as Tarod wished her to see them—nondescript, irrelevant. Her voice carried clear above the rumble of their progress as she called out, "Aeoris be with you, good people!" and she made the Sign, with just a hint of patronage, in their direction.

Cyllan saw Tarod bow his head as though in recog-

nition and thanks, and hastily followed his example.
As the gilded palanquin swayed past she peered
harder, curious to glimpse the Matriarch; but the
curtains didn't so much as twitch. Then the cavalcade was drawing away from them along the road
into Shu-Nhadek.

Tarod watched as the riders diminished. He had,
without realizing it, touched his right hand to the
ring on his left index finger, and in response the
ring's stone flared and shimmered like a small, white
eye. He had made the decision to restore the Chaos
stone to its silver base after their flight from Prospect; and as the ring's contours flowed once again to
clasp the jewel he had felt a bitter mingling of despair and triumph. He was, truly, whole again—but
as he slipped the ring back onto his finger and sensed
the old familiarity of its presence, he had realized
afresh how dangerous its pervasive influence might
prove to be. He would need an iron will, a steel
control, to keep to his resolution now, against the
living power of Chaos. Yet over and beyond that he
would need the power the ring granted him—the
power of his own soul—if he wasn't to fail in what he
set out to do. And the presence of the Matriarch in
Shu-Nhadek made the goal that much more urgent
than before.

The thought was like a goad, and without warning
he urged his mount forward. Cyllan followed, confused by the anger that she'd seen in his eyes in the
moment before he set off.

"Tarod! Tarod, what is it?"

He looked back and said something that she couldn't
hear. She kicked hard at the grey mare's flank. The
animal put on a turn of speed and danced alongside
Tarod. Even in the gloom, Cyllan could see that his
face was taut and bitter. "Tarod, I don't understand!
You said that Keridil had called a Conclave—what
does that *mean?*"

No one outside the Circle could possibly understand the full implications of what the High Initiate
had done. But if his suspicions were right, then Keridil
had set something in motion that, if he didn't act
quickly, could bring catastrophe on them all.

He realized suddenly that he'd been on the verge of
cursing at Cyllan, taking his anger out on her simply
because there was no one else at hand. With an effort
he controlled the rising tide of emotion in him.

"I can't explain it now," he said. "But we've no
time to lose—and the Gods help us if we're too late!"

Shu-Nhadek was in a ferment. By one means and
another, news of the High Initiate's decision had
flooded into the town ahead of the three rulers' par-
ties, and with it had come a steady stream of devout
or frightened people, anxious to congregate as near
as possible to the site of the holy alliance and seek
sanctuary or blessing in its shadow. By the time
Tarod and Cyllan arrived, the Matriarch's cavalcade
had disappeared, whisked away to the Margrave's
residence to await the arrival of Keridil Toln and
Fenar Alacar—and, as Tarod had anticipated, every
inn and hostelry in the town was full to overflowing.

They finally reached the market-square and stopped
to rest their tired horses. The square was abnormally
busy; torches burned in the porticoes of all the larger
buildings, casting a peculiar, flickering hellglow across
the flagstones; people had congregated simply to wait
and watch and see whatever might be seen; at the
harbor side of the square a group of minstrels were
singing pious songs in the hope of earning a coin or
two.

Cyllan looked to where black openings gaped at
intervals among the buildings, and fancied she saw
the cold glimmer of the harbor waters at the far end
of an unlit alley. She shivered at a sudden, unwanted
memory, and edged her horse a little closer to Tarod's.

"This atmosphere . . ." She pitched her voice to a whisper that only he could hear. "It unnerves me."

"I know." He patted the chestnut gelding's neck. "It's as if the whole town had caught a fever. But at least we're not too late. The town's still awaiting Keridil—we're ahead of him, and that gives us some leeway. We'll find somewhere to rest the night, then see what we can discover in the morning."

Cyllan shivered again. "There's not an inn that hasn't barred its doors to new trade."

"Maybe." Tarod smiled, an old smile that hinted at something she preferred not to question. "We'll see."

Within half an hour he had found lodging for them, at a respectable tavern only a few moments' walk from the market-square. Cyllan had been dubious at first, afraid that they might be courting disaster by settling so close to the hub of activity, but he had soothed her fears, knowing that they were in no danger—at least until the Circle party should arrive. Money, a little intimidation, and a touch of his power had secured them a good room, and a meal was served to them there. Cyllan didn't want to eat—her nerves, like the strings of an overtuned instrument, felt on the verge of snapping—but Tarod's calm confidence soothed the worst of her terrors.

As they ate, Tarod explained the nature of the Conclave, and described what its outcome could mean to them.

"If Keridil succeeds in summoning Aeoris on the White Isle," he said, "then the powers of Order will have only one aim—to eradicate every trace of Chaos in the world."

Cyllan looked at him through her lashes, aware that her heartbeat had quickened uncomfortably. "But isn't that what you want?" she asked.

"Yes." She thought that Tarod had hesitated momentarily, though his answer was decisive enough. "But I fear that the White Lords will pursue that aim single-mindedly, without thought for the consequences that might befall mere mortals." He touched his tongue to his lips. "How is it possible to comprehend, let alone explain, the reasoning of a god? Yet I feel . . . I feel I know, far better than Keridil, the true nature of the power he means to unleash." He closed his right hand over the restored silver ring, aware of the Chaos stone pulsing beneath his fingers, and saw that Cyllan was watching him intently. "Although He is the patron and protector of humanity, Aeoris transcends human limitations to such a degree that individual lives and deaths—which are of vital importance to the mortals concerned—are so trivial to Him as to be beyond His consideration—and so much more so when weighed against the threat posed by Yandros." He paused, then smiled wryly. "Imagine that you stood in a meadow, confronted by an enemy who meant to slay you. In fighting that enemy, would you be concerned for the tiny insects that might be crushed out of existence beneath your feet as you battled?"

Cyllan nodded. "I understand you."

"Then you understand the danger in what Keridil means to do. And if Aeoris should find Yandros a powerful enemy, not easily overcome, the destruction they wreak will be all the greater. It mustn't come to that, Cyllan."

She turned her head to gaze out of the window. Across the rooftops the light of Shu-Nhadek harbor gleamed, reflecting broken mirror-images on the sea's calm surface. Mist was stealing in as the night deepened, and the peacefulness of the scene made a bizarre contrast with her thoughts.

"Then if it's to be prevented," she said, "we must

reach the White Isle before the Conclave can take place." She looked round at him, her eyes dark with emotion. "And you must do what you've been planning."

"Does the thought distress you so much?"

"I—don't know. My conscience tells me it's right, but—" She closed her mind to the sudden image of Yandros's face, and the memory of their bargain that rose within her. "I don't know, Tarod. I'm so afraid of the consequences. More afraid, I think, than of what might happen if Aeoris and Yandros should clash. What you said, what you described—it's too remote to affect me. Here, in this room in Shu-Nhadek with you, it doesn't *mean* anything; but if you surrender the soul-stone it—it'll dictate our future, and I feel that keenly." She gripped her hands together until the knuckles turned white. "I'm so afraid of losing you forever."

As she spoke the White Lord's name, Tarod noticed, she hadn't made the Sign. For anyone brought up as she had been that was an unthinkable omission, and he sensed the other forces that were at work in her. Yandros had touched her with far more than a physical scar, and, against his will, he felt a surge of pride in her.

My brother, she is worthy of us. . . .

The voice spoke silently in his mind, and it shocked him back to cold reality. Yes . . . it would be all too easy for them both to be seduced by that ancient power—and he, far more than Cyllan, had good reason to feel an affinity with it. But it mustn't be. He *had* to hold fast to his resolution; and if it resulted in the ultimate sacrifice, that sacrifice must be made.

"Cyllan." He reached out across the table, pushing aside the remains of the meal to take her hand in a grip that hurt. "Cyllan, I won't let myself be swayed. I came here to fulfill a pledge, and I'll fulfill it, whatever the consequences. While the Chaos stone exists, Yandros can challenge the rule of Order—but *only* while he has that foothold in the world. With the stone in Aeoris's hands, the Conclave will never be called—and this insanity can be stopped.''

She gazed at him, her expression bleak. "And you're sure, in your own mind, that this is the only way?"

There was another—but he daren't dwell on that thought for a moment, lest it should take root. . . .

"I'm sure," he said.

Cyllan nodded. "Very well. If it must be, it must." With her free hand she rubbed fiercely at her eyes, and Tarod couldn't tell whether or not she was crying. If she was, then knowing Cyllan they'd be tears of anger rather than despair. At length she blinked, sniffed, and said with determined conviction, "I was brought up to believe that Aeoris is just and fair. I can only pray that his High Initiate's blindness doesn't stand in the way of that justice."

Tarod smiled. His grip on her fingers relaxed a little, and he lifted her hand to his lips and kissed it. "Remember my analogy of the insects in the meadow?" he said. "If Aeoris is what we believe Him to be, Keridil's arguments will no more sway Him than they could do."

Despite their brave words, both Tarod and Cyllan suffered monstrous dreams that night. Cyllan was haunted by tormenting images of an unthinkable future in which she saw Tarod sacrificed on an altar stone that ran black with blood, while she, hampered by the white robes of a Sister of Aeoris, could only stand by and scream his name over and over again, knowing that nothing she could do would prevent his destruction. She threshed in her sleep, reaching out clawing hands and snatching at invisible assailants; then at last she settled a little, as she sensed Tarod

beside her, and fell finally into a deeper if just as
dismal slumber.

Tarod lay unmoving and unaware of her distress,
but his sleep wasn't natural. Nor—or so he thought
later—were his dreams dreams in the usual sense. It
was more as though his mind, troubled by his waking thoughts, had reached out beyond mortal dimensions to a place of atavisms and ancient memories.
And there something awaited him.

The familiarity of the proud, cruel but beautiful
face with its welcoming smile made him ache to the
roots of his soul with a feeling he couldn't define.
Yandros emerged from a column of coruscating light,
and as he moved, the atmosphere about him shifted
subtly between a myriad dimensions, changing color
and form in ceaseless, patternless motion. Around
him something was pulsing—a vast heart, its note
too deep to be anything more than a slow, earthshak-
ing vibration; and it too had no pattern, the rhythm
changing each time Tarod's senses tried to attune to
it. And he felt rather than saw other presences;
shadow-shapes drawing towards him out of this formless place, entities he had once known and with whom
he had shared a shattering affinity.

Tarod. Yandros's silver voice had a flat quality, a
sound recalled rather than heard, with no true existence beyond memory and imagination. Light flared
at the Chaos Lord's heart and focused to the image of
a seven-rayed star. *Still you try to forget.*

There was no reproach in the voice, only a detached interest which made Tarod realize the extent
of Yandros's weakness. This, he understood suddenly,
was no true manifestation of the Chaos realm. He
still retained his links with the mortal world, and in
that world he was the stronger of the two.

He smiled and saw the green of his own eyes reflect momentarily in the Chaos Lord's gaze. *I don't
forget*, he said calmly. *But I have made my choice.*

Yandros considered for a moment, then inclined his head as though acknowledging a viewpoint which, though he opposed it, interested him. *You choose a strange path, Tarod. You have seen injustice, bigotry, persecution, murder, all perpetrated in the name of Order—and yet, despite the high principles you profess, you still give fealty to Order's ways.* His eyes—changing now from blue through purple to a disturbing crimson—flickered with amusement. *I am intrigued by your logic.*

Logic has never been your favorite weapon in my experience, Yandros.

The entity laughed. *Oh, I choose whatever weapons suit my purpose at the time—as you know full well!*

Images ... old loyalties, pleasures, triumphs ... Tarod forced them away. *Then perhaps you should choose more carefully. What I have seen is no true reflection of Order. It's merely the panic-stricken reaction of those who know no better. And if I knew no better, I'd suspect your hand behind it.*

You flatter me. Yandros smiled malevolently.

Hardly. For in this world, I have the advantage of you—the advantage of humanity. And I wield the greater power. I banished you, Yandros; and while I continue to live, your power won't gain a hold here.

Yandros didn't reply, but seemed to be considering Tarod's words. Far off in the distance a voice began to scream at a pitch which had never been mortal; Yandros glanced in its direction and the sound abruptly ceased.

At last, the Chaos Lord nodded. His eyes were oddly quiet and contemplative and he said, *Yes. You banished me. And for your fidelity to the Lords of Order you were damned by those same Lords' servants. Yet still you cling to that fealty, and you believe that though the puppets might condemn, the puppet-master will praise.* His eyes flared white-hot. *That is a very*

*human sentiment. I might have expected better from
you.*

Better? Tarod smiled cynically. *Better by whose standards, Yandros?*

Again the Chaos Lord laughed, but this time there
was an appalling irony in the laughter, as though he
were the victim of some celestial joke. Tarod, knowing him of old, was unmoved, and finally the laughter subsided, leaving only echoes which seemed to
take on a life of their own before whirling away into
nothing.

By whose standards? Yandros repeated. *Ah, Tarod,
you've forgotten so much!* He turned suddenly to face
Tarod full on, and despite the gulf which separated
them Tarod felt a powerful psychic jolt as the Chaos
Lord's finger pointed accusingly towards him. *Go
your way, then,* Yandros said. *Bow to the corruption
of Order, and learn the lesson to which mortal life has
blinded you! You are beyond my power to control—I
must admit it, for you know it as well as I, and in the
old days there were no secrets between us. Go, then.
Bespeak the demon Aeoris. Throw yourself on his mercy,
and where there were seven there will be six!* He hunched
his shoulders, and the column of light in which he
stood drew inward, darkening, so that at last Yandros's
bone-white face stared with cold disdain from a fog
of blackness, only his brilliant golden hair lending
any color to the disturbing scene. His voice carried
softly, sibilantly, insinuating in Tarod's mind as the
dream began to fragment and drag him back towards
the physical world.

We shall mourn your passing. . . .

He woke to a stillness that struck at the core of his
being. No screaming, sweating explosion out of the
realm of nightmare; no muscular spasm hurling him
from the depths of sleep—simply the quiet dark of

the room in the Shu-Nhadek inn, and a pattern of moonlight tracing meaningless pictures on the ceiling. From below, he could hear muted murmurings and the occasional clatter of pewter; it seemed that the tavern-room still stood open to trade and would remain so through the night.

At his side, Cyllan slept. Her cheeks were streaked with tears long since dried, but whatever night-borne horrors had assailed her seemed to have passed now; her breathing was gentle and even. Tarod reached out to touch her and realized his hand was shaking; on his index finger the Chaos stone glared as a stray moonbeam caught in the facets.

Yandros's last words burned like fire in his brain. Whatever term he might choose to give to the encounter, it hadn't been a dream; and it had struck hard at his confidence and resolve. *We shall mourn your passing.* . . . But Yandros was the master of lies; no man knew that better than Tarod. His greatest skill was to play on the fears of the unwary, causing the heart to doubt, the mind to question.

An involuntary shudder left him feeling chilled; he withdrew his hand from Cyllan's hair and saw the tiny light within the soul-stone wink out as his finger moved into shadow; and suddenly he smiled. He had one weapon which Yandros could never counter—his own will. And whatever his subconscious mind might try to argue to the contrary, while consciousness held sway the blandishments of Chaos were impotent. He had the stone, and the stone gave him power. Power that had stood against Yandros once, and could do so again. And though in the dead hour of night it might seem a cold consolation, it was enough.

His hand was steadier when he reached out again to touch Cyllan. She stirred in her sleep and murmured something unintelligible, but her voice was calm. Tarod leaned over her and let his lips brush her face gently. He didn't want to wake her—her presence was enough to hold him to the real world.

He settled back, one arm protectively across her slender body, and closed his eyes, knowing that sleep would come and there would be no more dreaming.

Chapter 9

The *Summer Sister* was sighted off the coast shortly after noon on the following day. Within minutes, a diverse flotilla of craft from fishing-boats to small dinghies and skiffs had put out, forming an impromptu escort to welcome the High Margrave to Shu-Nhadek, and by the time the tall, graceful ship with her gold-threaded sails came dipping and curtseying in to harbor a large crowd had gathered on the dock.

From the ship a voice shouted orders that were echoed and relayed from bows to stern, and men swarmed into action on the deck. The waiting throng shuffled and parted as harried militiamen struggled to make some semblance of order out of the confusion, and at last a broad gangplank was lowered from the ship's rail to fall with a noise like thunder on the jetty, where two burly men roped it fast.

The crowd fell silent. The *Summer Sister*'s master had ordered his sailors into a tightly-formed guard of honor on deck, and abruptly they all stiffened to attention as Fenar Alacar emerged from his cabin and stepped onto the plank.

Isyn had taken care to instill into his young master the importance of first impressions. This was the first time in his life that Fenar had set foot on the mainland, and the first chance that all but a privileged few had had to see their High Margrave in person. And so Fenar had dressed for the occasion, in trousers and coat of fine tapestried silk, with a brocade cloak thrown over and a narrow, jeweled gold circlet on his fine brown hair. An appreciative breath rustled through the throng as he appeared, and, as Isyn had coached him, paused at the top of the gangplank; then the rustle swelled into full-throated cheering, while a myriad hands jubilantly traced the Sign of Aeoris in the air.

The High Margrave raised an arm in acknowledgment of his welcome and took a careful pace down the sloping plank. Behind him walked Isyn, and immediately at Isyn's back came the Guard of the High Margravate, a handpicked body of swordsmen whose task, while they were on the mainland, would be to protect Fenar from the smallest hint of danger.

Fenar's relief as he finally stepped from the vibrating plank to land was profound; he paused a moment to allow the throng to get a closer look at him, then moved forward along the hastily-cleared aisle to where an open carriage waited to convey him to the Province Margrave's residence. Up the steps of the carriage, another pause, another wave, and dust rose from the turning wheels as the caparisoned horses set their heads towards the center of the town.

From the open window of their room at the tavern Cyllan could see only the *Summer Sister*'s tall mast as she rode at anchor; but the noise from the harbor carried clearly on the light spring breeze, and the people thronging the market-square just a street away were clearly visible over the low rooftops. She watched as there was a sudden commotion in one of the wider roads to the far side of the square; then, as the High Margrave's carriage came into view, she turned from the window to where Tarod reclined on the bed.

"Have you ever seen the High Margrave?"

He rose and came to join her, crouching at the low window to look out. The carriage was making slow progress across the square, hampered by the jostling press of people anxious to glimpse or possibly even touch their ruler, and Tarod's eyes narrowed slightly as he looked at the gorgeously-dressed youth in the carriage.

"Gods, he's no more than a child. . . ." He remembered Keridil's description of Fenar Alacar after the High Initiate had visited the Summer Isle for the formal and traditional ratification. A sound head on his shoulders, Keridil had said; but his first sight of the young man did nothing to dispel Tarod's doubts. Any hopes he might have had that Fenar would prove strong enough to stand against the combined opinions of the High Initiate and the Matriarch faded; this boy would be too intimidated by his two elders in the triumvirate to do anything other than follow where they led.

The carriage was by this time weighed down by tokens and offerings—spring flowers, sweetmeats, charm-necklaces and all manner of artifacts—that the crowd had showered on their ruler. As it finally maneuvered its way out of the square and away towards the town's outskirts, Tarod sighed and turned away from the window. "Two out of three," he said. "They only wait Keridil's arrival—and I suspect he'll be here before sunset."

Cyllan rose, stretching a cramped leg. "You sound very sure."

"I'm sure enough." He smiled. "In the old days, when we counted ourselves the best of friends, Keridil and I had a rapport that at times was near telepathic; and no degree of enmity can altogether destroy that. He's near. And when he reaches the town, I'll know it."

"And will he know of your presence, too?" Cyllan asked uneasily.

"If I relax my guard, he will."

"Then perhaps we should find some other place to—"

"No." He interrupted her with a slight shake of his head. "I must be vigilant, that's all—Keridil won't be a threat to us if we take reasonable care. But his arrival means time is growing short—we *must* reach the White Isle before the barque arrives to take the Conclave."

They had spent the morning, in their adopted guise, enquiring among local fishermen and other boat owners for a craft that might be hired. Cyllan's upbringing in the Great Eastern Flatlands had given her a sound knowledge of seamanship; and the currents here in the south were far less treacherous than those around Kennet Head, so that she could handle a reasonably sized vessel without need for a crew. But there wasn't a vessel to be found. Every last craft that was remotely seaworthy had already been hired or commandeered by people anxious to follow the fabled white barque when it set sail, and neither money nor status was enough to buy them passage.

Tarod had refrained from using his powers to secure them a boat, as least thus far; he was wary of causing argument or arousing suspicion, and would have preferred to solve their problem by more mundane means. But it was beginning to look as though he'd have no choice—and time, as he had said, was not on their side.

He said, "We'll look again early tomorrow when the town is quieter. By that time Keridil's party should be settled at the Margravate, and they'll hear no word of us until after we've departed."

"And if we still can't find a boat?" Cyllan asked.

His laughter was soft in the quiet room. "We'll find one."

*   *   *

The party from the Star Peninsula arrived in the middle of the afternoon. They were eight riders altogether, headed by Keridil and Sashka, with Gant Ambaril Rannak and three of his servants, plus two high-ranking Adepts whom the High Initiate had selected to accompany him.

They had made astonishingly good time on the long journey, aided by good weather conditions, which Keridil, with some relief, interpreted as a favorable omen. The Margrave's decision to ride with their convoy had disconcerted him at first, but Gant had argued that, with the land in a ferment, his first duty was to his Margravate—and besides, it was unthinkable that he shouldn't be present to play host to the full triumvirate of rulers when they lodged at his home for the first time in history. The Lady Margravine, still suffering from her shock and grief at Drachea's death, would remain behind at the Castle until she was fitter; but Gant would leave for the south with the Circle party. Reluctantly Keridil had seen the sense in his arguments, and as matters turned out, the Margrave had been far less of an encumbrance on the journey than he'd feared; the old man seemed to possess reserves of physical as well as mental stamina, and proved no hindrance to their progress.

He had anticipated a warm welcome in Shu-Nhadek, but was nonetheless astonished by the level of relief and joy that greeted them. Sympathy for the Margrave was running at fever pitch in the wake of his son's murder, and his arrival in the company of the High Initiate fueled the fires almost to the point of adulation. They made as rapid progress as they could through the town without giving offense to the hundreds who had turned out to greet them, but Keridil could only begin to relax when at last the gates of the Margrave's residence closed behind them and the noise of the crowd fell away into the undisturbed quiet of the formal grounds.

Gant reined in his horse, trying not to drop an elaborate flower garland thrust into his arms by a well-wisher, and stared at the gracious house at the far end of its long drive. Turning in his saddle, Keridil could see the sudden acute pain in the Margrave's eyes, and imagined what he must be thinking. For as long as Gant lived, this place would hold bitter memories.

"Come, Margrave," he said, speaking gently but firmly. "It has to be faced sometime. Best to get it over with."

Gant glanced at him, then his lips quirked in an ironical smile. "Ghosts take a long time to die, High Initiate," he said, and urged his horse onward.

"I can't describe how thankful I am that I no longer have to be beholden to the Sisterhood!" Sashka stretched like a cat and shook out her long auburn hair so that it rippled like water over her shoulders and back. The sun, arching low through the tall window of Keridil's room, seemed to set the tresses on fire.

Despite his bleak mood, Keridil smiled. "You should honor the Lady Matriarch, love. Wasn't that the first lesson you learned as a Novice?"

She turned from the window and regarded him with narrowed eyes. "She's senile, and you know it. Fusses and tantrums; she's worse than Lady Kael at West High Land, and I'd have found that hard to believe before today! And as for that appalling woman from the senior Shu Cot—what's her name?"

"Lady Silve Bradow."

"Yes, her. Lisping and stammering like a terrified child, and she doesn't know whether it's night or day, she's so inept . . . *ah*," Sashka shuddered with exquisite emphasis, and Keridil laughed, then hastily quelled it. Sashka's irreverence was a tonic, lifting the sense of burden that had sat more and more heavily on him as they approached their journey's end, and he realized afresh how thankful he was to have her at his side now. Downstairs in the Margrave's drawing room, as the three rulers exchanged stultified greetings, she had been the perfect foil to his official role; kissing the Matriarch's imperiously extended hand, bowing in the manner of the Sisters to the High Margrave, accepting their good wishes on her betrothal with a sobriety that matched the occasion. Only now, alone with Keridil, did she allow her true feelings to show, and he envied her ability to be so mercurial. He was still touched—tainted might be a better word—with the stilted dourness that had attended the first brief meeting. Far worse, he knew, was to come, and Sashka's levity provided a welcome relief.

He said, "Well, we must suffer them all again when we dine tonight."

"I know. And I'll be a model consort, Keridil." She moved across to the bed where he was unpacking—he had sent away the servants Gant had despatched to help him, wanting to be alone with her for a while—and slipped her arms round his neck, stopping him in his tracks. "I hope I shall always be that."

"You know you will." Her lips tasted faintly of the perfume essence she used because she knew it pleased him. "And when this is over, you will really *be* my consort—in name as well as in body and spirit."

"When it's over . . ." She repeated the words slowly, thoughtfully. "Poor Keridil. This is a burden, isn't it, that you'd rather not have to bear? But it won't be long now; it can't be long. Once the Conclave has decided—"

He interrupted her, but gently. "I don't want to dwell on that, love; especially not now. The moment's so close that I'd prefer to forget it until I have to remember." *The white barque would come when the Guardians judged the moment to be right; they had their own ways of knowing. And when it appeared out of the southerly mist, a horn would be sounded in Shu-Nhadek and a rider would gallop pell-mell to the Margravate with the news.* . . . He shivered, pushing the thought away. Time enough for that later. . . . There was more than an hour before they would all be summoned to dine and the ordeal of protocol must start all over again.

He kissed Sashka once more, this time letting his lips linger on hers as his sense of urgency eased a little, and murmured, "Do you need time to change your gown for the evening?"

Her fingers tangled in his hair. "No."

"Good." He released her, rose. "Then let me lock the door for a little while. . . ."

Midnight had long passed, and the harbor was deserted and silent as Keridil emerged from a dark, narrow alley onto the jumble of piers and jetties.

He'd been unable to sleep, despite Sashka's warm presence at his side—the evening's formal dinner had only served to increase his awareness of the ordeal that lay ahead. He had tossed and turned in the unfamiliar bed, racked by thoughts and worries dredged up by his subconscious, which held him in a distressing limbo between wakefulness and rest. At last, knowing he couldn't cope with the feverish, form-less torment any longer, he had risen and dressed in his stained travelling clothes before slipping out of the darkened house and walking down to the town. Sea air, he hoped, would clear his brain; and the walk would help to relax his muscles.

Sashka slept on, and although at first he thought he might wake her and ask her to come with him, Keridil decided against it. He felt an overwhelming need to be alone for a while, and even Sashka's com-

pany would strike a wrong note. Though the incident
was small and insignificant, he still recalled the avid
hunger—there was no better word—with which she
had followed his efforts to track down Tarod and
bring him to justice. Her hatred was so strong that
Keridil found it hard to believe that her feelings
stemmed simply from loyalty to himself and loathing of Chaos. Granted, it was natural that she should
feel the taint of her own previous involvement with
Tarod; but nonetheless her reaction had been far
stronger than seemed justified; almost as if the old
attachments still lingered, though in a twisted form.
And though he tried to rationalize, Keridil couldn't
help but feel a twinge of jealous suspicion. It was
intuitive, no more; but he couldn't erase it, and it
stirred up a terrible cauldron of doubt and guilt and
uncertainty. Just for a while he needed to be free of
those ghosts, and solitude was his only escape.

His ingrained sense of duty had, nonetheless, constrained him to inform one of the Margrave's tireless
servants that he would be out for a while. That done,
and his conscience salved, he had made his way
through the quiet streets of Shu-Nhadek, thankful to
encounter no one on the way who might recognize
and detain him. Now, sitting on one of the great
stone capstans to which docking ships were tied, he
looked out at the slowly swelling sea, where wavelets
reflected a pattern of light from the first rising moon,
and tried to find something of the sense of peace that
the scene should have imparted to him.

The fact that he still had doubts about the task
ahead troubled Keridil more than any other facet of
this whole unhappy affair. As the Castle party travelled south from the Star Peninsula, he had been
appalled by some of the scenes he had witnessed in
towns and villages along the way—he hadn't imagined that his decree would light such fires in the
minds of the populace, and those fires were now

burning out of control. So much hatred and suspicion, simmering under the surface of every community and only waiting for a spark to set it blazing ... surely the long centuries under the rule of Order should have eradicated such barbarism?

He was able of course, as High Initiate, to override the judgments of prejudiced or frightened town elders and bring some semblance of sanity to the witch-hunts, and as they travelled south he had done what he could, where he could. But it wasn't enough. For every false accusation, every mockery of a trial in which he had intervened, ten or twenty more were taking place over which he had no jurisdiction. What he had seen had made Keridil all the more determined to complete the task ahead of him, and swiftly—but it had also sowed the seeds of a doubt that nagged at the back of his mind and wouldn't let him alone.

He had unleashed, though unwittingly, a wave of fear that had exploded out of all proportion; and he was about to take a further step that could—*could*, he reminded himself—escalate the terror that held the land in its grip utterly beyond the realms of human imagination. To call the gods themselves back to the world ... did he run too far, too fast? Fasting, prayer and contemplation had convinced him he was right; but he still couldn't be sure enough to face the next few days with a clear conscience.

It would have been so much easier if he hadn't made the one fatal mistake of underestimating Tarod. One lesson should have been enough—he'd witnessed at first hand the power his adversary could command, and when he and the girl who abetted him had been captured, Keridil should have refused to bow to the demands of tradition and accepted ritual, and executed them both before anyone could argue. Now, in the wake of the turmoil that had spread through the world like a plague, Chaos must be satis-

fied with the victory it had claimed over its ancient
enemy. . . .

The thought brought a sudden and unexpected resurgence of the anger that had sustained Keridil
through his darkest hours of doubt and dilemma. It
washed over him like a cold, clean breath of air—
anger against Tarod and all he stood for, against the
blindness of the girl who, infatuated by the Gods
alone knew what manner of madness, had pledged
herself to the powers of dark and evil; anger, even,
against the cloud that Sashka's past relationship with
Tarod had cast over his love for her. If that demon
had been apprehended, there would have been no
need for this. . . .

He rose from his makeshift seat and paced moodily
along the dock. From a black-mouthed alley came
faint sounds of revelry; some diehard carousers in
one of the taverns that littered the harbor area, intent on making up for the anticlimax that all felt in
the wake of the triumvirate's arrival. Keridil was
tempted to join them; in his present mood, the effects of a night's drinking would be a blessing after
the Margrave's abstemious table, and only the fear
that he might be recognized held him back. Instead,
he paused in the shadows near the entrance, listening to the noise. The tavern wasn't a savory place;
unsteady light spilling through the door and the grimy
windows showed a crude sign worn with age and
never repainted, and the smells wafting out into the
alley weren't altogether pleasant; but all the same
the obvious good humor of its customers made Keridil
feel faintly wistful. A sharp, salt-laden gust of wind
blew along the alley and he hunched into his coat,
turning and pacing moodily back towards the harbor. Far from soothing his mind, this solitary mean-
dering had only served to stir up the uneasy thoughts
that he'd been trying to forget. Still, the peace of the
night was a relief after the atmosphere in the Mar-

grave's house. . . . He'd walk for a little longer before
turning back.

As he approached the end of the alley, beyond
which the sea gleamed faintly under the strengthen-
ing moon, Keridil started as a shadow moved suddenly out of the deeper darkness ahead. It hesitated,
silhouetted against the sluggish tide, and he realized
that it was nothing more untoward than a woman
crossing the jetty—doubtless one of the whores who
haunted the dockside to ply their trade.

And yet . . . an instinct made Keridil freeze into
the darkness, staring more intently at the indistinct
figure. Something about the way the woman turned
her head stirred memory and with it recognition;
and he thought he'd glimpsed pale hair as the moonlight caught it. . . .

Telling himself he was imagining things, the coincidence far too great, he nevertheless started towards
the jetty, keeping well hidden in the alley's over-
hanging shadow. The woman moved abruptly, crossing the rectangle of light and vanishing; but she
hadn't seen him; she was simply walking on. Keridil
quickened his pace—the noise from the tavern covered his light footsteps—and, reaching the alley's
mouth, peered cautiously out.

The woman was a mere fifteen or twenty yards
away, and the moonlight reflecting from the sea like
silver on lead showed her small, slight figure in stark
relief. She was climbing carefully down a slippery
flight of steps that led from the jetty to where several
small boats—dinghies, a wherry or two—bumped sullenly at their moorings against the wall; and though
she had changed the dress in which he'd last seen her
for a rough shirt and trousers, and there were peculiar streaks of auburn in her white-blond hair, the
High Initiate recognized her instantly.

"*Cyllan Anassan . . .*" His lips formed the name
silently and with venomous astonishment. It seemed

an impossible stroke of fortune that she should be here in Shu-Nhadek, but he couldn't deny the evidence of his eyes. And, since the bloody affray in Prospect town, it was a certainty that wherever Cyllan was, Tarod wouldn't be far away.

Keridil bit his lower lip, still watching her. She seemed to be going from one boat to the next, struggling with the wet knots of their painters, and it was obvious she meant to steal a craft for her own use. Well and good . . . it would take her a while to find what she wanted and free it, and in that time he could summon the help he'd need to capture her. To attempt to take her unaided would be foolish in the extreme; there were too many bolt-holes in and around the harbor, and if she once evaded him she'd be away for good. But if he went for help, there'd be no time for lengthy explanations and questions. As he gazed at the harbor he saw the solution to his problem: a fishing boat, riding at anchor just beyond the flotilla of smaller vessels . . . and from here he could just make out the name painted on her bows. The *Blue Dancer* . . .

Keridil eased back into the alley, then ran to where light and noise were still spilling from the tavern. He shouldered the door open and looked through the haze of smoke and fumes at the crowded bar. Mostly seagoing men, by the looks of them—which was precisely what he wanted.

He raised his voice above the throb of noise and shouted, "Can anyone tell me where to find the owner of the *Blue Dancer*?"

The babble slackened off immediately and the drinkers turned to stare at the stranger with the outland accent who had interrupted their revels. After a few seconds, a swarthy, middle-aged man with a walleye rose from a corner table.

"I own the *Dancer*, friend. What of it?"

Keridil pushed through the crowd towards him,

relying on his height and build to prevent any retaliation from the indignant drinkers in his path. "Then
you'd best get to the harbor," he said. "There's some
wharf-brat down there trying to steal her!"

"What?" The swarthy man slammed his tankard
down with a resounding crash, and Keridil saw with
relief that he wasn't as drunk as he looked. He swung
an arm, pointing to three of his companions in turn.
"You, you and you! Come on; don't just sit gawking!"

The three scrambled from their places and headed
for the door with the walleyed sailor at their head, and
Keridil followed. The simple stratagem had worked—
now, he must just see to it that the four seamen
didn't break their quarry's neck before he could take
charge of her.

Cyllan's fingers were raw from the brine-soaked
rope as she struggled with the complex knot that
secured the dinghy to its mooring ring. It was the
fifth craft she'd tried, and the only one whose owner
had been foolish enough to leave a set of oars stowed
under the plank seats, but the knot was proving far
more stubborn than she'd anticipated.

She wished she'd brought a knife, but wishing was
of no use to her now. Somehow, she *had* to free this
painter and get away with the stolen boat before
anyone discovered her—or before Tarod woke and
found her gone.

She'd said nothing to him of the plan that had
been formulating in her mind all evening, knowing
that if he found out he'd prevent her from going.
Instead, she had forced herself to stay awake until at
last she could be certain he was sleeping, then had
changed quietly into her old clothes and slipped out
of the inn by the servants' way.

He'd be angry with her when he found out what
she'd done, but his anger would stem only from concern for her safety—and it wouldn't last when he

learned what she had achieved. Once she succeeded in freeing this irksome knot, she'd take the dinghy out of harbor and then row along the coast to some empty cove, well away from Shu-Nhadek. Then, tomorrow, they could return to it at their leisure and set out for the White Isle with no one the wiser.

Her fingers slipped suddenly and she swore aloud as the rope grazed her hand. It was coming, slowly but surely . . . another effort was all it would need—

The quiet was broken by yelling and the stamping of feet, and Cyllan jumped with shock, almost losing her footing on the slimy steps. Regaining her balance, she peered over the jetty wall in time to see several men come running out of an alley and head straight towards her, and, appalled, she tried to duck down again—but she was too late.

"There!" A hoarse bellow echoed across the harbor. "There he is!" The feet pounded more loudly and Cyllan looked wildly around for a way of escape. Short of jumping into the harbor, there was nothing; unless—

"I'll break his head!" one voice bawled above the others, "Steal my boat, would he—I'll flay the flea-bitten cur alive!"

Silhouettes lurched into view above her, and the men surged toward the steps. Cyllan had less than a second to judge the distance between herself and the nearest boat before, panic-stricken, she jumped. She landed on the nearer gunwale of a dinghy, which rocked wildly, almost pitching her into the black water, and, trusting to nothing but luck, leaped to the far gunwale and launched herself across the awful gulf to the next craft. She didn't know where she was going; her one thought was to get as far away from her pursuers as she could—and as she sprang and scrabbled over the side of the third boat in the line she realized that she had reached a dead end. Ahead, a wide stretch of sea gaped menacingly; behind her one seaman was starting to climb across the bobbing boats after her while the others leered and shouted from the harbor wall. She was trapped.

She turned, facing her assailant and clenching her fists, knowing she couldn't fight but nonetheless prepared to try. But the man had stopped and was standing upright in the next dinghy, grinning broadly and unpleasantly. And then Cyllan felt the boat beneath her rock convulsively, before it began to move.

She should have realized what they'd do—and mortification mingled with the fear she felt. But she could only cling impotently to the sides of the dinghy as the men on the jetty reached down, took hold of its mooring rope, and began to pull it, hand over hand, in to the wall.

The dinghy bumped against the stone of the jetty, and rough fingers grabbed the collar of Cyllan's shirt, hauling her, kicking and fighting, up onto solid ground. She sprawled on the harbor, gasped as a kick was aimed at her back, saw heavy boots closing in on her—then someone said, his voice thick with shock, "Straits take all of us, it's a woman!"

They shuffled back in chagrined confusion, and she took the only chance she might have. Her muscles contracted violently and she sprang up, launching herself forward at the same time so that her captors couldn't collect their wits before she had darted between them and was running desperately for the black safety of the alley.

She was three paces from sanctuary when someone stepped out of the darkness to block her path and, unable to swerve, she cannoned into him. Hands locked on her arms and she swore aloud—then the oath died on her tongue as she looked up into the angrily triumphant eyes of Keridil Toln.

"*No!*" Cyllan twisted and might have broken away, but as she turned, a silhouette loomed behind her. Something—it looked ludicrously like an empty ale-tankard—flashed metallic in the moonlight, but before her spinning mind could identify it, it slammed with sickening violence against her forehead, and she pitched into silent, lightless nothing.

Keridil stared down at her sprawled figure, and as the *Blue Dancer*'s owner made to kick Cyllan again he held up an admonitory hand.

"No. Don't do her any further harm."

The man glowered at him, and one of his companions spat accurately at the unconscious girl. "Throw her in the harbor. Best place for flotsam like that; no one'll miss the bitch."

"I said, no." Keridil hadn't wanted to flaunt his authority, but the seamen were spoiling for blood, and he pushed back his coat so that the High Initiate's gold insignia was clearly visible at his shoulder. It took a few moments for the badge's significance to register, but when it did the sailors' leader swore, apologized, and made the Sign of Aeoris before his own face.

"This girl," Keridil said, staring at Cyllan dispassionately, "is wanted by the Circle. She's a criminal and a fugitive." He looked up. "I don't think I need say any more."

The men, understanding, backed away a fearful pace or two, and one of them muttered something that sounded to Keridil like a charm against evil. He smiled thinly. "I'm sorry that I had to mislead you, but there was no time for explanation. I will, of course, compensate you for your trouble." He touched his belt-pouch, and coins clinked pleasantly. "The girl won't do you any harm, so there's no need to fear her. I want her taken to the Margrave's residence before she regains consciousness. That way, we'll—" And he stopped, as a low, chilling sound came ranging across the harbor from somewhere to the west, distant but carrying on the still air. A horn, ethereal, sounding a warning note.

The seamen had all turned their heads at the eerie summons, and a good deal of the high color drained from their faccs. Kcridil, who had never heard the sound before, felt his spine prickle with alarm—and then he realized that the men were all staring at him, with an awed respect in their eyes.

"The white barque . . ." The *Dancer*'s master spoke in a strained whisper at the same moment that the significance of the horn sank into Keridil's mind. He should have anticipated this—the Guardians, who shunned contact with the mainland beyond bare necessity, wouldn't choose to bring their strange ship in from the White Isle with the eyes of every man, woman, and child in Shu-Nhadek upon them. The dead of night would suit their ways far better, and they'd care nothing for the convenience of their passengers, however exalted.

The horn sounded again, mournfully, and Keridil shuddered. He didn't want to look oceanward, but the fascination was too great; and if he strained his vision to the limit, he thought—or did he merely imagine?—that he could just glimpse a nacreous shimmer far, far out on the sea; a shapeless phantasm that deceived his eyes, one moment there, the next vanished back into the dark.

They wouldn't hear the horn at the Margrave's residence—word must be sent to them, and quickly. Common sense came to Keridil's rescue, freeing him from the formless dread instilled in him by the horn and the distant ship; he turned to the *Blue Dancer*'s master.

"I must get a message to the Margravate—"

"It'll be taken care of, sir." The seaman looked uneasy.

He'd left word with a servant; the man had wits enough to tell his companions where to find him. . . . Keridil nodded. "The barque will put in to shore?"

The man shook his head. "Not in my experience,

sir." He hunched his shoulders, thrusting both hands deep into the pockets of his coat. "Not that she's been near the mainland for five years, since the last time they brought the women back to us. . . . She'll drop anchor a mile or so out." He licked his lips. "It'd be my privilege to take you to her in the *Dancer*, if you'd forgive the smell of fish belowdecks."

Keridil had the feeling that the man volunteered reluctantly, but he wasn't about to refuse the offer—and besides, ten gravines or so would doubtless ease the sailor's burden. "Thank you," he said, glancing out to sea once more and then looking quickly away. "I appreciate your generosity."

The seaman looked down at the ground, then nodded at Cyllan's huddled, motionless figure. "And what of her, sir?"

He'd forgotten Cyllan. . . . Keridil stared at her, considering. Left at the Margravate in the care of servants, she'd either trick her way to freedom, or make telepathic contact with Tarod and summon him to her aid. He could be searching for her already, and the thought of the Margrave's defenseless household at his mercy wasn't pleasant. There was no time for him to magically bind and isolate her; and that left one alternative.

The High Initiate smiled. The incoming barque would take them to the one place in all the world where Chaos could have no influence. Should Tarod follow them there, he would find himself stripped of his power, helpless before the ultimate justice. And the one lure that could force him to follow was in Keridil's hands.

"Take her on board the *Blue Dancer*," he said. "She sails with us to the White Isle."

Chapter 10

This time, there were no cheering crowds to wish them good speed. They had crossed the precarious board between the jetty and the deck of the *Blue Dancer* in a constrained silence, broken only by the slap of water against the quay and the subdued grunts of the crew as they made ready to cast off. Now Keridil stood at the fishing boat's rail, listening to the crack of sail and boom as the vessel tacked about ready to head for open water, and aware of the hunched, unhappy figure of Fenar Alacar a short distance away. The young High Margrave's face was pale and tight in the darkness, his profile made harsh by the faint glow of a lantern in the wheelhouse where the skipper steered steadily on his new course. Though the others were old enough and experienced enough to hide their disquiet, they all shared the boy's unspoken fears; even the Matriarch had ceased her complaints and sat silent and brooding in the cabin belowdecks.

The wind strengthened suddenly, filling the sails, and Keridil felt the hull beneath his feet buck and then surge forward in a new rhythm as they cleared the harbor's shelter and the full power of the tide took hold of them. Nothing now between themselves and the phantom waiting ahead in the dark; nothing but black swell and the deep straits. . . .

As though the boy had picked up his uneasy thoughts, Keridil saw Fenar Alacar shiver suddenly and turn away from the rail. They had, as they must, left all but their closest companions behind; and though old Isyn accompanied him, the High Margrave needed more than one familiar face to bolster his courage. For a moment it looked as though Fenar was about to approach him and speak; then the boy thought better of it and instead stumbled along the deck to the dimly-lit companion-hatch. He disappeared, and for a moment his footfalls clattering down the steps broke the smooth rhythm of sea and sails until they faded and were gone, leaving Keridil alone.

He didn't want to peer ahead into the darkness, but a fascination he couldn't fight made him turn and stare beyond the ship's bows. And there she was . . . indistinct still, but closer, a white ghost of a ship rocking gently at anchor. The dark shrouded her and made it impossible to judge her size; sometimes she seemed to tower into the night murk, sometimes he thought that even the *Blue Dancer* might dwarf her. At her stern a cold, colorless witchlight flickered uncertainly, but there was no other sign of life. She might have been something out of a disturbed dream. . . .

"Sir?" The voice that spoke behind him was softly pitched, but nonetheless Keridil started. He turned and saw one of the crew standing at a respectful distance, cap in hand.

"Captain's compliments, sir, to say as there's hot mulled ale ready below, with a tot of something stronger in it to keep the cold away." The sailor smiled, gap-toothed and fearsome in the ragged glow from the wheelhouse. "Be half an hour, thereabouts, before we get where we're going, sir."

His father would have called it coward's courage ... but in the circumstances, Keridil thought, he would also have understood.

"Thank you," he said, taking his chilled hands from the rail and rubbing them. "I'd be glad of it."

The mulled ale was good despite a faintly fishy flavor, and for a while the group in the cramped and primitive cabin was able to maintain a spirit that kept their private thoughts at bay. Keridil sat beside Sashka, who held his hand in a clasp that communicated how tight a hold she was keeping on her composure. He had never known her to feel fear before and the discovery touched him in a new way, awaking in him a protectiveness that lessened his own apprehension. Fenar Alacar sat hunched in a corner, gripping his cup as though it were his most precious possession, while, flanked by two handmaids, Lady Ilyaya Kimi kept up a flow of murmured and trivial conversation, seemingly unconcerned as to whether or not anyone listened.

And in the hold, guarded by one of the captain's men and still unconscious, was Cyllan.

The news of her capture, when he had delivered it to his companions as they assembled at the harbor, had shocked them all. Only Fenar had questioned Keridil's decision to carry her with them to the White Isle, arguing that it might be better simply to execute her and have done—a sentiment that echoed Keridil's own doubts. The Matriarch, however, would have none of it.

"The High Initiate is quite right," she said in a tone that brooked no argument. "The girl is far less important to us than the Chaos-demon she abets, and there is no better way to secure his capture. Besides," she added with a faint gleam of relish in her eyes, "the girl's immortal soul will fare no worse in the afterlife if she suffers the rightful terror of Aeoris's judgment *before* she dies."

Keridil had looked at Sashka, who thus far hadn't spoken, and asked in an undertone, "What do you think, love?"

Sashka met his gaze. "However much she suffers, it can be nothing by comparison with what she deserves." For a moment she looked more malicious than he had believed her capable of being, though her expression quickly altered and he thought it must have been merely a trick of the light. And so, as Fenar's dissent was halfhearted, Cyllan's limp body was carried on board and dumped unceremoniously among the fish-boxes, nets, and ropes below deck.

Now, as the *Blue Dancer* sailed on, they had all had a respite from what lay ahead. . . . But all too soon they felt the motion of the boat beneath them change subtly, losing rhythm, and muffled orders were shouted above their heads. Keridil tensed, hearing a moment before his companions the sound of feet heading down towards them. The cabin door opened, and he saw the captain's bulk framed in the doorway.

"We're there, sir—or at least as close as they'll allow us to get. I've ordered the dory to be made ready."

Keridil rose, having to stoop in the low-ceilinged cabin, and saw the flicker of near-panic on Fenar Alacar's face before the youth could get himself under control once more.

"Thank you, Captain." He glanced at his companions in turn. "I believe we're all ready. . . ."

He didn't dare look up. From his seat in the stern of the *Blue Dancer*'s dory, the hull of the white barque filled his field of vision, blotting out sky and moons and horizon like a giant fog bank. He could hear the creaking of her aeon-old timbers, the ominous, rattling moan of her towering sails as they shifted and flapped with the wind. Everything about her was white—a dim and sickly white, making her, at close quarters, more an apparition from a ghost realm than ever she had seemed from shore. Once Keridil *had* looked, trying to glimpse the tip of her mainmast, but vertigo and another, less explicable feeling had swamped him and he turned away hurriedly, left only with the disturbing impression of a vast, phantasmic wing of sail and a single cold star glaring in the black sky above.

Beside him on the dory's damp, narrow bench seat, Sashka huddled into her coat and stared at the curving floor. In front of them Fenar Alacar seemed to be shivering uncontrollably, and their other companions fared little better. Only Ilyaya Kimi stared at the slowly approaching monstrosity with a peculiarly resigned calm, as though it had no power to affect her.

The dory was nearing the white barque's side: a wall of white toppling out of the sky towards them. The bump as they touched the ship was inaudible against the groan of water under her hull. Keridil jumped when, apparently from nowhere, a rope came snaking down and struck the ship's side with a dull *crack*. One of the sailors who had rowed them across snatched the rope's end and lashed it to the dory's prow; then a shadow fell across them and Keridil looked up to see a crude sling that dangled like a hangman's noose being lowered slowly from the barque's deck.

The Matriarch shifted stiffly in her seat and smiled an old, ironic smile. "If I read my scriptures rightly, High Initiate," she called back, "the privilege of boarding first is yours."

"*Keridil*—" Sashka couldn't disguise her fear and held onto his hand as he rose cautiously to his feet. He disentangled her fingers with what he hoped was

a reassuring squeeze, but couldn't bring himself to
speak before stepping carefully over the seat and
making his way towards the prow. As he reached it
he heard Fenar's voice above the sea-surge, a terrified whisper.

"I've forgotten the words—Gods help me, Isyn, I've
forgotten what it is I must say to them. . . ."

The High Initiate shut his eyes tightly for a moment, then grasped firm hold of the waiting sling.

The ascent seemed an endless dream, but at last a
moment came when Keridil glimpsed light flaring
from above, and seconds later he swung inwards to
stumble free onto the deck of the white barque. For a
few seconds he was near-blinded; then, as his eyes
adjusted, he saw them.

There must have been twelve or fifteen of them,
ranged in a semicircle on the pale boards of the deck.
The shifting sails overhead cast bizarre moon-shadows
across their motionless figures, and for an instant
Keridil had the hideous sensation that these were
not true men but dead things reanimated, old beyond
reckoning and unthinkably alien. The words he had
so carefully rehearsed caught in his throat—then one
of the figures moved, and the spell—or at least its
worst element—shattered.

Like his fellows, the Guardians' spokesman was
dressed from head to foot in white; a sailor's garb,
though he was like no sailor Keridil had ever seen
before. A seamed, milk-white face, untouched by the
sun; unkempt grey hair swept back from his skull;
his face utterly without expression. He looked at the
High Initiate with empty eyes, and Keridil had the
disconcerting feeling that the Guardian either didn't
see him, or deemed his presence irrelevant.

It was his place to speak first—but the words codi-
fied in the Circle's law-scrolls seemed very different
now to when he had so carefully rehearsed them

with Gyneth playing the role of Guardian. Keridil resisted an almost overwhelming compulsion to cough, and said: "Keridil Toln, High Initiate of the Circle, comes in peace and humility, and craves the sanction of the Guardians to set foot upon the White Isle."

The Guardian continued to gaze through him. "What is the High Initiate's purpose in so doing?"

"To join with the High Margrave Fenar Alacar, and the Lady Matriarch Ilyaya Kimi, in the Conclave of Three."

"By the laws of Aeoris, the Conclave of Three may be convened only when all other sanction has failed. Does the High Initiate attest that this is so?"

Feeling as though he were taking part in some mumming drama on a plane far beyond anything earthly, Keridil replied firmly, "It is so."

Silence but for the creak of timber and sail followed his words, and Keridil sensed that the Guardian communicated with his fellows, though no obvious sign passed between them. Then, after what seemed an interminable wait, the pale man spoke again.

"The petition of Keridil Toln, High Initiate of the Circle, is heard and granted. Let those willing to share in his duty be brought aboard." The Guardian stepped back, distancing himself from Keridil with the movement, and the High Initiate saw the sling swing ponderously over the white barque's side once more to begin its downward journey. Involuntarily he looked back over his shoulder to see how his companions fared, but from this height the dory was invisible.

He cleared his throat, drawing the Guardian's attention. "We have a prisoner," he began, still unsure of his ground despite the fact that the formalities were done. "She—"

The pale man interrupted him with a wintry smile. "The girl may be brought aboard. She will be confined in the appropriate manner until her presence is required."

What they knew of Cyllan, or how they knew it, Keridil didn't care to speculate. He merely nodded an unspoken acknowledgment, then turned to the ship's side as, with its second passenger secured in its folds, the sling began to rise slowly, slowly towards the deck.

The blow that had stunned Cyllan insensible had left a violent blue-black bruise on her forehead, and her skull beneath the bruise throbbed sickeningly as consciousness began to return. At first she was reluctant to open her eyes, knowing only that she was emerging from an ugly dream in which conflicting images had become confused: Tarod sleeping in their room at the tavern, a wet rope that grazed her hand, and, ludicrously, Keridil Toln's face seen against the backdrop of the moonlit harbor in Shu-Nhadek ... wild, mad nightmares. Her limbs were numb with cramp; she made an effort to sit up—and fell back painfully onto a hard surface with a jolt that jarred her eyes open.

She was surrounded by whiteness. White shrouds formed vast, menacing wings all around her, climbing above her to such a height that for a moment her confused mind thought they must be clouds. But clouds didn't descend to earth ... and the surface beneath her was moving in a way she found disconcertingly familiar.

Alarmed, Cyllan tried to scramble to her feet, and sprawled again. *Her wrists and ankles were tied. . . . And the movement beneath her was the steady, rhythmic motion of a ship beating its way out to sea. . . .*

It was then that she saw the motionless figure standing behind her. Clad in white like some phantom sailor he stared into the middle distance, apparently unconcerned by her efforts to free herself. His

sheer impassiveness chilled her marrow as she realized that, though he guarded her, he was utterly
indifferent to anything she might try to do; that he
knew, even if she did not, how helpless she was.

White . . . white ship, white sails, white-garbed crew
. . . The truth began to dawn hideously in Cyllan's
mind. *Keridil!* So his face hadn't been her dream; he
was here—

Here? she asked herself, and instantly knew the
answer to the unvoiced question. She had been taken,
caught in a trap and brought to this ship; a ship
which, with bitter irony, was bearing her to the very
place which she and Tarod had so desperately needed
to reach.

But not this way—Gods, not this way!

Knowing that she'd have but one chance, and it
was her only hope, Cyllan gathered all the mental
strength she could muster, her mind reaching back
towards Shu-Nhadek and the darkened room in the
tavern. From some distance away she heard a choked-
off imprecation, then someone whose colored garb
was in startling contrast to the white all about her
appeared and ran towards where she lay.

Tarod!! Frantically the mental cry went out, though
in her panic and confusion Cyllan didn't know if she
could hope to reach him. The white-clad sentry shifted
from one foot to the other but gave no other sign
that he had sensed her call—then he moved aside
to make way for the other man, who stood looking
down at her with anger and contempt.

Keridil knew what she had done; she read the
understanding in his eyes. Then he smiled, and she
felt despair.

"Call your demon-lover if it pleases you," the High
Initiate said almost gently. "Chaos wields no power
here, and he can't reach across the water to your
rescue." He paused, then the smile widened. "Yes;

call him. Let him follow you, if he's fool enough—
and if he dares!"

He turned and walked away, and she watched him
go with misery in her eyes. Of course, that was exactly what the High Initiate wanted—for Tarod to be
drawn to the White Isle in pursuit; to the absolute
source of Aeoris's power. And Tarod *would* follow
them; and when he arrived, what would he find waiting for him . . . ?

She turned her head aside, staring over the rail of
the barque to the slate-dark sea beyond. She wouldn't
cry—nothing would induce her to give them the satisfaction of seeing her tears—but within, her soul
was tearing apart.

Tarod!

The cry ringing in his mind was as loud as though
someone had screamed his name in the room. Startled violently out of sleep Tarod sat up, his consciousness still vibrating with the sound—and in the
same moment that he recognized the agonized voice,
he realized that Cyllan was no longer beside him.

"Cyllan—" Her name formed on his lips in a sharp
hiss of alarm and he rose quickly, lithely from the
bed, drawn by an unrecognized instinct to the window, where he hacked back the curtain.

The street and the market-square beyond were
empty. The first moon had sunk below the level of
the rooftops and the second, smaller satellite was
following, a dim and worn crescent in the west. Dawn
wasn't far away and, but for a faint scatter of stars
mirrored by a few remaining lights in the harbor,
there was nothing to be seen.

Tarod swung round and stared at the room's bland
shadows. Mentally he sought the source of the cry,
but found nothing. His only certainty was that Cyllan
had gone.

Swiftly he turned his concentration to the bounds

of the inn itself, and let his mind probe and seek. Other lodgers asleep in their beds; a couple, back to back, who had quarreled before retiring; an austere merchant sharing his bed with a dockside whore whom he'd smuggled in; the tavern-keeper, his pallet made uncomfortable by the coins stowed beneath it . . . downstairs, the deserted taproom, silent dining room; outside, the stables filled to capacity with dozing horses . . . but not a trace of Cyllan.

Tarod's left hand throbbed suddenly and the stone of his ring glared, drawing his attention. With the throbbing came the surge of an unhuman intuition that made his skin crawl, telling him that, wherever Cyllan was, he'd not trace her by normal means. He sank back onto the disordered bed, covering the ring with his right hand. He was reluctant to use sorcery, but there was no other choice open to him if he was to find her. And this way—he had to steel himself to the thought—he would know whether she was alive or dead.

His green eyes closed and he felt the ancient power begin to awaken in him. It was painfully, exquisitely familiar and despite his misgivings he welcomed it, letting it rise through the many levels of awareness, finally to take hold of his consciousness. His eyes opened fractionally again, narrow emerald slivers that glittered now with an alien intelligence as Chaos-born understanding mingled with and then eclipsed the mundane. Scrying was a talent he'd developed during his years as an Adept, but this way bore no resemblance to the Circle's formalized practice. He needed no glass, no invocation; and the planes on which his mind moved ranged far beyond anything his one-time peers might have aspired to.

Darkness. The darkness moved, slowly and rhythmically, like the flank of some huge, amorphous beast as it breathed. A knife blade of cold light stabbed across it, shivering and breaking with the swell, and he knew he looked down at the sea under the moon's last rays.

It sailed on the sea, and yet he couldn't reach it. ... He sensed the presence of something out there on the deep, but it was occluded, protected by a force that resisted his will, so that it slipped mockingly away when he thought he had it fast. Anger licked at his mind like fire; the proud, cold anger of an entity that would not tolerate being thwarted. He felt the power focus as he cast off the last links with the human body in the tavern at Shu-Nhadek; and that which sought out and finally, triumphantly grasped the elusive presence on the sea was nothing mortal.

White sails swelled ghostly in the dark as the huge white hull cleaved black water. The tongues of angry fire in Tarod flared to hatred and contempt as the great ship's aura met and clashed with his own; it was inimical to what he had become, the vessel and the symbol of his despised enemy, and only a great exertion of will kept him from recoiling in revulsion.

He could see no detail of the ship, but he needed none—this astral image was enough. The barque had taken her passengers in the dead of night, and now she sailed for the White Isle and the Conclave of Three. And Cyllan was on board. ...

The fury erupted in him as Tarod's mind smashed back to the body he had left behind in the dark bedchamber. Muscles contracted and jackknifed him to his feet, and a black aura flickered into life and blazed about his frame. He couldn't contain the rage; it was too great, too unhuman, out of control—but he *had* to contain it, had to hold fast to his humanity, fight the Chaotic will—

With a choked-off shout he reeled back and fell onto the bed, and as his body struck the pallet something seemed to wrench free from his skull and disintegrate with a sound that was no sound but a jarring, sickening sensation. His head spun dizzily and he clawed at the pillow beneath him, needing something real and earthly that would give him an anchor. After a few moments the spinning receded, though it left him sick and drained. Slowly, painfully, Tarod sat upright.

He hadn't been prepared for the power of the primeval hatred that had surged up within him as he encountered the white barque of Aeoris. It had been an enmity too ancient to comprehend, and he had reacted with all the loathing and contempt locked away in millennia of preternatural memories. Clinging to his identity at the last, he had fought the power and conquered it; but he had paid a price for the victory. And though he might have found Cyllan, he couldn't cross the barrier that separated them.

Still dazed, and hardly knowing what he was doing, Tarod reached for his clothes and began to dress. Everything took too long; he was acutely conscious of being hampered by the constraints of a physical body, and memory of the power that still lurked, though dormant now, in his soul tore at him.

It would be so simple. . . . He paused, staring at the ring on his left hand. Chaos was a titanic force—but on this earthly plane he was master of Chaos. Once he had banished Yandros, destroying his one sure foothold in this world, and the golden-haired lord couldn't return unless Tarod were to revoke the banishment and summon him again. If he did, the white barque and all its crew would be no match for such an adversary. . . .

Appalled rejection came hard on the heels of the thought, and Tarod was shocked to realize how close he had come to falling prey to the temptation. With the aftermath of the Chaos force still making his skin tingle he had felt the old affinities rising; he had *wanted* Yandros's presence as ally and long-time companion . . . and he knew that such a temptation was the opportunity for which the Chaos Lord had been waiting all along. Yandros would answer the summons, should he utter it. And with his return, all Tarod's hope of petitioning Aeoris would be ashes. If he was to prove his loyalty to Order, then to call on Chaos now, even in desperate need, would be the ultimate betrayal.

Even to save Cyllan's life . . . ?

The silent question was as insidious as it was deceitful. To summon Yandros might save Cyllan from the peril she faced aboard the barque, but beyond that it could achieve nothing. The Circle wouldn't harm her, not yet; with the White Isle and the Conclave so close, Keridil would have other plans for her. And that gave him time—little time, true, but enough.

Tarod's hands were steadier as he continued to dress. Though the unholy thoughts were banished, the dark seemed to have closed in about the room; had he not known better, he might have imagined that a presence stood motionless in the deepest shadows of the far corner, watching. If he attuned his mind he could almost convince himself that he wasn't entirely alone.

He made to gather up his cloak, then thought better of it. There was no need for disguise now. As he moved quietly to the door he paused, and smiled towards the dark, silent corner.

He said softly, "Not this time, Yandros . . ."

The door swung gently to behind him.

The second moon's distorted crescent was sinking into the sea, and, with dawn less than an hour away, mist had stolen up from the water to drift patchily through the town and lie in pale, deceptive pools about the streets and the market-square. Tarod, dark as a shadow in the plain black clothes for which he'd abandoned the richer merchant's garb, moved silently down a long alley, past shuttered taverns, and emerged on to the harbor docks.

The harbor was deserted. With only the last scatterings of starlight to relieve it the dark was almost absolute; only the silhouette of a fishing boat hunched at its mooring and rocking lightly showed blacker against the leaden water. Tarod moved towards it, found the jetty steps, and climbed down until a faint shifting glimmer and a sullen, rhythmic slapping sound told him he had reached the tide level.

He crouched on the algae-coated stair and gazed at the water, clearing his mind of all but the one, immediate thought that concerned him. To his left and above a shadow moved; he saw the eyes of a feral cat reflecting the sea's faint phosphorescence as it peered curiously over the wall at him; then, noiselessly, it ran away. Tarod took a fresh hold on his concentration, and sent out the soft mental call. . . .

He had never attempted to communicate with such creatures before, but something beyond even his normal instincts told him that they would come. They had aided Cyllan once when without them she would have drowned in the ferocious seas off the Castle stack. And he felt intuitively that they would aid him now.

When the first sleek head broke surface a short distance out from the dock, Tarod released the pent breath that had been tightening in his lungs and smiled with relief. He had thought he might sense their presence before they arrived, but the fanaani had allowed him no forewarning. Curious, but aware that his was a mind of an order they had never touched before, they had made their approach in secret, and only when three of the beautiful, catlike sea beasts had risen to the surface did Tarod feel the first faint brush of telepathic contact.

Strange . . . The word was the nearest interpretation a human being could make of the thought that reached him from the fanaani's alien minds. They were unsure of him, and nothing he could say or do would persuade them to hasten their judgment, or influence it. These sea-creatures were a law unto themselves; no one could fathom their thoughts or motivations. But, if a mind was truly open, it was possible to communicate with them in their own bizarre way.

He let his thoughts touch them in turn, sensed the curiosity again.

Will you aid me? Like them, Tarod used concepts rather than words, images that he translated into a form they might understand far better than speech. The nearest of the three creatures rolled in the water, hardly creating a ripple; it was man-sized and he had a glimpse of deep intelligence in its eyes as it solemnly regarded him.

Secret. The thought was accompanied by a quiver of voiceless laughter, and he realized that the fanaani had read in him the need to reach the White Isle unbeknown to anyone, and were amused by the idea. Then came another concept: a land-animal slipping down through green depths, not breathing, fading, dying. Tarod smiled faintly as he realized that he was that land-animal and the fanaani were commenting pityingly on his inability to swim a distance which was, to them, nothing.

He responded with the idea of a fanaan attempting to walk on land, completing the image with an ironical query. The fanaan blinked, rolled again, then slid beneath the sea's surface with barely a ripple. When it reappeared some seconds later, there was a new concept in its mind.

Why?

It was probing his purpose, and Tarod sensed that any attempt to dissemble would alienate it and its fellows. The fanaani demanded honesty in return for their aid, and he opened his thoughts to them, allow-

ing them to probe his intentions and his purpose and
make what sense they could of them. The wait seemed
interminable; but at last he felt the strange, seeking
minds withdraw from his. And then:

Too soon. Light above.

Tarod glanced involuntarily upward. The stars were
gone, and the sky had begun to lighten. When he
looked again at the fanaani he saw that their dense,
brindled fur was losing its night phosphorescence.

Dark above. Come then. Come to this place. . . . And,
clear in his mind though the image was from a sea-
ward viewpoint, he saw a cove where waves rushed
on a narrow bar of grey sand. To one side the cliff
jutted aggressively out, and here the tide's constant
assault had worn away a soft stratum and cut a
soaring arch through the rock spur. It was an unmis-
takable landmark, and it was all he needed.

Two of the fanaani, who throughout the exchange
hadn't come close to the jetty, were already turning
and moving slowly out to sea. Tarod exchanged a
last look with the third creature and projected gently,
My thanks.

They were gone with scarcely a ripple. He rose,
flexing cramped muscles and satisfied with what had
been achieved. Uncertain allies though they were
reputed to be, the fanaani hadn't failed him; and
when the sun set tonight they would return to fulfill
their promise.

A line of color like dark, dried blood lay along the
eastern horizon now. Tarod climbed the jetty steps,
paused a moment to look back at the slow swell of
the sea, then walked away towards the tavern.

The cove that the fanaani had shown him lay some
nine miles east of Shu-Nhadek, where the previously
gentle shoreline changed to form the far higher and
less hospitable cliffs that dominated the coastlines of
three provinces before finally falling away to the

Great Eastern Flatlands. The place was known locally as Haven Point and had been the salvation of many a fisherman caught far from harbor in bad weather; but it was only rarely used, and there was no habitation nearby. Tarod had left the tavern early, telling the landlord that he intended to spend the day riding for pleasure, while his wife, who was feeling tired, would remain in bed. By the time anyone tapped on the door to ask if the vintner's lady required food or drink he would be long gone, and the money he had left in the room, when added to the value of Cyllan's abandoned mare, would more than pay for their lodging.

He was glad to leave the busy town behind for the peace of the countryside, and took the narrow track along the coast. His horse was skittish after being confined in the inn stables and he gave it its head, enjoying the sensations of a ground-eating canter as he rode towards the climbing sun.

He saw the cove's location long before he reached it; a long spur of rock jutting out into the sea ahead, with an almost perfectly symmetrical arch cut through its narrow finger. He had perhaps a mile or two more to go, and slowed the gelding to a walk, allowing it to loiter and crop at the lush spring turf. He had the day ahead of him with nothing to do but wait; there was no need to hurry.

Half an hour later Tarod reached the cove, and sat in the saddle gazing down the steep, crumbling cliff to the triangle of beach below. Noon was approaching and the bay was filled with red-gold light; from here he could see a narrow gulley in the cliff that formed a steep but negotiable way down to the sand.

He slid to the ground, and with relief shrugged off the heavily-embellished cloak, which had helped him maintain his assumed role as a merchant of substance. He also discarded his soft leather boots and his belt-pouch, dropping them all carelessly on the

grass, knowing that from now on he'd be better served
by going barefoot. Then he turned his attention to
the horse, unsaddling it and leaving the harness beside his cloak. He rubbed the animal's nose, and it
whickered softly at him before turning its attention
eagerly to feeding. It didn't as yet realize that he had
given it its freedom; rather than sell it for money
that he'd have no use for, Tarod preferred to let it go.
Doubtless in time someone would find it and take it
for their own, as they'd find the clothes and coin he
had left behind. If the abandoned possessions were
recognized as belonging to the vintner who had stayed
in Shu-Nhadek there would no doubt be speculation
as to his real identity and his fate—but by then he
would be beyond caring.

The gelding raised its head and watched with mild
curiosity as Tarod walked away towards the head of
the gulley, then it lost interest and resumed grazing.
He didn't look back at it, but stepped on to the steep
path and began the precarious, slithering descent. It
was easier than it had looked, and within a few
minutes he reached the beach and walked out across
the narrow strand to where the sea licked and surged.
The sand was cold and damp underfoot, and sharp;
composed of the tide-worn remains of uncountable
millions of tiny shellfish. He stood at the water's
edge, staring out to where he judged the White Isle
must be, but the horizon was lost in haze and he
could see no trace of it.

By now the barque must have reached its destination. . . . Thoughtfully, Tarod turned back to where
tumbled boulders provided a resting place. He believed Cyllan must still be alive and unhurt; knowing
Keridil as he did, he doubted that the High Initiate
would make any hasty decision on her fate. More
likely he saw her as the perfect bait to lure his enemy
to the Isle—and he was right; though the manner

of Tarod's arrival wouldn't be quite what Keridil anticipated.

And when he did arrive, he asked himself, what then? He had made his plans and was determined to see them through; but prior to this moment he had always turned aside from thinking too deeply about the consequences of what he meant to do. Now, though, with the long afternoon stretching before him and nothing to do but sit and watch the sea, he had little defense against the questions and apprehensions that lurked unanswered in the back of his mind.

He was gambling not only his life but his very soul on the hope that he could appeal to the ultimate arbiter and be heard with sympathy. But so much had happened since he had first pledged to surrender the Chaos stone on the White Isle that he was no longer sure he could trust his own judgment. Innocent people had died at his hand and at Cyllan's; and however great his justice or his mercy even Aeoris could not overlook those deeds or excise them. His own word must stand against Keridil's when he made his plea—would the greatest of the Seven Gods be willing to hear an accused servant of Chaos, when the accuser was his High Initiate?

Tarod turned abruptly, angered by his thoughts. There was no room for doubt; he daren't let it get a foothold, for once it did it would take root and grow too fast to be contained. He had made his decision and mustn't waver now; and besides, the choice was clear. Order, or Chaos—there was no middle way. He had begun on this path; he would see it through.

Nonetheless, his mood was far from happy as he returned to the rocks and settled himself for the long wait.

He realized later that he had slept a good part of the afternoon away, and when he woke the last light

Louise Cooper

was glaring sullenly in the west, setting the cliff edges on fire. The cove was plunged in shadow; with the tide at the ebb it looked dank and chill and unfriendly, and cold was striking through Tarod's thin shirt.

He rose, flexing his limbs to ease stiff muscles, and walked slowly down the beach to the tideline. Foam showed as a pale fringe at the water's edge, but beyond the waves all was dark, sea and sky no longer distinguishable. He wondered when they would come, and suppressed a shiver that had little to do with the bitter air.

Tarod couldn't calculate how long he stood on the shore while the light faded finally into complete darkness. But at last he heard a faint, eerily sweet note, far away but discernible amid the hush of the sea. Moments later it was joined by another and then another, a bitterly pure harmony that thrilled through his bones and made his throat constrict. The song of the fanaani . . . They were here, and they were waiting for him.

Tarod drew a deep breath and opened his mind to the first stirrings of the alien thoughts that probed his. At first they were composed of nothing but strange, phantasmic sea-images, but gradually they coalesced until clear words took form in Tarod's mind.

Come . . . join us . . . join us. . . .

The dark was all but absolute, but as a wave rose to break at his feet he could see them, blacker shapes against the swell. Doubt and fear assailed him; he forced the feelings down and walked forward.

The sea swirled around his ankles, around his knees. The beach shelved steeply, and the first wave that broke over him was an ice-cold shock that set his teeth on edge. Tarod waited for the following wave and dived to meet it, surfacing in its backwash and shaking water from his hair and eyes. He had one

last glimpse of the silent, brooding cove, then he
struck out strongly for open water.

The fanaani met him as he cleared the cliffs' embrace; three of them, as before, though whether they
were the same creatures with whom he'd communicated at Shu-Nhadek harbor he couldn't tell. Sleek,
lithe bodies flanked him and he felt one beast brush
against his body; treading water he reached out and
laid an arm over its back to grasp the powerful,
thickly-furred shoulder while a second swam to his
other side to complete the link. Ahead of them now
he could see the third clearly; a bigger animal, its
coat dappled and its eyes, as it turned to regard him,
calm and wise. He smiled, formed words of thanks in
his mind, and the leading fanaan uttered a series of
shivering, silver notes on an alien scale. As though
the sound were a signal, the two creatures to either
side of him surged forward. Tarod felt the heavy
muscles bunching under his hands, saw the sea's
swell surging to meet him; then the fanaani were
swimming easily and swiftly away, bearing him towards the black, empty horizon.

Chapter 11

The most eerie thing of all, Cyllan thought, was the profound silence with which the white barque sailed slowly into harbor. There were no shouts or cries from her strange crew, no rattle and thunder as her towering sails were furled and the lines made fast; she seemed almost to have a life and a will of her own, for the ease with which she maneuvered to her resting place and finally docked was unnerving.

A gaunt, indifferent Guardian had loosed the knots that bound Cyllan's ankles, and though her wrists were still tied she had been able to kneel on deck and watch the sacred island approaching in the first cold light of dawn. Mist shrouded it until the ship was almost under its lee; then the sun's weak rays slanting in from the east had severed the mist and the Isle rose before them with shocking clarity. Grim rocks that seemingly offered no landing-place loomed out of the sea, dominated by a single titanic crag at the island's center; the huge, brooding shell of a long dormant volcano, a black silhouette against the paling sky. Cyllan had felt something of the aura that radiated from the place and turned her head away with a fearful shudder.

The barque sailed on, her crew caring nothing for the treacherous rocks that lurked just beneath the ocean's surface and sometimes showed savage teeth above the creaming water. Then with no warning she turned landward, heeling in straight towards the cliff face so that Cyllan shut her eyes and hissed an imprecation under her breath. But there was no grinding, jarring impact, and when she dared to look again she saw that the vast rock face before them had split countless centuries ago to create a narrow channel through which the tide surged, and the barque was heading into its maw. They slid between giant, spray-soaked cliffs, whose surface she felt she could almost reach out and touch; then gradually the tide-race quieted until the barque sailed in deep, calm water, silent as a white ghost.

And before them was their final destination. . . .

Overhead the cliffs towered and almost met, the sky a thin, vicious dagger of brilliance far above. The shadows were so deep that the pier where the barque had come to rest was half hidden in gloom; but nonetheless Cyllan could see that everything about this harbor, such as it was, had been hewn to a scale that bore no relation to human dimensions. The stones of the pier were monstrous blocks that an army of laborers would have been hard pressed to move an inch; and now men, pale as phantoms, were emerging from some unseen place to secure the ship to a gigantic capstan that dwarfed their figures. Behind them a flight of steps had been cut into the rock face, so huge that they might have been the work of giants; and she shivered as she recalled the nature of the unhuman feet that trod those stairs a millennium ago.

There was movement on deck, and she turned her head to see the barque's other passengers emerging from whatever quarters they had inhabited below. At

first she didn't recognize Keridil Toln; he had changed
his clothes for more formal garb, and on his shoulders was a heavy ceremonial cloak, the fabric invisible beneath the weight of its gold-thread embroidery.
The cloak's high collar shadowed his face, but she
could see the gold circlet that banded his fair hair,
and in his hands he carried the staff of office of the
High Initiate. He walked slowly towards the barque's
side, flanked by two of the Guardians, and Cyllan's
lungs and throat constricted; however much she hated
him, however great an enemy he might be, she
couldn't help but be awed by the figure he presented.

Behind Keridil came Fenar Alacar, whey-faced and
looking pitifully young in his ceremonial garb, his
cloak a cascade of white fur over crimson and the
huge single ruby that was the High Margrave's badge
glittering at his right shoulder. And lastly, with the
careful tread of old age and infirmity, the Matriarch
Ilyaya Kimi. As always she was dressed in the white
robe of the Sisterhood, but her usual belt had been
replaced by a silver sash, and on her head she wore a
silver filigree circlet from which a cloth-of-silver veil
swept almost to her feet.

Cyllan stood rigid as the small procession passed
by only three paces from her. For a brief moment her
gaze met Keridil's; she saw the strain in his face and
thought he gave her a look that mingled pity with
contempt; then he was past and she turned away
from the scrutiny of his companions.

The massive wall of the pier was on a level with
the barque's deck, and as the three members of the
triumvirate crossed over, the waiting Guardians
formed a tightly-ranked escort to flank them as they
stepped on shore. Cyllan stared after their retreating
shapes until only a dim blur of white in the gloom
marked their whereabouts—then her pulse lurched
sickeningly as a hand, cold and light as a spider's
web, touched her shoulder.

The pale-eyed crewman didn't look at her and didn't speak. He simply gestured towards the rope-railed gangway that separated the ship from the dock, and before she was aware of what she did Cyllan found herself walking unsteadily towards it. She heard movement at her back but didn't dare look round; then she was crossing the narrow divide over still, black water, to set foot, afraid and awestruck, on the White Isle.

Another hand touched her shoulder—she shuddered at the contact, finding it repulsive—and she was guided to the foot of the monstrous steps that wound up and out of sight. Keridil and his companions were no longer visible and she wondered if they had been taken this way—it was hard to believe that the aged Matriarch would have the stamina for such a climb. The stairs drew her gaze, frowning and fearsome; again she felt the chilly touch of the island's aura, and shivered.

Other people were now being escorted from the ship—two men she'd not seen before, wearing the badges of Adepts; another, older man whose garb suggested a scholar; two Sisters of Aeoris; and—Cyllan felt her jaw tighten—a tall, patrician girl with auburn hair that rippled over her shoulders. Sashka Veyyil . . . Tarod's one-time lover, who had betrayed him to the Circle and who was now enjoying her triumph as the High Initiate's new consort. They had met once before, at the Castle, and the encounter was still a goad in Cyllan's memory.

Sashka saw the fair-haired girl staring at her, and a flicker of a scornful smile crossed her beautiful face. Then a white-clad Guardian moved between them, and gestured silently towards the gigantic stairs.

Cyllan had steeled herself for an exhausting climb to the Gods alone knew what destination at the top of the terrible flight, but it was not to be. Instead, the small party had toiled a bare hundred stairs when their escort led them off into the black maw of a tunnel that gaped out of the dark rock. For a while they walked in darkness, the quiet broken only by the stertorous breathing of the old scholar as he tried to regain his wind; then the tunnel opened into a high but narrow chamber, lit from some undetectable source above and furnished only with a wooden table and several benches. They moved into the chamber, uncertain what was required of them, and one of the dispassionate Guardians spoke.

"The Conclave of Three is about to begin." His voice echoed thinly in the vault. "Those who have accompanied the triumvirate will remain here until summoned."

One of the Sisters spoke up, though diffidently. "The High Margrave's adviser has been adversely affected by the climb, Guardian. He needs something to help him recover his strength."

"Sustenance will be given." The Guardian's manner didn't waver and Cyllan was unnerved by the way in which these strange men—if men they were— seemed incapable of addressing anyone directly. He started to turn away, but suddenly Sashka stepped forward.

"Guardian." She clearly wasn't hampered by the Sister's diffidence, and there was an indignant edge to her voice. "You're surely not intending to leave this creature here?" One finger pointed imperiously at Cyllan. "She's the High Initiate's prisoner, and an ally of Chaos! She should be confined somewhere where she can present no threat to the rest of us!"

The white-clad man turned his disinterested gaze on her and appeared to stare straight through her; and two spots of color flamed high on Sashka's cheeks.

"All will remain here until summoned," the Guardian repeated flatly. "There will be no opportunity for mischief." And turning on his heel he left the chamber, closing the door behind him.

Sashka whispered something under her breath and swung angrily about, pacing towards the far end of the vault. The Sister intercepted her path and spoke to her, clearly intending to soothe. But Sashka snapped a harsh word and the other woman retreated. Cyllan sank down near the door, squatting on her haunches and ignoring the others as they milled about and murmured uneasily to each other. Sashka's remark to the Guardian had stung, but was no less than she might have expected; at their first encounter intuition had told her that there was more to the auburn-haired girl's enmity than met the eye. No matter; Sashka was nothing to her . . . and she had far more immediate and deep-rooted worries to concern her.

The Conclave was taking place at this very moment; and Tarod's future hung in the balance of its outcome. Since the moment when Keridil Toln had mockingly challenged and encouraged her to call on Tarod and bring him to her aid she had known that her presence here was playing into the High Initiate's hands, and she bitterly regretted the fact that Tarod's love for her would make him seek her out, no matter what the risk to himself. If he had heard her psychic call, the scruples that had so far prevented him from using his power would count for nothing. He'd use it and he would come to find her—as Keridil well knew. It was a perfectly baited trap, and nothing she could do would put matters to rights. Even as the white barque glided slowly in to harbor she had sensed the peculiar isolation of this island, and knew that any attempt she made to contact Tarod again and warn him would fail. He'd follow her here, and when he stepped onto the White Isle's shore his enemies would be waiting.

Her unhappy reverie was broken by the sound of
the door beside her opening, and she looked up to see
an empty-eyed youth in the now familiar white garb
of the Guardians entering the vault. He carried a
tray laden with a pitcher, several cups and a plate of
what looked like coarse black bread, which he set
down on the table. He didn't utter a word, no one
spoke to him, and seconds later he was gone and a
key grated metallically in the lock.

Glad of a diversion, however small, Cyllan watched
as the Sister who had asked for sustenance filled a
cup from the pitcher's contents and took it, with a
piece of the coarse bread, to the old scholar. Their
hushed voices reverberated in the rock chamber although it was impossible to discern what they said,
and Cyllan looked away again, slumping forward
and resting her head on her folded arms.

"You must be thirsty." The voice impinged on her
thoughts, and she looked up with a start to see Sashka
standing over her. She held a cup in one hand and
the faint traces of a smile touched her features. "Or
do you have other matters on your mind?" the girl
added with undisguised malice.

Cyllan ignored her, and with a graceful movement
Sashka seated herself on a convenient bench. She
sipped at the cup's contents, grimaced, and said,
"Water, and brackish water at that ... I suppose we
can expect no better in these barbarous surroundings. Although I'd advise *you* to make the most of it.
It's quite probably the last drink you'll ever taste."

Her taunt was a clear indication of her temper,
and gave Cyllan an insight into the depths of Sashka's
anger and resentment. She allowed a small bark of
laughter to escape her lips, and the other girl's cheeks
colored.

"I'm glad to find you in such good heart, Cyllan.
Lightness of spirit is a rare quality in one on the
brink of death—you're an example to us all."

Cyllan's only response to her sarcasm was to lean her head back against the wall and close her eyes. Sashka's mouth tightened into a vicious line. "So you're not moved by the idea of dying?" Her voice had risen in pitch and some of the others were watching her curiously; she ignored them, caring nothing for their opinion. "You're very courageous. I'm sure that courage will prove most entertaining when you watch Tarod destroyed before your turn comes!"

That provoked the reaction she had hoped for. Cyllan's eyes snapped open, filled with a mixture of rage and misery, which gave Sashka considerable satisfaction. She would have been more gratified had it been Tarod rather than Cyllan bearing the brunt of her venom—she had often lain awake at night, imagining how she would taunt him, what she would say—but this was pleasurable enough, and a small revenge.

"Ah," she said softly. "So you *are* afraid. . . . Have you only just realized that your lover isn't invincible? That he will die, and his death will be no less ugly and agonizing than your own?" She stood up, took three slow paces until she was directly in front of Cyllan, and sighed theatrically. "I believe I rather pity you."

Cyllan wanted to maintain her stony silence, but the churning, bitter rage inside her was too strong.

"Save your energies," she said ferociously. "I want none of your taint."

Sashka made a moue and studied her fingernails with an air of infinite, martyred patience. "It's a shame that you're so stubborn, Cyllan. You could still save yourself, you know." She looked up, saw Cyllan glaring at her, and smiled with sweet kindness. "Even after all you've done, I believe the High Initiate could be persuaded to show clemency towards you, if you were to renounce your—let us say, your misguided loyalties."

Oh yes, Cyllan thought; *that would serve your vanity very well!* Not only would Sashka succeed in depriving Tarod of his one true ally, she would doubtless take great satisfaction from letting him know that ally had deserted him; and her motives were painfully clear. Mingled with Sashka's hatred of Tarod was a warped echo of the desire she had once felt for him, and perhaps felt still. And though she claimed to loathe him, she nonetheless couldn't bear the thought of his allegiance turning elsewhere. She wanted him to love her still, so that she could have the pleasure of hurting him by her rejection. Suddenly, Cyllan could almost feel sorry for Keridil Toln.

Disappointed by her lack of reaction, Sashka shrugged carelessly. "It's of no moment to me, of course. But you can hardly be blamed for lacking the wisdom to understand matters such as these." She smiled again, and added with a patronizing confidentiality, "I suspect I know Tarod better than you could ever hope to do, and he has always had a talent for persuasion. But there are those who are capable of seeing through his deceptions, and those who are not. In truth, Cyllan, I feel it's a little harsh to condemn you for what is, after all, only unwitting ignorance."

For one blinding moment Cyllan wished with all her being that she had the Chaos stone in her hands once more. She remembered the blazing glory of its power when it had flooded and overtaken her; the indescribable thrill of revenge and bloodshed when Drachea Rannak had fallen before her Chaos-driven fury. . . . Getting a grip on herself she drew a deep breath and banished the images to the dark recess where they belonged. Sashka Veyyil was no Drachea, no threat; she was no better than a jealous and spiteful child, and to make more of her taunts than was warranted would be folly.

But whatever wisdom dictated, her self-control refused to bow to it. Nothing she could say or do would harm Sashka; the girl was triumphant and relishing her ascendancy. Yet—for Tarod's sake if nothing else—Cyllan couldn't bear to allow her vindictiveness to go uncountered.

She looked up, her eyes glittering, and said huskily, "Have you ever looked upon Chaos, Sashka Veyyil?"

The words had come unbidden to her tongue, and as she spoke she felt an alien sensation, like a psychic charge, welling within her, fueled by her anger. It was akin to the uncontrollable and unpredictable power she had sometimes been able to command as a fortune-reader, but stronger; far stronger. And it made Sashka tense with sudden unease. . . .

Cyllan smiled coldly. "No . . . I thought not. But you will. One day." She felt the psychic charge taking a tighter grip on her, as though some unnameable power were speaking through the medium of her voice, and the soft laughter that issued from her throat wasn't pleasant. "That's my promise to you, Sashka—and it's my curse on you."

Sashka blanched, and the hand that held the cup shook. For a moment stark fear showed in her eyes—then fury replaced it, and with a violent gesture she hurled the remains of the water directly into Cyllan's face, whirled, and strode away.

The shock of the water shattered the hold of the peculiar power, and brought Cyllan jarringly back to reality. She blinked, shaking her head to clear her eyes—her bound wrists made it impossible to do more—and looked towards the far end of the vault, where Sashka had retreated. In the dimness she could just make out the color of the other girl's gown, and the faces of the rest of the company, who were all staring curiously at her. She looked away, resuming her slumped posture. The brief surge of furious psychism had left her feeling desolate, and her threat to Sashka now seemed a hollow sham. She had no power to curse, and hatred alone couldn't translate her words into reality. She had had the momentary pleasure of seeing terror in Sashka's eyes, but it gave her no comfort.

She wondered whether Yandros knew what had become of his plans and of the promise she had made to him. Here on the White Isle, the seat of Aeoris's strength, he could bring no influence to bear; even Tarod, were he to be willing, might find his power so diminished in this place that he was unable to call on the Chaos Lord. And without some aid from a plane beyond this earthly world, what hope was there?

A shuffling footfall close by made her look up, and she was surprised to see the elderly scholar bending over her.

The old man smiled a lopsided smile. "You seem to have greatly displeased our High Initiate's consort," he said dryly. "And I saw that you didn't receive a drink, at least not in the accepted sense." He proffered a brimming cup. "There's more than enough to go around."

Nothing in his tone suggested mockery or sarcasm, and Cyllan returned the smile hesitantly. Then she held up her bound hands. "I'm afraid I can't take advantage of your kindness."

"Allow me." He held the cup to her lips, waited while she drank, then smiled again. "Better, I imagine?"

Cyllan swallowed. "Yes—thank you." She hesitated. "I hope you're recovered from the climb."

"Well recovered—though you're the only one apart from Sister Malia who's been courteous enough to ask." He studied her for a few moments before adding, "You're not entirely what I'd been led to expect."

Cyllan's initial feeling of gratitude towards the old man soured a little at that; and her tone took on a frosty edge. "And what had you been led to expect?"

"Oh, the usual products of superstition," he told her, unperturbed. "Something less and yet more than human. Certainly not an obviously intelligent and—forgive me—ordinary girl who might be anyone's daughter or sister."

Cyllan bit her lip hard. "If you're about to tell me that I've reached this pass through no fault of my own, and that it isn't too late to save myself, you might as well save your breath." Her amber gaze flickered to meet his in angry resentment. "I made my choices a long time ago."

"I don't doubt that for a moment." The old man's wry smile returned briefly. "I'm simply interested by your story. I'm a scholar, you see—Isyn by name—and I have a particular interest in the wide varieties of human nature. I'm always seeking to extend the boundaries of my knowledge and understanding."

Cyllan's lip curled. "You'll find little for your researches here, Isyn. I have nothing to offer you." Her anger was returning, though in a quieter form. "Unless, of course, Tarod should come here in search of me. That might satisfy your desire for new knowledge."

Isyn chuckled. "I trust not! But tell me—and I ask only in a spirit of understanding—aren't you afraid?"

"Afraid?" said Cyllan dully.

He gestured towards the vault door. "Of what lies ahead of you. For want of a better word, your fate."

Cyllan realized suddenly that to Isyn—perhaps to all of them—she was a curiosity, like the unfortunate mutants sometimes exhibited at Quarter-Day fairs; something to be tormented, or exclaimed over and discussed in erudite language, depending on the viewer's proclivities, but not a thinking, feeling creature in her own right. She had joined the throngs of market-square gawkers often enough in the past; she knew, now, how such mutants must feel. And suddenly she understood, in a way she had never done before, Tarod's contempt for them all; Circle, Mar-

gravate and Sisterhood alike. She must hold to that
feeling—whatever else might befall her, she must
hold to it.

She said with dignity, "No. I'm not afraid."

Cyllan's stony indifference at last deterred Isyn,
and Sashka made no more efforts to taunt her. She
was left alone with her thoughts, while the others
kept ostentatiously away. And she couldn't judge how
much time passed before the sound of a key turning
in the lock drew the attention of everyone in the
vault.

Two Guardians appeared in the doorway; beyond
them Cyllan could see at least two more in the tunnel. One spoke in the now familiar flat tones.

"The Conclave is ending. The attendance of those
who have accompanied the triumvirate is required."

Glances were exchanged; slowly the vault's occupants got to their feet. Only Cyllan didn't respond,
and one of the Guardians moved to stand over her.

"The attendance of *all* is required. There are no
exceptions." He stared at the wall as he spoke, and
Cyllan felt an impulse to lash out and kick him, just
to see if it was possible to provoke a reaction in one of
these bloodless zombies. She resisted it, along with
the temptation to ignore him and simply sit here
refusing to cooperate. If she didn't go with the party
of her own volition she would doubtless go by force;
and the loss of her dignity wasn't worth the hollow
satisfaction of resisting.

She struggled to her feet, hampered by her tied
wrists, and followed the rest of the party through the
door and along the dark tunnel beyond.

As they emerged from the tunnel's mouth, they
were bathed in the dim and deceptive light of approaching dusk. Full day had come and gone while
they waited in the underground gloom, and the sun
was an angry crimson ball against the sky's murky

backdrop. The Guardian who led them stared directly at the red inferno for a few moments, then turned to his charges and gestured to where the giant stairs continued on and up. Cyllan looked at the flight stretching away ahead and climbing the island's humped shoulder, and saw that it seemed to terminate at a thin and razor-sharp ridge, barely discernible in the fading light. Beyond the ridge, a wall of dull grey-brown rock towered into the sky, its summit lost in darkening mist. The crater of an ancient and long-extinct volcano . . . and there, she knew, lay the sacred shrine, and the casket, which had remained unopened since the seven Lords of Order had fought the last battle against Chaos.

The Conclave was over, and the decision had been taken. Night would fall long before the party reached that brooding summit, but when they did she would learn which way the decision had gone—and learn, too, what fate lay in store for her, and for Tarod should he fall into the trap set for him.

She had clung thus far to a fierce pride and determination not to weaken, and they had sustained her through the voyage to the island and the long wait in the vault. But now, gazing up at the volcano's unrelenting and lifeless slope, and knowing what lay beyond, she felt fear eating into the core of her soul.

The fanaani had let him go as the pinnacles of the Isle loomed out of the dark; waves crashed glaringly white against their sheer slopes. He felt the fanaani's sleek bodies slide away from beneath his hands, heard a thrilling cascade of notes above the sea's roar, then he was striking out towards the towering rocks under his own volition. A powerful crosscurrent caught him and bore him at tremendous speed towards a savage gash in the cliff, where titanic boulders had smashed its symmetry in an aeon-old fall. He glimpsed the yawning mouth of a cave half-submerged under the tide, then fanged rocks rose out of the blackness and he had to exert all his physical strength to avoid being dashed against them. Seeing clear water momentarily ahead he struck out towards the cliff fissure; another wave, breaking, swept him into the shore and, twisting about at the last moment, he felt his hands graze on rock as he struck hard against the cliff. The rock was rough and broken enough to grip; he hung on as the huge undertow drew back, and before the next wave could come thundering in he had pulled himself clear of the sea.

He was on a steeply sloping ledge, and, gaining a foothold, he climbed higher until he reached a point where the tide could no longer wash over him and drag him back. Salt water streamed from his hair; his clothes clung to him and his body was bruised and lacerated by the impact; for some minutes he could only crouch on the precarious ledge struggling for breath.

A sound, faint but clear, mingled with the rolling thunder of the sea; the fanaani's shivering, farewell song as they swam clear of the island. They were away to whatever strange depth or shore was home to them; he raised a hand in a salute of thanks though he knew they could no longer see him, then their bittersweet voices faded, faded and were gone.

Both moons were up; one a thin, chill crescent, the other a vaster, dimmer sphere at the full. The speed at which the sea-creatures bore him here had been awesome; there were hours yet to go before dawn began to break . . . He turned his head, gazing up at the stone ramparts rising behind him. The dead volcano at the center of the island was invisible, hidden by the night and the cliffs, but the cliffs could be climbed, and he knew he could reach his final destination before the sun came out of the east to reveal his presence.

He felt the answering tingle of power in his left

hand as the stone of his ring flared with sudden brilliance. Yes . . . here, he could trust himself to use the strength of Chaos, knowing that it couldn't overtake him or sway him from his goal. He flexed his fingers, and felt a new and unhuman strength course through his blood, negating tiredness and exhaustion. Tarod smiled, and, rising to his feet, moved silently across the ledge to where the cliff fissure gaped black and waiting.

Chapter 12

The High Margrave Fenar Alacar rose from the centermost of the three carved stone chairs. The peculiar light that suffused through the musty, windowless chamber etched lines of shadow on his young face, making him look older than his years; but it couldn't disguise the uncertainty in his eyes as he cleared his throat and then, nervously and with frequent hesitation, spoke the formal words that ended the Conclave.

"I, Fenar Alacar, elevated by grace of our lord Aeoris to rule as High Margrave, declare that the triumvirate has spoken as one, and that all have set their seals to this resolution. The decision of the Conclave is that the casket of Aeoris shall be opened. And I charge and call upon the High Initiate, Keridil Toln, to be the instrument through which this sacred task shall be undertaken." His gaze flickered to Keridil's impassive face and he licked his lips nervously, certain that he had spoken the words correctly but still unsure of himself in the presence of his older and more experienced peers.

Keridil returned the gaze for a moment, then he too rose from his seat and stepped forward until he faced the young Margrave. Slowly, stiffly, he bowed low before Fenar.

"I am sensible of the honor done me, and sensible of the grave responsibility which I undertake." Now he turned to face the third and final member of the triumvirate, who was also rising, though with some difficulty, from her chair. He bowed to her in her turn. "I ask the blessing of the Lady Matriarch, mother and comforter of us all, to grant me succour in this momentous hour."

Ilyaya Kimi, magnificent in her silver veil, reached out an arthritic hand to touch Keridil's brow as he made a knee before her. "The clear light of Aeoris shine upon you, my son and my priest. May you walk always in His path of wisdom."

Keridil straightened, and both he and the Matriarch turned to face Fenar once more. The High Margrave nodded.

"It is done," he said. "Let the portal be opened and the decision of this Conclave made known."

They made a strange threesome, Keridil thought with a curiously detached part of his mind as he led them across the faintly shimmering stone floor; an old, old woman barely able to walk, an unfledged boy, and a man who, whilst he presented a properly confident face to the world, was besieged by doubts and fears which he couldn't even name. But they were the best the world had to offer to its gods. The ultimate temporal power had been invested in them, and, whatever their misgivings, they must do their utmost to be worthy.

He reached the portal—a huge stone slab which pivoted on some hidden and indescribably ancient mechanism—and raised his right hand to rap, once, on a diamond-shaped section of crystal set into the otherwise blank stone face. A terrible grating, grinding sound rumbled beneath their feet, and slowly the portal began to turn. Cool, clean air rushed into the chamber—he heard Ilyaya drawing a deep and grateful breath—and they stepped out to meet the deputation of Guardians who had kept vigil through the long hours of Conclave. Each pair of pale, expressionless eyes was focused on Keridil, and the Guardians clearly read the result of the Conclave in his face without a word needing to be uttered. Their spokesman inclined his head in acknowledgment and said in his toneless, distant voice, "The triumvirate will be conducted immediately to the shrine. Those who have waited behind are now gathered outside and may stand witness to the rite if the triumvirate so wish."

Fenar cleared his throat again and glanced at Keridil with the odd mixture of deference and resentment that he always seemed to feel for the other man. "I promised my adviser, Isyn, that he might accompany me if it was permitted. . . ."

In other words, his confidence was flagging and he needed his old tutor's support. Keridil could hardly blame him. He was about to smile back at Fenar but thought better of it; with his nerves in such a state the boy would probably interpret a smile as patronage.

"It's entirely your decision and privilege, High Margrave," he said.

"Yes . . ." Fenar's face cleared. "Yes, of course."

"I will need two of my Sisters at my side," Ilyaya Kimi declared fussily. "If I am to endure another lengthy ritual, I will need their support, quite literally. I never thought I'd be called upon to undergo such trials of exertion at my time of life."

Of them all, Keridil thought, the Matriarch was the only one who seemed capable of accepting this extraordinary and daunting situation with ease. She was involved in the making of history, yet she behaved as though she were merely undertaking one of the more tedious everyday duties of her office. He envied her—whether her calm pragmatism stemmed from self-confidence or senility, it was a feeling he would have liked to share.

Keeping his feelings to himself, he nodded. "Two of my Initiates will guard our prisoner, but aside of them I shall ask only my consort to accompany me."

Ilyaya was adjusting her veil with small, impatient movements of her hands. "And what *of* that girl, High Initiate—our prisoner?" She pursed her mouth. "Our baited trap doesn't seem to have yielded up a victim. I'm beginning to wonder if the Chaos-demon has decided that discretion is the better part of valor, and abandoned her."

They were walking along a narrow, unadorned tunnel that burrowed through the shoulder of the volcano. Guardians walked before and behind, carrying torches, and there was a faintly sulphurous smell in the stale air. Keridil thought for a few moments before replying to the Matriarch's barbed remark.

"No, lady. He'll come; I'm sure of it." He knew Tarod well enough not to have wavered in his conviction that the trap would work. Earlier, before the Conclave began, he had requested a few minutes alone and, escorted to another of the seeming myriad of empty rooms and vaults that honeycombed the mountain—and whose function he couldn't begin to imagine—had cleansed his mind of all extraneous thoughts. After a short Prayer and Exhortation, he used the techniques of mind-searching that he had first learned long ago as a new Initiate, in an attempt to discover Tarod's whereabouts. He had found nothing; but the fact that his enemy was untraceable was in itself, he thought, a favorable omen. If Tarod was seeking to invade the White Isle and rescue Cyllan, secrecy would be his greatest weapon; and though he still couldn't locate him by magical means, Keridil sensed in his bones that he was near.

Ilyaya Kimi sniffed. "And if he does not?"

"If he does not, his fate—all our fates—will no longer rest in our hands."

The High Margrave shivered and made a poor job of disguising it. "I still say that girl should have been executed without the need for all this subterfuge," he said. "It could have been done in minutes, and we'd have had one less risk to worry about. But I was overruled." This time, the hot look he gave Keridil mingled the old resentment with a new and more personal dislike, and Keridil choked back the temptation to suggest that, if the High Margrave was so set upon that course, he might like to take a knife or sword and show the courage of his convictions by cutting Cyllan's throat himself. It was easy now for his peers to carp and criticize, he thought angrily; Ilyaya Kimi cast aspersions on his judgment in the matter of Tarod's capture, Fenar on his wisdom in allowing Cyllan to live as a lure to their adversary. But he had made his decision, and he wouldn't be influenced by arguments made from the relative comfort of their positions. Theirs weren't the hands that must unlock the casket and lift its lid; theirs weren't the shoulders that must bear the full brunt of responsibility for summoning the White Lords to the world. If he refused to give way to them, that autonomy was surely the least they could grant him in exchange for undertaking such a burden.

A paler rectangle showed ahead, indicating that they approached the end of the tunnel. As they emerged onto the volcano's gigantic flank Keridil saw that the sun had set, leaving only a last, pallid shimmer in the sky. Twilight had drained all color from the blank rock faces, and the Guardians with their white skins and clothing looked like great, phantasmic moths in the gloom. Ilyaya's veil shone with a weird inner radiance of its own; Fenar's circlet

glowed nacreously, and for an instant something about
the scene struck Keridil as unhealthy, tainted with
an edge of corruption. . . . He shook the thought off
hastily, aware that it was little short of blasphemous.

They were conducted along the narrow walkway
by which they had come from the great staircase to
the vault of the Conclave, and where the parapet
ended, the rest of the party awaited them. Sashka
saw Keridil and didn't wait for anyone's consent
before she ran forward and embraced him. She didn't
speak—something in his face told her it would be
wiser to stay silent—but she took his hand firmly in
hers as they walked together towards the stairs. The
others greeted their companions with less of a show;
all but Cyllan, who stood at the back of the group,
between two tall, thin Guardians. Just once she caught
Keridil's gaze, and he blanched at the cold, controlled hatred that burned behind her amber eyes.

Sashka squeezed his fingers. "It's done?" she
whispered.

He nodded. "It's done." He didn't need to tell her
what the outcome had been, and heard her draw in a
long breath. Then: "And now? Will they let me come
with you?"

Keridil had been staring ahead to where the monstrous stairs wound ever farther up the flank of the
mountain. The sky was almost dark, but he could
still make out the menacing truncated peak of the
ancient crater at the volcano's summit. They would
climb those terrible steps, on and on, and when finally they reached the end there would be nothing
before them but the shrine itself. Now he looked at
Sashka, searching her face for signs of fear and finding none. With her beside him, he wouldn't feel so
appallingly alone. "They will," he said. "That is . . .
if you'll consent?"

She could almost pity him for being so naive as to

think that she'd not grasp this giddying chance. She, Sashka Veyyil, would witness the opening of the casket—and when the historians came to write their accounts of this momentous night, her name would be inscribed alongside Keridil's as the consort of the High Initiate who had summoned Aeoris to the world.

She clasped his hand more tightly in hers and gave him the sweet smile that could always win him over. "Of course I'll consent, my love," she said softly. "Nothing would keep me from your side now!"

Cyllan climbed with one Initiate before her and one at her back, blocking any escape route, but was incapable of giving her attention to anything beyond the huge, endless stairs. She seemed to have been climbing for hours, each step a strain that made her muscles throb in protest, and her mind was numb with the ceaseless, toiling effort. Ahead, Keridil Toln led the procession, flanked by two more of the white-clad zombies—a new escort, for it seemed that only a small and carefully-chosen few in whatever peculiar hierarchy existed here were allowed within reach of the mountain summit. Behind him came the High Margrave, then the Matriarch, now carried in a strange, carved chair by two more Guardians. Torches glittered like small, feral eyes, a snake of light winding higher and higher into the night and dwarfed by the threatening peak.

And when they reached the shrine, what then? She had given up praying that Tarod would not come to her, for the fear that had begun to eat at her when they were brought from the vault now had a stranglehold that she couldn't fight. She was too alone, too lost, and too threatened not to long for his presence, for no one else would help her. And if he came too late—she didn't once consider that he wouldn't come at all—she would be dead, and her soul, having failed both Order and Chaos, would be damned forever. . . .

She was so enmeshed in her fearful thoughts that she wasn't aware of the procession ahead of her coming to a halt until she collided with the Guardian before her as he stopped. Blinking, Cyllan looked up.

The cone of the volcano, which before had seemed so distant as to be unreal, now loomed with terrifying immediacy ahead and above. She could see the crater like a vast, insensate mouth edged with jagged teeth, reaching up as though trying to devour the sky; she could see the ugly scar of a fissure where, aeons ago, lava had come blazing in a river of fire from the earth's heart, the malformations of rock torn and twisted and melted under unimaginable heat and pressure. It was prehistoric, savage, an aberration; and her fear began to transmute into a palpitating sickness.

It seemed that they were waiting for some signal, and after long minutes it came. A horn, sounding from somewhere near the heart of the crater itself, amplified by the towering rock walls so that it echoed like the call of some supernatural denizen of a ghostworld. The sound wound on and on, finally dissipating out over the sea and swallowed by the night, and as the last echo faded, the party began, slowly and with a new purpose, to move again. Onward, upward . . . and the gigantic stairs were at an end.

The gateway had been hewn into the rock face of the crater; a plain, foursquare portal formed of a single massive lintel supported by perfectly angular uprights. At the lintel's exact center a design had been cut and filled with gold; an unblinking eye from whose iris a single bolt of lightning emanated. It was the ultimate sign of Order, the sigil of Aeoris Himself—and it marked the entrance to the heart of the crater, and the shrine.

The two Guardians who had led the procession with Keridil stepped aside and took up new positions, one to each side of the huge gate. Their fellows joined them, and the white-clad figures formed a rigid guard of honor at the entranceway.

Keridil realized that these strange men would come no farther. From now on, he and his companions were alone. He stared ahead and saw a chasmlike tunnel stretching away, lit by a faint and sullen glow that appeared to seep from the rock itself, then he heard movement at his side as the High Margrave and the Matriarch, who had dismounted from her makeshift litter, moved up to join him. Keridil swallowed, took a deep breath, and glanced at the nearest of the stiffly attentive Guardians; and with what might—unless imagination deceived him—have been the ghost of a smile, the man raised his right hand and made the Sign of Aeoris.

It was the signal to embark on the last stage of this ritual journey, and Keridil knew he couldn't delay it any longer. He stepped through the maw of the gaping portal, heard Fenar and Ilyaya a pace behind him, and forced down the sudden inrush of dread that tried to grip him. It must be done—it *would* be done. Quickening his pace as determination overcame the fear, Keridil strode forward into the chasm.

The rift, which millennia ago had been torn in the volcano's side by an eruption of lava, and which now formed the one and only entrance to the ancient crater, was not a long passage. It cut directly through the cone, following an uncannily straight path, and after only a bare few minutes Keridil saw a pinpoint of light ahead. He couldn't identify its source, though instinct and knowledge of lore prompted him to guess, and his throat constricted with apprehension. Only a short way more . . .

The chasm opened abruptly and shockingly, and

they emerged onto a wide ledge that overlooked a vista, awesome in its sheer simplicity.

All around them, dizzying, the crater walls rose in vast ramparts, pitted and scarred and creating a terrible sense of vertigo. Perhaps two or three hundred feet below lay the bowl, a plain of pumice and basalt fused in incredible patterns and lit by the faint night radiance filtering down from the open sky. In the bowl's center was a single, gigantic slab of volcanic stone, which some long-dead hand had carved into a perfect cube to form an altar—and here, the pinpoint of light that Keridil had glimpsed from the chasm revealed itself as a golden chalice in which burned an unwavering, eternal white flame. This votive light, he knew, had shone since Aeoris and His brethren left their awesome gift to the world; it was the Guardians' task to tend it; one they had never neglected. And before the chalice, shimmering blindingly in its spilling light, was a simple casket no bigger than a man's clenched fist, also made of solid gold. The casket of Aeoris . . .

Fenar Alacar made the Sign with awed and clumsy haste while the Matriarch lifted one edge of her veil to her lips and kissed it, murmuring a prayer. Keridil couldn't begin to define the feelings that this first sight of the shrine awoke in him—awe, yes, and fear and reverence, but also a sense of destiny that was impossible to put into words, but which made him forget everything beyond the short ritual, and its culmination, which lay ahead.

From the ledge a steep but far from impossible path wound down into the crater's bowl, and the High Initiate turned to his companions. "Those who wish to witness the ritual at close quarters may come to the shrine with us," he said quietly. "Though if any of you would prefer to remain here and watch from a distance, you're perfectly at liberty to do so."

Silence greeted his words. Though he had the impression that one or two of the party felt trepidation, no one would be first to back away. Only Cyllan seemed unmoved, standing now with two of Keridil's Initiates flanking her. Her gaze, when he reluctantly met it, was blank and empty.

"Very well. I ask only that you all keep silence until the rite is over." And with a small bow to Fenar and Ilyaya in turn, he began the descent to the crater floor.

Beyond the volcano's wall, the Guardians who had escorted the triumvirate and their company still stood in twin rigid rows at the portal. They had brought their charges this far, but the laws laid down for this eventuality centuries ago forbade them to go farther. Their duty now was to wait, and they would fulfill it with the same impassive stoicism with which they approached every task. If they were curious or apprehensive about what might befall before the night ended, their distant expressions gave nothing away.

The slight movement in the shadows, some minutes after the last of the company had vanished in the gloom of the chasm, caused the two Guardians farthest from the portal to turn their heads in surprise. Both moons were now well risen, illuminating the titanic stairway cascading back down the mountain slope—and on the first stair they sensed an untoward presence. Their fellows picked up the psychic disturbance an instant later, but before any of the Guardians could react or issue a challenge, the air before them shivered as though disturbed by an invisible hand—and a figure, silhouetted against the moonlit staircase, stood before them.

As one, the Guardians moved to block the way, still keeping to their precise formation.

"Those without sanction are not permitted to set

foot on the island." Their spokesman's tones were clipped, but there was a trace of disturbance in his voice. The intruder laughed softly, and something glinted with a starburst flicker of brilliance on his left hand.

"One without sanction has already done so. The Guardians will stand aside."

To touch their minds was child's play, making a mockery of the awe in which they were held. Centuries of isolation, undisturbed in their stronghold, had caused the Guardians to overestimate their invulnerability—any occult skills they had once possessed but never needed had atrophied as their complacence grew, and to a will such as Tarod's they presented no obstacle.

"The Guardians will stand aside." This time the words were a sibilant command, and the white-clad figures shrank back as the interloper took a pace forward, then another. He looked from one pale face to another and another; slowly, like hypnotized children, they drew back to their old positions, reforming the double guard of honor as all motivation drained from them. The stranger waited until the formation was complete. Then he walked quietly between them, and away into the towering rift towards the crater.

The opening words of the ritual were, to Cyllan, like a death sentence. She didn't want to listen, but a terrible fatalism made her concentrate on the High Initiate's gold-robed figure as he offered up a solemn prayer to the gods, while behind him the Matriarch and the High Margrave knelt in homage before the shrine of the casket. Her last hope was gone, and she bitterly regretted that she'd not thrown herself over the appalling drop as they neared the top of the staircase, or, perhaps better, hurled herself into the sea from the deck of the white barque before it reached

its grim destination. Now it was too late. She must
live through this nightmare and face what was to
come as best she could. Tarod had failed in his attempts to find her, she could not contact him; she
could only pray—and not to the White Gods—that,
somehow, he would survive the insanity being loosed
against him.

Despite the night's cold the atmosphere pervading
the crater was stifling, and growing more claustro-
phobically intense with every moment. It was like
the rising tension before a storm; a sense that something was coming, lurking beyond the horizon and
marching nearer, building up its power towards fever-
pitch before the first roll of thunder would boom out
and shatter the breathless, unnatural calm. Keridil
spoke—a prayer now that Aeoris might forgive what
he was about to do, echoed by the chanting of Fenar
Alacar and Ilyaya Kimi as they lent their voices to
his—but the words lacked all resonance, swallowed,
or so it seemed, by the thick air almost before they
could take full form.

Cyllan looked fearfully around at the other witnesses,
who formed a rough semicircle at a respectful distance from the triumvirate at the altar. The old
scholar, Isyn, craning forward to hear the ritual words;
two Sisters with their veils to their faces, silently
mouthing prayers; and farthest from her the tall, graceful figure of Sashka, whose eyes were feverishly alight,
face avid with excitement and pride. There, Cyllan
thought, was the greatest betrayer of all—the fickle
and greedy heart whose self-interest had brought them
all to this. . . .

Suddenly a hollow silence fell as the prayer Keridil
had been intoning ended. Fenar and Ilyaya raised
their heads, and the High Initiate stepped forward so
that the light pouring from the sacred chalice fell on
him, setting his gold robe and circlet on fire with
brilliance and casting a vivid halo around his fair

hair. Cyllan heard someone—she thought it must be Sashka—gasp with poorly-controlled eagerness, and then Keridil raised both hands high to begin the Exhortation to the Ultimate, the final words that he would speak before raising the lid of the gold casket. The High Initiate tilted his head back to gaze heavenward—and stopped, movement arrested as though a dagger had pierced his heart and struck him dead. Everyone heard his sharp, involuntary intake of breath—then he turned, staring up past the company, back to the opening of the chasm in the rock wall.

Cyllan knew what he must have seen even before she read the confirmation in his face. And there, on the ledge overlooking the crater's bowl, a solitary figure stood staring down at them. Barefoot, dressed only in a black shirt and trousers, his hair salt-matted and dried to wild tangles by the wind, he had none of his enemy's magnificence—but a quiet, deadly power radiated from him that dwarfed Keridil's ceremonial splendor to a hollow parody.

Amid shocked silence the High Initiate took a step forward. His right hand reached unthinkingly for a sword that wasn't there, but he was the only one of the company who moved as Tarod crossed the ledge to the path and began to descend. He reached the crater floor, and for long moments the two adversaries gazed at each other from a distance while a myriad emotions crossed Keridil's face. Then, slowly, Tarod approached.

Cyllan felt her upper arms suddenly and painfully gripped by the two Initiates beside her, and as Tarod drew nearer she was pulled roughly back, away from him. He stopped. For an instant venom glittered in his green eyes, then he looked at the High Initiate once more.

"Tell your Adepts to stay their hands, Keridil. I wish no harm to anyone here."

"How did you—" Keridil started to say, then stopped. The whys and wherefores of how Tarod had duped or evaded the Guardians to reach the crater undetected were irrelevant—he was here; that alone mattered. But though he had planned for this moment, the manner of Tarod's arrival had thrown Keridil's scheme in disorder and caught him unawares. He didn't know what to do. . . .

Aware of Keridil's discomfiture, Tarod turned and walked to where Cyllan was held by her guards. The two Initiates fell back as he approached; with no direct command from Keridil they were unsure of themselves, and afraid of the man before them. Tarod took Cyllan's wrists; she felt a small tingling shock, and the cords that bound her fell away, writhing to the ground, before Tarod raised her hands to his lips and kissed her fingers in a brief but significant gesture. As he raised his head again Cyllan saw, over his shoulder, Sashka staring at them. Her face was frozen into a look that confirmed everything—hatred, blind jealousy, rage, the final realization that she had lost all sway over Tarod, and her utter refusal to accept that such a thing could be true. By his simple gesture to Cyllan, Tarod had delivered Sashka a vicious blow, and her pride couldn't bear it. As Tarod turned back to the company she continued to stare at him, ready, it seemed, to tear him apart with her fingernails in sheer fury; but he looked through her as though she didn't exist, and his eyes focused on Keridil.

"There's no more need for conflict," he said. "And no need for what the Conclave has resolved to do."

Keridil's face went white. "You *dare* to presume that you can stop it? Gods, I thought you arrogant, but never as arrogant as this!" He had recovered from the initial shock of Tarod's appearance, and his confidence was restored. "We're not in the Castle now. This is Aeoris's sacred place—the greatest stronghold of Order; you have no power here, whatever your dark masters might have deluded you into believing!"

Tarod shook his dark head and smiled thinly. He looked tired, Cyllan thought—tired and drained and troubled. "I am not deluded, Keridil," he replied, "and you misunderstand my meaning. I haven't come to challenge you."

Keridil's eyes narrowed. "You wear the ring of Chaos, and you expect me to believe that?"

"Yes," Tarod said. He looked at the High Initiate for another moment as though trying to calculate whether or not he would intervene. Then he drew the silver ring slowly from his finger and, holding it in the palm of his hand, turned to where Fenar Alacar was standing staring as though transfixed at him. This was the first time the young High Margrave had set eyes on the Chaos-demon, of whom he had heard so many horrifying tales, and when his gaze met Tarod's he blanched visibly.

Tarod took two steps towards him, then, to Fenar's and Keridil's astonished chagrin, bowed formally and with the greatest courtesy.

"High Margrave. I pledge to you my loyalty and my fealty, and my word that I serve you in the name of Aeoris." He made the Sign and straightened, his eyes suddenly intense. "I have been accused of a great many crimes, High Margrave—in some instances I am guilty; in many I am not. Above all, my fealty to our Gods, the Lords of Order, has never wavered. I don't serve Chaos—I renounce it and reject it, as I have done since the day of my Initiation. And I surrender this stone as proof of my good faith."

Fenar Alacar, his eyes wide, backed away as though Tarod held a Warp in his hand. Tarod hesitated, and his fingers closed over the stone once more.

"Yes, sir; it's an evil gem; I won't deny it. But whatever might have been said of me, I don't want to bring Chaos back to this world—I've already seen the madness that the mere *fear* of Chaos has loosed on the land, and if the Conclave's resolve is carried out, and Order and Chaos conflict, that madness could erupt into full-scale destruction. Enough harm has already been done. I have the means to destroy this stone by commending it into the hands of Aeoris Himself—and I ask you to stop this rite and allow me, instead, to carry out that pledge."

"M-madness?" Fenar's voice squeaked on the second syllable and his face flushed angrily. "You speak of madness, but the only madness I see is that which *you* have perpetrated—and which you try to perpetrate with your lies now! You think that a few cleverly chosen words can sway us from our rightful and holy duty. You're wrong, demon! You're *wrong!*" He licked his lips and looked to his peers for confirmation. Keridil's expression was indecipherable, but the Matriarch nodded grim encouragement.

"You come too late to use your trickery, creature of Chaos," Ilyaya Kimi told Tarod with venom. "You have been the source of much evil in this world, but that evil will be tolerated no longer! Aeoris shall return—He will destroy you, and when you are destroyed He will root out all who have strayed from the ordained path, and they will be punished! There'll be none of your wicked spawn left behind to carry on your work when you are gone!"

Tarod had a sudden and terrible insight into the Matriarch's vision of the Gods' judgment. "How can you say that Aeoris will punish His own people, when their only failing has been that of fear?" he demanded. "There has been no crime!"

Fenar, whose confidence was growing by the moment, said contemptuously, *"Ha!"* and Ilyaya's eyes glinted coldly.

"There has been *sin*," she said implacably. "We have seen its corruption throughout the land, and we have seen the brave efforts made to bring its perpetrators to account—but it's not enough! It must be utterly expurgated, and the greater the sin, the greater the expurgation."

Tarod stared at her, appalled, and remembered the sickening injustices he had seen as he travelled: the burning fields, the slaughtered animals, the mockeries of trials that sent innocent folk to their deaths. And the Matriarch spoke of *brave efforts* . . . He said, his voice harsh with emotion, "But there's no call to resort to such savagery! The stone can simply be destroyed—surely you can see the wisdom in that? This way, there will be bloodshed and misery of such an order that it doesn't bear thinking about. It could be avoided!"

"Aeoris will extract His price," said Ilyaya stubbornly. "And we, who are His chosen, will be the instruments of His justice and mercy."

"*Mercy?*" Tarod's face was haggard.

"Yes, *mercy*." She all but spat the word back at him. "And those whose souls are pure need not fear, for though they suffer greatly in the trial, they will not be found wanting."

It was blind dogma—the Matriarch spoke nothing but meaningless cant, and yet, Tarod realized, no reason in the world would shake her. As for Fenar Alacar—perhaps he could expect no better from an arrogant and inexperienced boy in the throes of his first true taste of power, but the High Margrave's refusal to listen made mockery of Tarod's hopes. He was about to entreat them one last time to consider what he had to say when a new voice spoke harshly behind him.

"Kill him, Keridil." He knew the tones only too well. "He lies, and he attempts to blind us, as the High Margrave and Lady Matriarch have already seen. Kill him now. Send him to Aeoris, and let's see how his protestations of loyalty fare when he confronts the god he professes to worship!''

A shocked silence followed Sashka's outburst, but as everyone turned to look at her, Tarod saw a glint of approval in Ilyaya Kimi's eyes. The girl was staring at Tarod, every fiber radiating loathing and fury, and before Keridil could react Ilyaya Kimi said, ''Your consort speaks out of turn, Keridil, but she speaks good sense nonetheless.''

''Yes, Keridil.'' Fenar Alacar was determined not to be in the minority. ''Your lady is right—and you yourself have warned us often enough of this demon's duplicity! I say, kill him.''

Tarod was looking at Sashka, his eyes contemptuous. ''I'd expect little better counsel from the High Initiate's consort,'' he said almost gently. ''And, to me at least, her motives are pitifully clear.'' He bowed sardonically to the girl. ''I'm sorry, Sashka, that I disappoint you by my refusal to wring my hands in anguish at your rejection of me.''

Sashka's mouth tightened into a vicious line and her cheeks flamed; Tarod saw Keridil's quick, chagrined glance in her direction and realized just how successfully Sashka had blinded her new lover to her true nature. It seemed that the High Initiate was about to make an angry outburst, but Tarod forestalled him.

''Very well. Kill me now, Keridil—or try. But there is an alternative, if what I've already said can't move you.''

Keridil stared at him. ''It cannot. And any alternative you may suggest is pointless.''

''Is it? Even if I were to ask that I be allowed to plead my case to Aeoris Himself?''

The slight frown that appeared on the High Initiate's face rekindled the last slender hope that remained. Unreason might prevail amongst his peers, but Keridil had never been one to allow dogma alone to sway him, and he could see that his adversary's offer left no room for trickery.

Before he could speak, however, the Matriarch hissed deep in her throat and said, "The demon has a silver tongue! I counsel you not to heed him, Keridil. He must die. There is no more to be said."

Sashka smiled, and Fenar Alacar nodded vigorously. "Kill him."

Keridil glanced at the auburn-haired girl beside him and saw the unholy light that gleamed with a clear message in her eyes.

"He deserves far worse than death," she said. "But death is a beginning. . . ."

And Keridil, though he wished with all his heart that he could have remained in ignorance, began to understand. . . .

Tarod watched them all, his unquiet gaze flickering from one to another. It took great self-control to keep silent, but he knew that to speak now would be to wreck this one final, perilous chance. Keridil's hatred of him was intense, but beneath the High Initiate's prejudice reason was struggling to find a foothold. And Tarod was gambling on his one-time friend's unwillingness to be pressured into a decision to which he might be irreversibly committed.

Encouraged by Keridil's silence, Sashka said suddenly, "My love, if—" but got no further as, to her discomfiture, Keridil looked quickly at her with suspicion and anger in his eyes.

"No," he said, then raised both hands as his other companions made to protest. "No. If Tarod is willing to face the ultimate arbiter, I won't deny such a request." He looked at them all in turn, his eyes suddenly cold and challenging. "I haven't the *sanction* to deny it. What temporal power may refuse any man"—he touched his tongue to his lips—"*any* man, whatever his nature, the right to plead directly to the Gods who rule us all?" He looked at Tarod, his eyes suspicious and unhappy. "Ironically, you and I seem to agree on one matter at least—that it is better if needless suffering can be avoided. I grant your request."

Sashka hissed, *"Keridil—"* and the Matriarch's face reddened with impotent anger. "Keridil, think what you're saying! This demon has duped you before, and it's plain to me that he means to dupe you again! You cannot do this; I forbid it!"

The High Initiate turned to her. Something within him had turned to ashes, and the bitterness—which, as yet, he couldn't even begin to comprehend—brought anger and a sense of personal injustice in its wake.

"You cannot forbid it, madam." His tone was cold, bleak. "Unless, that is, you would care to stand before that votive light and raise the lid of the casket with your own hands . . . ? Or you, High Margrave . . . ? No; I thought not. That responsibility is mine alone, and if I am to accept it—as I do—then I'll brook no interference." He smiled faintly but with no pretense at humor. "Besides, to believe that any duplicity Tarod might be planning could prevail in the face of Aeoris's power would be, I think, tantamount to blasphemy."

Ilyaya's jaw dropped and the High Margrave paled. Sashka moved towards Keridil, one hand outstretched as though to touch his arm, then thought better of it. Keridil faced Tarod once more.

"I give you this one chance, Tarod. Not for your sake, but because I've seen what's afoot in this land and I want it to end. I hope . . ." He hesitated then shook his head. "No matter. Let it be done."

He had been about to say, *I hope Aeoris extracts payment threefold for the evil you've done*, but suddenly the words seemed hollow, meaningless; and Keridil was no longer sure of their validity. This wasn't the time to question his own subconscious motivations; all he knew was that a goal that once had seemed so bright had been tarnished, and at the heart of the tarnishment was doubt. Sashka's eyes as she gazed at Tarod, mixed hatred with a desire that betrayed the High Initiate's deepest-rooted suspicions; his peers' determination to have revenge at any price and without thought for the consequences ... He had learned a good deal on the long journey south through stricken villages and frightened towns and ruined farmlands, and the harshest lesson of all was the fallibility of human judgment, not least his own. If it wasn't too late to redress the balance, history might at least grant that achievement to his credit.

He said: "I ask you all for silence. If anyone is not yet prepared in mind and heart for what is to come, I exhort you to prepare yourselves now."

No one spoke. The two Initiates had relinquished their hold on Cyllan, but she didn't move. Tarod stood motionless, the silver ring with its deadly stone glinting in his cupped hands as Keridil turned his back on the assembly and walked, with the slow deliberation of one in doubt of his own strength, towards the votive altar at the center of the great bowl. The light from the eternally burning chalice spilled over and around him, casting a grotesque shadow; for perhaps two or three minutes he stood with his head bowed. Tarod's arrival had interrupted the Exhortation to the Ultimate, the final rite that tradition dictated must be completed before his hand touched the casket. Keridil had carefully memorized the formalized phrases, the long, elaborate sentences ... and suddenly he thought: *damn tradition*. Briefly, silently, his lips formed the words of a very private prayer. Then he reached out both his hands and brought his fingers to rest on the glittering casket.

It felt cold and yet hot together; a sensation his senses couldn't assimilate and which defied description. No human hand had touched this artifact since the day Aeoris Himself had commended it into the custody of the first High Initiate of all. . . .

Keridil's fingers tightened on the golden surface, and he lifted the lid.

Chapter 13

Overhead, in the circle of visible sky, the stars went out.

The towering walls of the volcano's crater lost their color and texture, fading through the brown of long-dried blood to grey to an utter absence of hue, as though something were draining their pigment, their solidity, their very existence. The figures grouped about the altar seemed to lose their reality, becoming two-dimensional, ghost images with no semblance of life. Only Keridil, now framed by a glaring and brilliant halo, was real; Keridil, and the blinding radiance that had begun to issue from the open casket, a light that eclipsed all in its path, gaining strength, growing, slowly taking form.

A sound like titanic wings clashing together, a noise beyond thunder, beyond anything imagination could conjure, crashed against the ears of the mesmerized watchers, and in its wake came a slow, clopping, terrifyingly measured tread, as though some monstrous supernatural horse bore an unnameable rider towards them, stepping between dimensions and threatening to break into a world too small to contain it. The two Sisters who had accompanied Ilyaya

Kimi fell to their knees, sprawling in the dust of the crater bowl; one cried out, but her voice was no more than a tiny, wounded cry against the vast cliff of noise.

The brilliant light that poured from the casket intensified, pulsed, intensified again until no one could bear to look at it—no one save Tarod. Even the High Initiate recoiled from the radiance as it threatened to burn his eyes to ash in their sockets, flinging his hands up to protect himself while behind him his companions turned away and covered their faces. Only Tarod stood still, staring fixedly at the incredible brilliance swelling above the casket. And only Tarod bore full witness to the manifestation when it came.

The wall of sound suddenly ceased. Onc moment it dinned and echoed throughout the crater; the next it was gone, and the shocking peace was broken only by a last, incredibly pure harmonic before that too faded and died. The white light still burned, but its edges were turning to gold, and at its heart a face was forming; proud, wise, beautiful. Then the sphere of radiance seemed to rise above the altar stone; there was a moment of utter silence—

A single bolt of white lightning sheared from the core of the light in silent glory, and the great stone split in two. For a moment even Tarod was blinded; then his vision cleared, and he could see the stone once more.

The casket and the votive chalice were gone. The altar was severed into two perfect halves. And before it stood Aeoris.

The greatest of the Lords of Order had chosen to take the form of a tall and perfectly proportioned warrior. His clothing was a simple white jerkin and trousers, over which a light white cloak had been cast, falling almost to His feet. A plain golden circlet held back long white hair that framed a strong, impassive, stern face. He might have been human—but for His eyes. They had no pupil, no iris; instead, the deep-set sockets were filled with pulsing golden light.

Keridil dropped to one knee, bowing his head almost to the ground in the ultimate gesture of obeisance. All around him Tarod glimpsed others following his lead; even Cyllan—stunned and awed by the implacable aura that radiated, both physically and astrally, from the White Lord's figure—sank, fearful and trembling, to her knees in the dust of the crater. Tarod, too, should have knelt—this was the god he had revered all his life, the supernal being, ultimate judge of all in and beyond the world—but he couldn't do it. However loudly reason and right cried out to him, he couldn't make the gesture—and he didn't know why. Instead he stood, immobile and alone, facing Aeoris.

The White Lord stepped forward, until the light that burned around him also encompassed the hunched figure of the High Initiate. He reached out, and his right hand came to rest on Keridil's brow. Tarod saw the shudder that racked Keridil; heard his whispered words: *"My lord Aeoris . . ."*

"You have called me, High Initiate, and I am here." Aeoris raised his head and surveyed the scene before him. The terrible, featureless gaze, which looked blind and yet saw far beyond physical dimensions, lingered on Tarod's face for a moment, then dropped to the ring cupped in Tarod's hand. His aura drowned the Chaos stone's small brilliance, but nonetheless Tarod felt the gem pulse hot against his palm.

Keridil spoke again, more clearly this time, and there was real and painful fear in his voice. "My lord Aeoris, I beg your forgiveness if I have transgressed, or shown haste or rashness in my judgment. I believe— we all believe—that only your justice and your mercy can save our land from the dark threat of Chaos."

Summoning all his courage, he dared to look up. "We have done all we could, and we have failed."

Aeoris was still gazing at the gem. His eyes were cold, remote; his mouth set in a harsh line. "You were not wrong to call upon me," he said. "For I know that evil walks abroad once more in this world, and must be expunged." The golden eyes pulsed. "And I see before me the quintessence of that evil."

Tarod took a deep breath. His throat was dry and speaking was painful; but he forced himself to break the silence.

"My lord, you see before you a loyal and faithful worshipper of the Order that was your greatest gift to this world. I come before you in humility and truth, to commend this stone of Chaos into your hands, that it may never again taint or threaten our land."

There was an ugly taste in his mouth. Did his words ring false? They surely couldn't; this was the goal for which he'd striven since the day when he'd first understood the Chaos stone's nature. . . .

"A loyal worshipper who does not kneel to his god?" There was an edge to Aeoris's voice; sharp, angry, almost pettish.

"I face you as I am, my lord, that you may see me the clearer. Not a thing of Chaos, but a true follower of Aeoris."

"Yes; I see you the clearer." The god did not smile, did not unbend in any way. "I see the worm of corruption, the flouter of my law, the threat to my rule. There is no place in the world, or in the life beyond, for such a one. You have transgressed. And for those who transgress against me there will be no mercy!"

Cyllan's head came up sharply, her face ashen, and she cried out, "No! Tarod isn't evil! Lord Aeoris, I beg of you, grant him—"

"Silence!" The words had the impact of an Arctic

wind, and Cyllan recoiled in terror. The White God's gaze fastened on her with distant contempt. "I will hear no pleadings from the corrupt. You have sinned against my law, and there will be no forgiveness. You are damned."

"My lord, I ask you to hear me!" Tarod stepped a pace forward and the god's blank eyes turned to him. "I don't plead for myself; though I might seek to cleanse the taint of my own nature, I can't deny what I am. But I entreat you to show mercy to Cyllan. Her only crime has been to fall under my influence, and—"

Aeoris interrupted him. "That is crime enough. The girl has sinned, and sin will be punished. My word is law—I judge her guilty, and she shall be annihilated."

Tarod's jaw muscles tightened. "And is there no room for mercy in your rule, my lord?"

"You *dare* to question me?" Aeoris thundered. "I am Order, and Order is supreme! I have set the pattern of this world, and those who deviate from the pattern will know my wrath!" His voice dropped, but the menace in it was the greater for that. "Many have strayed away from the path. There will be a reckoning, and the transgressors will learn what it is to fear their lord and suffer his vengeance." He began, slowly, to walk towards Tarod, and the huddled figures about him cowered away. "The mercy of Order is *justice*. And justice lies in the punishment of those who have erred. There is room for nothing else!"

Tarod felt as though a shell of ice were forming around his heart, freezing and constricting him. Where was the clemency, the temperance, the open hand of kindness which he had been taught to expect from the greatest of all the gods? Instead, he faced an implacable and savage avenger; that which didn't conform rigidly to Aeoris's law, Aeoris would destroy; and there could be no compromise.

The White Lord had halted a few paces from Tarod, and now He extended his right hand in a commanding gesture. "I will take that evil jewel," He said coldly. "I will destroy it. When it is destroyed, the power of those who seek to oppose Order will be broken, and our rule will once again be absolute. You and your paramour will accept utter annihilation as your due punishment, and then my brothers and I can begin the work of retribution and the restoration of righteousness throughout the land."

Retribution and the restoration of righteousness . . . Tarod's fingers clenched convulsively over the silver ring. There was no righteousness in Aeoris's plan . . . He would scourge all who had strayed from His rigid path, with no care for the suffering and misery He would inflict. In the wake of this ugly revelation Tarod was reminded sharply of his own analogy concerning insects trampled by warring swordsmen; but this was worse, for the cruelty would be calculated and deliberate. If this was the justice of Order, Tarod thought with bitter fury, he wanted none of it.

We could challenge their sway. . . . The thought came unbidden to his mind, and in his hands the Chaos stone pulsed again. He forced the concept away, telling himself it was too late. He had come this far; he couldn't turn back now. There *must* be a way to break through the White Lord's rigidity, to appeal to his mercy.

He looked again at Aeoris, who still stood with His hand extended to take the ring, and hope died. The god would never yield, never forgive. He would smash the last vestiges of Chaos in the world, and then nothing could stand against him or temper his influence. The reign of Order *would* be absolute—and it would create a terrible imbalance that would set the world not on a shimmering road to peace and harmony, but on a dark, grim and inevitable path to entropy and death.

He remembered, though he'd been fighting to keep the memory at bay, the dream-encounter with Yandros while he lay sleeping at the Shu-Nhadek inn. *You have seen injustice, bigotry, persecution, murder, all perpetrated in the name of Order*, Yandros had said. Now, with the White Lord's cold gaze blazing before him, Tarod couldn't deny the truth of those words. *Throw yourself on Aeoris's mercy*, Yandros had said, *and where there were seven, there will be six*. Imbalance ... the realization, the understanding, struck at the root of his consciousness, and it horrified him. Chaos unchecked was the ultimate insanity— but at the other end of the spectrum, did not Order unchecked threaten to be the same? As a man, Tarod had worshipped Aeoris, loved this world, believed that Order must be supreme. But now he could no longer think as a man thought. There was more; so much more—unhuman experience and wisdom that warned him of the consequences of letting the balance slip beyond redress. Day must be countered by night, cold by heat, love by hatred ... and seven must be countered by seven.

Your cherished ways are crumbling back into the arid dust out of which they were born. It was as if Yandros stood beside him and spoke the words aloud; and though he had first heard them so long ago, and had rejected them, Tarod remembered them now with dreadful clarity. *Without Chaos, there can be no true Order....*

It had gone too far. There *must* be balance—for without one force to temper the other, the world would finally collapse into utter destruction. Yandros had been right....

"I still wait." Aeoris's voice cut into his tumbling thoughts, and Tarod felt an involuntary surge of hatred and contempt for the White Lord. He quelled it, licked dry lips. . . .

"Why do you hesitate, worm of corruption?" The god's voice was a challenging mockery. "Do you fear, at the last, the retribution which you deserve? *Well you might!*"

Beside him Tarod felt Cyllan stir fearfully. He reached down, took hold of her hand, and felt a terrible grief tear at him. He had been prepared to sacrifice everything for her sake. But the nature of the sacrifice he was about to make was greater than he'd dreamed; for it would divide them more surely than mere death could ever do. He would lose her, forever—and yet they would both live on with the eternal knowledge of that loss.

He looked at her and knew it had to be. For the sake of the world he loved, for the sake of life itself . . .

"Give me the jewel, demon of Chaos." Aeoris's face was darkening with the anger of one thwarted.

Tarod gazed back at him. His fingers relaxed so that the silver ring with its clear jewel shone, struggling against the brilliance of the White Lord's aura. Then, slowly and icily, he smiled, and said with soft malevolence, "I think not."

"What is this?" Aeoris's voice was thunder.

Tarod laughed softly. "You have become blind, Aeoris of Order. You have reigned unchecked for so long that you have forgotten what it is to be opposed. I think the time has come for you to learn that lesson afresh!"

At the periphery of his vision he saw Keridil rising to his feet. The High Initiate's face was a study in shock as intuition warned him of what was about to happen; beyond him the Matriarch and the High Margrave stared without comprehending. Tarod raised his left hand, which held the ring; he touched the stone against his heart and saw Aeoris's arrogant confidence replaced by astonishment—and then the first fires of the power within Tarod took hold.

He knew the door, and he knew what lay beyond it. Through all his years in this world he had barred that door fast, shutting out the knowledge and the memories to which it led, shutting out the titanic, nameless, ageless forces even as they cried for release. But no longer. In his mind—in his *soul*—Tarod felt the bar lifting. He was not human—he had never been human—and now it was time to relinquish the mask of humanity he had worn for too long. . . .

A cry that might have been the last protest of a fallible, mortal man was wrenched from his throat as the door that had separated him from his heritage smashed open and, as the long-dead volcano in which they stood had once erupted, the power exploded to life within him. A screaming, shrieking wind roared down on the crater bowl, the rock floor bucked and heaved, throwing the terrified company into sprawling tangles of limbs—and a light as black as Aeoris's aura was white began to emanate from Tarod's tall, gaunt figure. The semblance of humanity was slipping from him; the wild mane of his hair snatched and whipped in the gale about a white face in which every bone was etched to razor sharpness, and in their dark sockets his eyes burned like emerald flames, alight with an unholy, insane joy. Black tendrils smoked around his frame, forming a terrible cloak that hid all but one skeletal hand, and as his lips drew back in a smile he was the dark twin of Yandros, essence of Chaos incarnate.

Somewhere, a world away, Ilyaya Kimi began to wail on a thin, pitiful scale, rising and falling. Fenar Alacar crouched, retching with blind terror, beside her; others covered their ears, hid their faces. Cyllan, who had been flung aside by the monstrous power erupting from Tarod, could only stare like a trapped, mesmerized animal at the man—*being*—she had loved, as understanding threatened to split her mind apart. She had faced Yandros, but Yandros had been able only to manifest a fraction of his true self. What she witnessed now was Chaos in its triumphant entirety, and Chaos had a malevolent beauty and perfection that stirred pride, joy, despair and a savage longing to clash and battle together in her mind.

The wind died, and the silence was appalling. But it lasted only a moment before a deep, shattering throb, almost at the limit of mortal discernment, began far beneath the rocks of the crater, in the mountain's heart. The ring in Tarod's left hand started to pulse with its rhythm, growing stronger with each grim beat so that the stone's light began to challenge the aura of the White Lord. And slowly, gradually, the ring was changing. The intricate silver base faded, leaving only the soul-stone, unsupported, hovering over Tarod's heart. And then the stone, too, lost its solidity, seeming to merge with the smoking tendrils that shrouded Tarod's form. Stabbing points of brilliance radiated out from it in rhythm with the inexorable throbbing, and suddenly the jewel was gone, and in its place, pulsing like a monstrous heart, was a seven-rayed star—the emblem of Chaos.

Tarod raised his head and pointed towards the shimmering form of Aeoris before him. When he spoke, his voice was a shifting, sibilant whisper that drew its essence from dimensions beyond comprehension.

"Do you know me, Aeoris of Order?"

Aeoris's eyes turned from molten gold to white fire, searing Tarod's black aura. "I know you, Chaos! And I will destroy you!"

"If you can, White Lord. *If you can!*"

Aeoris raised a hand, and a single bolt of lightning smashed the crater floor at Tarod's feet, shattering rock and fusing it into a new and tortured shape. The White God smiled. "If I can?" His voice was mocking. "You presume a great deal, creature of Chaos, if you presume to challenge me! I am Lord of Life and Death. I and my brothers are sole masters of the forces that govern this world." His tone grew harsher. "Do you *dare* to defy the reign of Life and Death? The rule of the Lords of Time and Space, and of Earth and Air, Fire and Water?"

As Aeoris spoke, naming the ranks of the seven White Gods, six iridescent columns shimmered into existence at his back, in utterly perfect symmetry. They turned, spun, their facets reflecting brilliantly; then they coalesced into six appallingly beautiful human figures, white-haired, golden-eyed, each bearing a massive double-handed sword and each the perfect twin to Aeoris. As one, the Lords of Order smiled pityingly on their adversary, and their swords came up in a smooth, sweeping movement to reflect their own auras into a single dazzling coruscation of pure light.

Tarod raised his face to the ragged circle of sky, and the seven-rayed star at his heart pulsed anew. High above in the black void a pinpoint of light flashed into being out of utter darkness; a single, glaring white eye in the center of the firmament. It, too, began to pulse with the same primordial rhythm, until the two cold stars were as one in terrible harmony.

Long ago it seemed now, and far away, in the Marble Hall deep beneath the Castle of the Star Peninsula, Tarod had banished Yandros from the world. He alone had possessed the power then to thwart Chaos; and he alone had the power, now, to reverse that banishment and break the barrier which kept the dark Lord from returning to challenge his ancient enemy.

Where there were seven, there will be six. . . . Yandros's words rang again in Tarod's mind, and he smiled an old, knowing, and affectionate smile. The time for doubt was past. He had shed his humanity, allowed the mask to shatter and reveal what lay beneath, accepted the truth of what he was. The Lords of Chaos would number seven again—and, after long centuries of waiting, they would reclaim their place in the world.

He looked at Aeoris and the six glittering figures who flanked him, and spoke softly but with chilling pride.

"You seem to have forgotten, my lord of Life and Death, that you and your six brethren each has one who shadows him in the realm of Chaos." His gaze slowly raked the six shimmering figures ranged at Aeoris's back. "Which of these great princes, I wonder, calls himself the master of Time? I would be most interested to meet my own pale twin."

Aeoris's hot golden eyes blazed ferociously. "You *dare* to mock the gods who granted you your miserable life—"

"The gods of Order granted me nothing!" Tarod interrupted, his voice searing. "There is another lord of Life and Death, Aeoris; another who now comes to challenge you. And it is to *him* that I owe my allegiance." He raised his head again, staring through the dark to the threatening, pulsing white star overhead. Then he smiled and gently spoke a single word. The word was an acceptance and a summoning together, and it broke the strands of the web that had, for centuries, held two worlds apart.

"Yandros."

For a time that no mortal observer would have dared to judge there was silence: the stifled, oppressive silence that afflicts the elements in the moments before the breaking of a storm. Then maleficent laughter showered down into the crater, skimming around the rock faces to echo insidiously across the bowl. The empty space at Tarod's left side seemed, momentarily, to become an utter vacuum; he turned his head—and the gaunt figure of Yandros stood where the emptiness had been.

The great Lord of Chaos had taken human form. Gold hair, wild and unkempt, rippled over his shoulders; his eyes changed and changed their color, and his perfect features were made harsh and preternatural by the shivering rainbow of his own aura.

My brother of Time. You have learned—and you are whole again. A surge of kinship, amusement, affection, shared knowledge, accompanied the silent thought, and this time Tarod welcomed it, and the sense of triumph that suffused through him. He smiled in exquisite understanding. "I am whole, Yandros. And returned to my rightful place."

Yandros looked at the rigidly motionless Aeoris, and touched the tip of his tongue to his lips like a predator contemplating its prey. "And *you* . . . Greetings, old friend," he said softly. "It is a long time since we last met."

Aeoris's brows met in a savage frown. "And it will be long before we meet again, demon; for I will send you to a place from which you may never return!"

Yandros smiled. "Perhaps. But if you would reckon with me, Aeoris, you must also reckon with my kinsmen." He raised one hand in a calm gesture. "With Chaos that is Fire."

A sound like a heavy door slamming shattered the deep, throbbing rhythm that still beat far underground. To Yandros's left another figure appeared; an image of pride, disdain, incredible venom. Again, Yandros smiled.

"With Chaos that is Water."

A hiss this time, like a death-rattle. The fourth dark Lord lurked against the far wall of the crater. His hair was the color of rotting weed, his eyes insane; he made no move.

"With Chaos that is Air."

The rock floor shifted again. Something rose from

a fissure which moments ago had not existed; white-
haired, face like a bird of prey.

"With Chaos that is Earth."

Another, disturbingly akin to Yandros, his calm,
peaceable smile deceiving no one.

"With Chaos that is Space."

And the seventh . . . a dull noise like a single, dead
drum beat blotted out all other sound for an instant;
and when Tarod turned his head he saw, on a ledge
where the chasm mouth opened to the crater, a
shadow, darker than any blackness, etched into the
rock.

Yandros clasped his hands together, steepling his
fingers and contemplating them. "Life and Death,"
he said. "Fire and Water and Air and Earth and
Space." He looked obliquely at Tarod. "And Time."
Then his gaze flicked back to his adversary, and now
it was venomous. "Challenge us, old friend—or be
damned!"

While the Lords of Chaos took form, matching their
counterparts and enemies, Aeoris had stood motionless, gazing down at the veined rock beneath his feet.
But at Yandros's taunt he raised his head, and his
eyes burned with a power that could shatter suns.

"I pity you," he said thoughtfully. "I pity your
pride and your arrogance that compels you to stand
against the rightful rule of Order. Will you not accept the supremacy of my reign, and concede to me
now? For if you do, I might be moved to show mercy
to those unfortunate mortals who have been duped
by your false promises."

Yandros laughed, and the laughter fell like poison,
melting rock where he stood. "Order does not change.
Order *cannot* change. My brothers, our ancient adversary stands before us and pleads reason. What
does Chaos know of *reason*?"

Mirth shivered the crater; a vast sliver of stone
detached itself from high in the cone and crashed to

smithereens at Yandros's back. He glanced at the shards; they disintegrated and became dust. Then he smiled at Tarod.

"It is time," Yandros said.

Cyllan didn't know if anyone else was still conscious. She had watched the manifestation of the six Chaos Lords with a numbness that inured her to the worst shock; after such an experience, nothing could appall her now. But she heard the first rumbling of thunder in the distance, the herald of a storm moving in towards the island, and then in its wake a high, thin screaming that turned her blood to water.

A Warp . . . Chaos made manifest . . . Bile rose in her throat and she choked it back. Above the Warp's faraway howl another sound was rising, clashing with and countering the storm's terrible voice. A single note, pure and piercing, its harmonics vibrating in incredible accord as the Lords of Order summoned their power to meet the challenge of Chaos. She felt the ground beneath her shake with the onslaught of forces it could barely contain. And in the midst of the warring cacophony, she heard a voice—molten silver, fearsome with malignance—cry above the mayhem:

"Now! We Shall Destroy Them!"

His form was a star, and his dimensions spanned a universe. Screaming with the power that blasted from the furnace within him he turned and wheeled, hurling vast bolts of molten crimson at the stabbing, spearing comets of light that surged out of the blackness to maim him. Beside him a star exploded in a furious inferno; crimson through yellow through white through blue, tentacles hurtling across the void to snare the white comet-blades as they seared at its heart. Beneath him black emptiness gaped to swallow the singing, deadly bolts; iridescent fire splashed against the black and it twisted, whimpering, in on itself.

A new sun erupted into life no more than a handspan beyond the reach of his arm. Golden, blazing, Order incarnate, it burned steadily, eating the darkness around it. He howled a command, and black, formless creations of pandemonium zigzagged and gyrated from nowhere to attack and devour the gold brilliance. The sun flickered, faltered, gathered its failing strength for a last defiant surge; died. Voices shrieked in triumph, were drowned by a pure bolt of energy; something came at his back and he turned, flinging red lightning at its core, shattering, destroying. Chaos rampaged out of infinity to tear at the struggling remains of his broken enemy and he laughed, the laughter ricocheting from vast, invisible walls. This battle was older than form, older than time; in victory or in defeat it had never been resolved, but the joy of the primeval conflict was enough. He glimpsed faces twisted in malice or triumph or pain or all three together; sound dinned and howled beyond the threshold of bearing, hands clenched and clawed, and all the memories, the experiences, the knowledge and the understanding of the oldest conflict of all were fresh blood in his veins, new adrenaline, a power that could never be crushed but that would live, however battered and however bruised, to fight again and again.

Gold light blazed before him, but it no longer had the power to dazzle; and the laughter that greeted every victory was merging into an endless, shrieking cacophony of sound. He felt other presences touching and merging with his being, sensed the proximity of the greatest of his brethren and the satisfaction that burned at that being's heart.

They are falling back . . . they are defeated. . . . We have won, my brother of Chaos; we have won!

He heard the wailing cry of bitter defeat, felt a

backlash from the sting of shame as his ancient adversaries drew away, their light shining sullenly now, a poor mockery of its old glory. He joined with his brother-Lords to form the implacable dark that drove them back, twisted and broke their hold, compressed and compacted them within a pulsing ring of power through which they no longer had the strength to break. The sky darkened through purple to black. . . . It was done. . . .

Images flickered like half forgotten dreams across his consciousness, and at first he couldn't assimilate them or their significance. Bare rock; twisted forms that cowered and cried and prayed; a shattered altar. Laughter rang in his mind as his brethren poised themselves for the final blow—

"No!!"

His voice rang across dimensions, shattered the link between the seven Lords of Chaos, and he felt their shock as he hurled the full power of his will against their intent. The two forces collided, and a titanic upheaval snatched him and smashed him with the force of a hammerblow back to the mortal world he had left behind. He felt the sudden, violent constrictions of flesh, blood, and bone as his consciousness exploded back into human form; felt his body twist and wrench, rock flowing beneath him, towering walls falling out of the sky. Above and around him he heard the insensate screaming of the Warp, and in his mind the sound swelled and spread until other voices—a myriad voices, but human this time—joined the cacophony. It was as though his being encompassed the entire world. Oceans raged in his arteries and the roar of monstrous tides, whipped to frenzy by the warring powers of Chaos and Order, was the pounding of his own pulse. Mountains shook and cracked in his bones, opening mile-wide fissures that seared across the land and engulfed all in their path; he saw villages crushed and obliterated by

massive walls of moving rock. Storm-gales that were
his breath rampaged beyond control, smashing forests, destroying crops, leaving devastation in their
wake. And above the pandemonium still came that
vast throng of massed human voices, a ceaseless
wailing that seared him and tore at him and racked
him with its terror and its pain; a damned and desperate cry for salvation.

Man, demon, and god met and merged in Tarod's
mind, and in the crater-bowl he fell sprawling to his
knees as the raw, unleashed power threatened to
overwhelm him. *He had to stop it—he had to control
it, pull it back, or it would destroy the world—* He
gathered his will and felt the unchained forces fight
back. Sternly, though knowing he was at the limits of
his endurance, he commanded the raging seas, the
quaking earth, the thundering storms; taking their
fury upon himself, drawing it back, drawing it inward,
holding it, calming it—

He couldn't do it! The power was too vast and he
couldn't contain it, couldn't overcome the pain and
the destruction that beat against him like a ceaseless
tidal wave. Alone, he hadn't the strength; it would
destroy him. There was but one hope.

He cried out across the world, across dimensions,
seeking his kin. *"Yandros, this must not be! Help me—
help me!"*

In his mind the seven-rayed star blazed out of
darkness, and he felt the presence of his brothers.
Their minds joined with his; slowly, slowly, the
madness of the elements began to lessen, calming.
The rushing in his blood slowed, the mountains ceased
to shake; the crying, pleading voices were quieting at
last—all fading, fading—

Above the bowl of the ancient crater the Warp
howled once and flashed out of existence—and Tarod's
consciousness was slammed back into his mortal,
physical form. His mind reeled with shock and he

fought for breath; hardly aware of what he was doing, stunned by the terrible contradiction between his true self and the mortal memories that assailed him, he staggered to his feet and at last was able to open his eyes.

The crater was a wrecked wasteland. Huge slabs of rock had been torn from the walls and hurled down to shatter on the floor of the bowl; great fissures had ripped through the mountain cone; the volcano's north face had split, and gaped to the indifferent sky like the open mouth of a corpse. Aeoris and his brethren were gone. Yandros and his own kin were nowhere to be seen. The only witnesses to his return were a small group of fallible and pitifully human figures who had somehow survived the insanity and now crouched in the scant shelter of the smashed altar-stone. One by one they raised their heads to stare fixedly at him, like cattle sensing, though not truly comprehending, that the hour for their slaughter had come.

Yet there was one, just one, not bound by such mindless fear. Tarod's emerald eyes raked the gathering, and saw her. She got to her feet, unsteady but determined, and her amber gaze met his, seeking the humanity she had known behind the image of Chaos. What she saw, he couldn't tell; but in her face was a pain and a love that snatched him back to the humanity he had abandoned.

She said, her voice shaking, "Tarod . . . ?"

He couldn't bring himself to speak her name; memories hurt him like a knife-thrust. Instead he took a step towards her, knowing all the while that he dared not touch her, that the gulf between them was immeasurable. At last he said, with the voice she knew, "We are victorious. Order is defeated. . . ." He wondered why the triumph meant nothing to him.

"Oh, Tarod . . ." Understanding broke her composure, but despite what she knew she couldn't stop herself from stumbling forward, towards him, her hands reaching out as though in supplication.

Behind her, someone moved. Tarod didn't react immediately; he was too intent on Cyllan and her unspoken grief. Only when red-brown hair flickered in the cold light from above, and a figure interposed itself between himself and Cyllan, did he realize what was afoot—and by then it was too late to intervene.

Sashka was screaming; formless, wordless obscenities that spilled from her throat and lips as though she were possessed by the ultimate corruption. Cyllan started, swung round, tried to defend herself, but the knife in the other girl's hand was already shearing down. Where Sashka had found the blade Tarod couldn't begin to guess, and it was irrelevant—she had it, and the jealous, thwarted fury that possessed her was warped out of all proportion by terror and a mindless lust for revenge. Cyllan yelled as the blade came glittering at her unprotected body, a drover's oath that flung Tarod back in confusion to other, lost days—then the knife sliced her upraised arm, drawing a fountaining first sacrifice of blood before the blade bit deeply, greedily through her flesh and into her heart.

She didn't cry out again. Instead, she dropped her wounded arm to clutch at her breast, fingers locking round the hilt of the dagger protruding obscenely from her ribs. Her coarse shirt flowered brilliant crimson and she sagged to her knees, coughing, eyes filmed with shock. For a moment her amber gaze locked with Tarod's in what seemed a last, desperate plea. Then blacker blood vomited from her throat, cascading over her chin; she keeled sideways to sprawl on the hard rock floor, and her eyes stared at nothing.

There was utter silence. Tarod stood rigid, staring at Cyllan's corpse, his face utterly without expression. Sashka began to back away, her mouth working in a spasmodic, rictus grin of shocked pleasure. The oth-

ers stared like hypnotized sheep . . . until Keridil
broke the spell.

He got to his feet, moving like an old, crippled
man, and stumbled one, two paces forward. At first
it seemed he would turn towards Sashka, and Tarod
felt his whole body begin to shake with an emotion
he couldn't contain. But then Keridil stopped, looked
down, moved again. He dropped to his knees beside
Cyllan and covered his face with both hands. The
small part of Tarod's being that had retained its
humanity realized that the High Initiate was crying.

Green eyes, fathomless and filled with a savage light,
lifted their gaze from Cyllan's huddled body to the
girl who stood, shivering with an ugly blend of fear
and defiant triumph, not seven paces away. Sashka
met Tarod's stare; for a moment only her defiance
held, then it was replaced by a look of horror.

"*No . . .*" Her lips formed the word, but whether it
was plea or exhortation, Tarod neither knew nor
cared. He took a step towards her. Her eyes widened.

"Keridil . . ." She stumbled backwards, one hand
flailing, groping towards the High Initiate. "Keridil,
help me. . . ." Her fingers found his shoulder and
Tarod saw him flinch violently at the touch.

"*Keridil!*" Sashka shrieked, and spittle flecked her
lips. "Stop him—you've got to stop him! Help me,
damn you—*do something!*"

Keridil stared at her and his eyes were utterly
blank. She was gasping incoherently, terrified now,
but he made no move to aid her. Instead he shook his
head, incoherent, incapable of communicating what
he felt. Then, with a shudder that racked his entire
body, he pulled himself out of her reach and turned
away.

"Keridil . . ." This time Sashka's voice was barely
more than a whisper; she was too petrified to move.
Tarod's left hand started to rise, slowly, steadily,
fingers forming a symbol; with the gesture came a

resurgence of the power that had crushed gods, fueled by a loathing that transcended all human limitations. He raised the hand, outstretched his arm, spoke a single word in a tongue never before uttered by a human throat.

Sashka began to moan. She moaned as her cascade of rich, red-brown hair shrivelled as though consumed by invisible flames and fell in shredded clumps from her scalp. Her hands came up, snatching at her skull; Tarod smiled a savage smile of pleasure, and the skin and flesh of her hands lost their form and began to melt repellently into her wrists, leaving bones stark and white in their place. She touched her own face and screamed; this time there was no challenge but only naked, animal panic. Tarod whispered another word and her face began to disintegrate, layer after layer of skin peeling back to reveal raw, crimson flesh beneath; sinew and muscle and vein exposed to the stricken gaze of the company. Someone gagged, vomited; Tarod smiled. As the girl dropped to her knees, he caught hold of her mind, twisted it, drew from its struggling tendrils the full knowledge of what was happening to the beauty and power that she had wielded as a weapon for so long. He felt her hatred of him, her desire for him, writhing under his control; he turned them into groveling fear and let her consciousness flail in the emotion until he knew that agony and terror had devoured the last vestiges of her sanity and there was nothing more to be drained from her empty shell.

Keridil, kneeling on the uneven rock, stared transfixed at the scene, though he was shocked beyond all ability to move or speak. Tarod continued to hold the shrieking girl in a pain-wracked thrall, but bleak reason was struggling within him to be heard. There was nothing to gain from prolonging Sashka's suffering; his revenge was done and in ashes, and no savagery he might inflict on her could bring Cyllan back to life. . . .

His vision misted as tears filled his eyes, a legacy of mortality that ate at his soul, and he spoke for a third time. Sashka shrieked, once; then her body twisted and collapsed to the crater floor, blackening, losing form, her flesh falling away from staring bone, bone darkening, crumbling as the last echo of her scream died with her withering corpse. A white, bloated worm writhed briefly on the fused rock; he pointed, carelessly, and it was gone.

As Sashka's last traces vanished into the hell to which he had consigned her, the mortal man that had been Tarod struggled back to the surface of the Chaos Lord's mind. He looked down at Cyllan and found himself biting back a grief that couldn't be assuaged; that owed nothing to Chaos's legacy but stemmed solely from the humanity that had taught him what it was to love and be loved.

Keridil was moving away. He had abandoned all pretense of dignity, and crawled on hands and knees to put as much distance as he could between himself and the place where Sashka had been. The hideous manner of her death was burned indelibly on his mind, but as yet it had no power to affect him; he could only stare, mesmerized, at his one-time friend and old adversary. His breath rattled in his throat.

Around them, others were rising. Tarod sensed them, saw them moving uncertainly, sensed the crazed terror in their minds as they realized what he had done. He hated them all, and that hatred could make him destroy again. . . .

No. Not that. They didn't deserve such blind retaliation; to harm them without reason would make him no better than Aeoris.

He flung out a hand, felt the power surging in him. They dropped where they stood, like felled trees, cast into an instantaneous sleep that would bring few dreams and fewer memories. Now, only he and Keridil were awake and aware.

Tarod looked at the High Initiate's stricken face, and his loathing lost all meaning. What point was there in vengeance, when between them lay the dead body of the one human being who had mattered, whose life had been worth the price he had paid?

He reached towards her and gathered her into his arms. Her blood was warm and wet against him and he raised her head, kissing her stained face, willing her to respond. She didn't respond. Even Chaos couldn't call back the dead.

"Damn you. . . ." Tarod whispered, his voice breaking. *"Damn you all. . . ."*

Chapter 14

They faced each other across a mental abyss. Somehow Keridil had found the strength to get to his feet, though his body was shaking feverishly and his facial muscles twitched with uncontrollable spasms. Between them, Cyllan was a still, stark testimony to Sashka's last act of revenge. The knife she had used had been Keridil's own; he had tried to stop her as she snatched it, but in the confusion she had evaded him. Now Sashka was gone and he couldn't bear to think on what manner of torment Tarod might have committed her soul to suffer. She was dead; that was all he could ever know. And while his mind screamed out in grief for her, his heart was torn in two by the savage lesson he had learned. Sashka had betrayed him. His love had meant less to her than the chance to vent her unassuaged spite on Cyllan, and through Cyllan on Tarod. Keridil had doubted her motivations for some while, but had pushed the doubts aside and refused to face them until this moment. Now he felt shamed and used. The knowledge couldn't kill his love for her—memories of her sweetness, her lithe body, her beauty, haunted him and would continue to haunt him through whatever life he had left;

he would mourn her as any ardent lover would and should mourn. But he knew, now, what she truly had been.

And Tarod ... Bizarre though it seemed, Keridil knew that his friend-turned-enemy, despite the fact that he had shaken off any pretense of mortality, mourned for his lover just as he did. Though he'd never really known Cyllan except as an adversary, Keridil couldn't help but admire the loyalty and courage she had shown, and her steadfastness. She, far more than Sashka, had proved herself worthy of the one who loved her, and the knowledge was bitter wine. Keridil deeply regretted Cyllan's death—though how he could hope to convey that to the being who confronted him now—and hope to be believed—he didn't know.

He raised his head at last and said, stumbling over the words, "I'm sorry. She didn't deserve to die."

"No ..." The voice was so like the Tarod he had known in the old, lost days that its familiarity made Keridil shiver. He felt tears springing to his eyes, and they weren't for Sashka but for something deeper; a trust, a kinship, something betrayed and gone beyond recall. There was so little left to salvage from this nightmare, yet he wanted to try. And if nothing else, he had a vestige of self-respect left to him.

He said: "So, you're victorious. At least now I know where I stand ... but I won't worship you, Tarod. I am what I am; nothing can change that." He looked up. "It's one trait, I think, that we still share."

A startlingly human pain showed in Tarod's green eyes, then he shook his head. The black aura still blazed around him, his face still bore little trace of humanity; but his resemblance to the one-time Initiate of the Circle was so strong as to be discomforting.

"I don't deny that, High Initiate; I've no reason to challenge it."

Keridil swallowed. "High Initiate? It used to be Keridil, in the old days."

"The old days are gone." A nacreous light glittered in Tarod's eyes. "We can't recall them."

Keridil nodded. "It could have been cleaner. Gods, I—" He paused, and smiled self-deprecatingly. "I must be careful. I no longer know which gods I call on."

"Does it matter?" Tarod's voice was cruel.

"Perhaps it doesn't; not when so much has been lost." He hesitated. "I sensed—at least, I think I did—something of what took place when you . . . defeated them. So much of it could have been avoided." He blinked, bit his lip. "Couldn't it?"

Tarod didn't answer. Instead he closed his eyes, sighed, and the sigh became a soughing wind that skittered across the crater. Far overhead the seven-rayed star still pulsed in triumph, but the victory was dust in his heart. He needed to forget, but he couldn't forget, not while he still suffered the terrible conflict between the essence of Chaos within him and the humanity that he had adopted and which held him in a tighter grip than he'd believed possible. That humanity had driven him to stop Yandros from destroying the forces of Order altogether, and it had driven him to risk his own destruction in a frantic effort to stem the forces unleashed on the helpless world by the warring gods. Yet he couldn't remain in this limbo between the two states of being; he had chosen a path, and it was impossible to turn back.

Silently in his mind he formed a name. The wind rose to gale force; above them in the sky the seven-rayed star flickered as though a cloud had passed across it. Then came a sound like a door softly closing, and Yandros stood at Tarod's side. His many-hued eyes were quieter than usual.

"Brother." Yandros laid a hand on Tarod's shoulder. "The world is calm now, and Order vanquished if not yet entirely destroyed."

Tarod smiled tiredly but affectionately at him. "And again I am in your debt, Yandros. If you'd not lent me your strength when I called to you, I couldn't have stemmed that tide alone."

Yandros made a dismissive gesture. "Why should we not have answered? We have no true quarrel with humanity, and certainly no wish to bring destruction on this world. And this world is now ours to command. Our only enemies are Aeoris and his insipid brood—and those mortals who have actively connived with them against us." His gaze flickered to Keridil, and the perfect, malevolent mouth curved in a smile that made the High Initiate flinch away. "It will please you, I think, to see them take a long while in dying."

Tarod looked bleakly at Keridil, then said, "No."

"No?" Yandros echoed the word. "My kinsman, I don't understand you. The battle's over; we have *won*. Order can be crushed to shards under our heel, and will never trouble us again. All that remains is for us to see to the destruction of their servants— beginning with vermin like this!" He pointed at Keridil.

Tarod hesitated, then shook his dark head. "No," he said again, and smiled sadly at his brother of Chaos. The barriers that had separated him from Yandros for so long were down now; there could be no more misunderstanding.

"I made a great mistake, Yandros," he said. "I turned my face from my heritage—my own nature— and I fell into the trap of believing in the ultimate righteousness of Order."

Yandros's lips quirked, but before he could comment Tarod continued. "I know what you're thinking— you warned me before I took incarnation on this world, and you've tried to warn me since. I would be tainted by those I moved among, and the purity of Chaos would be diluted by the catechisms of Order." His eyes narrowed. "You were right—and yet you were wrong."

"Wrong?" Yandros shifted a little; his voice held thoughtful amusement and the rock beneath his feet changed form with disturbing abruptness.

"Yes. I *was* tainted—and yet I learned lessons that, without the shackles of humanity, I couldn't have begun to understand." Tarod's eyes clouded for a moment. "I've brought us perhaps the greatest advantage over Aeoris and his kin that we've ever possessed, Yandros. The advantage of understanding, from experience, the hopes and fears and ideals that plague those not imbued with our immortality."

Yandros looked speculatively at Keridil, who was watching them uncertainly. He touched his tongue to his lips. "You intrigue me. When we first sought to infiltrate Aeoris's stronghold, I didn't imagine that such complications would result from the experiment."

"No more did I. But perhaps it isn't possible—even for the likes of us—to masquerade as mortals, and to take on mortal form and life, without gleaning something of mortal thought and emotion."

"Emotion?" Yandros raised his eyebrows.

Tarod looked back at Cyllan's body; felt something within him constrict. "Emotion, yes. Though that isn't the province of humanity alone."

The Chaos Lord acknowledged the point with an inclination of his head. "She served us well; she was faithful to you. It seems such a waste. . . ." He drew the coruscating brilliance that cloaked him more closely about his frame, and stepped around the corpse to confront Keridil directly. "And you. We meet again, High Initiate of the Circle, and under happier circumstances—at least for us. What have you to say, now that your gods are vanquished?"

Keridil didn't flinch. Once he had been afraid of

Yandros, and he knew that to face up to him now was insanity; but it didn't seem to matter. So much had been lost, so much had changed; if all he had left was his integrity, he could at least hold to that.

"I have served Order all my life, Yandros of Chaos," he said. "And whatever else I may be, I'm no hypocrite. I won't change my allegiance to save my neck; or to save my soul, for that matter. I'll admit to you—and if I'm damned for it I don't think I care anymore—that my conscience didn't rest easy with what Aeoris meant to do, and I"—he hesitated—"I'm not entirely sorry that Tarod chose as he did. But that doesn't mean I'm prepared to forsake all I've ever believed in, and worship Chaos simply because Chaos has triumphed." He looked at Tarod. "I like to think you might understand that."

"It's as it should be," Tarod replied softly, causing Yandros to look at him in surprise. His green eyes were narrow, but he smiled as he turned to his brother. "Keridil Toln was the first true friend I had in this world. He betrayed me, but he betrayed me for what he believed was a sound principle. He's learned a great deal since then, I think. Above all he's learned the meaning of equilibrium, and if we destroy him, we'll waste something that could prove invaluable."

"Equilibrium?" Yandros queried gently.

"Yes. Your own words, if you recall them. What use is Order, without Chaos to challenge its rule? And by the same standard, what lies ahead for us if nothing opposes our ways?" He looked up at the empty sky. Both moons had set, and the seven-rayed star no longer shone overhead. There was nothing but darkness. "Will we stagnate, as Aeoris and his brothers stagnated, so secure in our reign that we become anachronisms as he has done? The world sickened under that regime, and almost died. I wouldn't want to see us make the same mistake."

Yandros was watching him, and the expression in his deep-set, ever-changing eyes ran a full gamut of reaction. Amusement, anger, speculation, respect, affection; it was impossible to judge the thoughts behind his unhuman gaze.

Tarod said: "Perhaps Aeoris would have demanded an eye for an eye; but we know better. That's why I say that Keridil should live—wherever his loyalties lie."

Yandros considered for a few moments. "If he can learn, perhaps he deserves the chance to profit from his past mistakes. You speak of equilibrium, Tarod, and I think you are right. Order and Chaos are old enemies, but old enemies are also old friends. Aeoris must be taught that he has nothing to gain from tipping the balance so far in his own favor. The conflict between us can never be resolved—the balance must be maintained, for anything that is to grow and prosper must by nature contain its intrinsic opposite." He smiled wolfishly. "Opposition will prevent us from becoming complacent. Very well." He looked at the High Initiate with a new interest. "Keridil Toln may live."

Keridil shut his eyes tightly. He had been prepared and willing to die, yet the relief of his reprieve was indescribable. He couldn't assimilate the reality of his situation; part of him was still convinced that this was a nightmare from which he would, at any moment, wake.

He opened his eyes again and saw the two unhuman figures gazing at him. He was beyond fear now; all he felt was a strange, detached sense of sorrow to which he couldn't give a name.

He looked down at Cyllan and said involuntarily, "I wish—"

"No." Tarod's voice was savage. "Don't say it. Don't ever dare to utter it!"

Yandros regarded him, and a faint frown creased

his cruelly perfect features. "Did she mean that much to you? Don't answer me as a man or as a Lord of Chaos. Answer me as Tarod, who is both."

The green eyes narrowed with pain, and Tarod looked away. Yandros sighed. He gazed down at Cyllan, then held out his left hand. At first Keridil thought it must be an illusion, but his doubt didn't last. Cyllan's eyelids fluttered; a soft sound escaped from her lips and her body tautened. Then intelligence flooded into her amber eyes where there had been nothing but the glaze of death, and she whispered a word, just recognizable. *"Tarod . . ."*

Tarod turned quickly away, his face tortured. "Yandros, you can't—she's *dead;* I watched her die!"

"Peace." Yandros was still looking at Cyllan, but he reached out to touch Tarod's arm. "I've not reanimated her. This is not merely her soulless body which moves and speaks. She lives."

Tarod stopped, turned his head to regard the Chaos Lord in shock and confusion. The power to defy death, to reverse the stroke of its hand, was one that he knew Yandros alone in the Chaos realm possessed . . . but it was a power Yandros had not chosen to command for thousands of years.

Yandros took Cyllan's hand and drew her to her feet, though she could do nothing but stare back at him in mesmerized confusion. He smiled and laid one hand first on her bloodstained face, then on the ugly wound between her breasts. At his touch, the blood and the gaping gash vanished.

"I owe Cyllan a personal debt," Yandros said with gentle amusement. "And if by paying it I can also ease my brother's distress, so much the better."

Cyllan was beginning to recover from the inertia of shock; she put a hand to her face, tried to speak, but found no words that could express what she felt. Her eyes, suddenly wild, focused on Tarod and she made a violent movement to free herself from Yandros's hold.

He released her and she ran to the dark Lord, stopping only when they were face to face, as though at the last she lacked the courage to reach out and touch him. He said nothing but held out his hands towards her; hesitantly she went to him, and her shoulders began to shake as tears streamed down her cheeks.

Yandros approached them. "Make your farewells, Cyllan," he said. "Tarod and I must depart this world, and you must remain behind." He paused, smiled. "Unless, that is, you are prepared to make the sacrifice that will allow you to come with us?"

Slowly she turned to look up at him, not comprehending. Tarod, however, realized what Yandros was saying, but the Chaos Lord forestalled him as he made to speak.

"Chaos is in your debt," he said to the bewildered girl. "And it is within my power to grant you a gift that will, should you accept it, allow you to stay with Tarod." His eyes changed suddenly to a burning, searing crimson. "For all time."

Cyllan began to understand, and her skin crawled with a resurgence of hope, which she hardly dared acknowledge. Her throat dry as the dusty crater-bowl, she whispered, "You mean that I—I might—"

Yandros smiled again, this time with a touch of ironical humor. "Is the prospect of life in our realm so very daunting, Cyllan? You know more of Chaos, I suspect, than any other mortal in your world." He reached out and lightly touched her arm, tracing the scar that he had inflicted back in the Castle of the Star Peninsula. "And you would not experience our world in the vulnerable guise of a human being. You would become a *part* of Chaos, immortal in your own right. I offer you this in recognition of your courage, and your loyalty to my brother. Such a life is yours, should you wish it."

To leave her existence behind, leave humanity behind, and enter the unimaginable realm of Chaos itself . . . to become immortal, unbound by earthly things, untouched by time or by the prospect of death . . . Cyllan couldn't assimilate the gift Yandros proffered; understanding and even imagination failed her. But one fact stood out like a clear jewel in the miasma of her confused reactions. If she accepted what Chaos offered, she and Tarod would be together through eternity. If she did not, then she would never see him again.

Distressed, she turned to the dark figure at her side. Man, demon, god, whatever he might be, she loved him more than the world, and she needed his guidance now as never before.

"Tarod, what shall I do?" Her voice was close to breaking.

Tarod shook his dark head. "I can't help you, love. I haven't the right to try to sway you, not in this. But Yandros speaks the truth."

His green eyes, so unhuman now, were focused intently on her face. She knew that look so well, and it told her what she had hoped above all else to learn. Without him, there was nothing worth the having.

She let her fingers close tightly over his, and her amber eyes closed. "I'll come. If Tarod will have me, I'll come—and gladly." She blinked, looked at Yandros again. "How can I ever thank you?"

Yandros made a careless gesture, his face suddenly vulpine. "It's a whim; no more. Chaos has no logic, as you should know. It simply pleases me to please Tarod."

Tarod laughed softly. "If that's what you like to believe, Yandros, so be it."

Yandros inclined his head in faint self-mockery. "And now," he said, "there is one last matter. . . ." He turned on his heel, and faced Keridil Toln.

Keridil had watched the exchange between the three in numbed stupefaction, unable to move or to react in any way. He comprehended—or thought he comprehended—what Yandros had granted to Cyllan, and the knowledge of it awoke a sore, ravening hurt deep within him. Yandros had proved more merciful than Aeoris—and if the greatest of the Chaos Lords could restore the dead to life once, then surely he might do so again . . . ? Sashka's face, beautiful as it had been before Tarod wreaked his vengeance, materialized before his inner eye and made the pain worse; he thrust the image away though it took a great effort, and knew when he looked at Yandros again that what he had for a brief moment hoped, could never be. And perhaps—though he couldn't yet acknowledge it—he wouldn't have wanted it to be. . . .

Yandros and Tarod were moving towards him. Still Keridil couldn't quite accept the knowledge that the gods he had worshipped all his life were vanquished, and that these reckless, mercurial, and unpredictable entities had taken their place. Chaos had returned . . . and what future could there be for him, now?

Yandros read his thoughts, and the golden-haired Chaos Lord smiled. "The future, High Initiate, is what you will make of it," he said, and his silver voice seemed to strike sparks in the depths of Keridil's being. "The world will change. Order no longer rules—but we will be very different masters. We welcome conflict, and if you wish Order to have a role here, to stand against Chaos, it is your privilege to fight for it. Go back to the Star Peninsula, Keridil Toln. That is your rightful place. Make what you can of what we have left you. It's more than you yet realize."

Keridil couldn't answer him. He looked, momentarily, at the cruelly beautiful face, into the changing eyes, then had to look away. Tarod stepped forward.

"Where there is conflict, there can truly be growth and life," he said. "Understand that, and you'll understand everything. I believe"—he glanced at Yandros, and a private communication passed between them—

"I believe that you, above all other mortals, are equal to the tasks ahead, Keridil." To the High Initiate's surprise and confusion Tarod stretched out his left hand and took Keridil's right in a grip that sent a shock through his arm and into his shoulder. "I wish you well, old friend."

The hand that held his relaxed its grasp, the long, gaunt fingers curling as Tarod withdrew them. He smiled—and for a moment the smile echoed that of the thirteen-year-old waif who had come, a stranger and an outsider, to the Castle and befriended the son of the High Initiate. It echoed, too, the rebellious, black-haired Initiate who had grown and developed within the Circle; the Adept who, leaving that Circle behind, had wielded a power that smashed the barriers of Time; the demon who had challenged the ultimate, and won. It was the smile of a Lord of Chaos. Keridil watched, unable to speak, as Tarod drew Cyllan to his side and the three faced him. He thought he saw—afterwards he could never be sure, although the image was to haunt his dreams for the rest of his life—a landscape, so alien, so indescribable that his mind couldn't truly register it, superimpose itself over the harsh, dead rock of the crater; a place where color and form and sound clashed and mingled in mad pandemonium. *Chaos*—Keridil glimpsed it only for an instant; then, with a sound like a vast door being gently closed, the three figures before him were gone.

He stood still for a very long time. Behind him was the split altar where the casket of Aeoris had stood, but the casket itself had vanished now. All around him lay his companions: Fenar Alacar, Ilyaya Kimi, the old scholar Isyn, two Sisters, his own Adepts; they all slept on, and the silence that had descended on the dead volcano's crater was almost unbearable. Keridil looked around as though seeking inspiration or comfort from the towering rock walls, but there was nothing. All he saw was the first telltale glimmer of light in the sky high above, which told him that dawn was starting to touch the eastern horizon. In his present mood, it gave him little solace.

Someone stirred with a breath no stronger than a zephyr, and he turned to see the High Margrave moving slowly, like one in a trance, shivering as his consciousness rose up through the deep levels of the sleep geas towards morning. Others, too, were showing signs of waking, although the elderly Matriarch still lay motionless, pale, a shrivelled and fragile doll.

Fenar Alacar's eyes met Keridil's, but Keridil couldn't respond to the mute, bewildered plea that burned in the High Margrave's stunned stare, and turned away. Perhaps in time he could begin to answer the myriad unspoken questions; but not yet. Not yet.

So much was gone; so much that he had taken for granted all his life now swept away. And yet Keridil felt an unwarranted sense of release beginning to settle on him, as though a burden of which he'd never been fully aware had been lifted from his shoulders. As yet, it gave him no comfort . . . but there was a promise in it, echoing the promise of the dawn that crept slowly, quietly across the sky. Whatever the future might hold, he had been granted a chance to live and to rule as his conscience dictated, freed from any unquestioning fealty to Order or to Chaos. And he hoped—*believed*, he told himself sternly—that he could prove worthy of that responsibility.

Slowly, Keridil sank to his knees on the hard rock floor. His head bowed as he hunched over his own clasped hands, and he began to pray.

But he no longer knew which gods to pray to.

Epilogue

If he turned his mind to that dimension, he could see the Castle. Such an old edifice, built by hands that were not quite human, inhabited by ensuing generations, usurped by others whose vulnerability and mortality were painful to behold. Now, the circle had come full turn—or almost.

The watchers on the heights of the four dizzying spires were at their stations, faces stained by the last gory light of the sun as it slipped towards the western horizon. They were waiting, as they waited each evening, for the supernatural storm that would come wailing out of the north at the moment of sunset, hurling its chaotic flares of lightning across the heavens while the great, pulsing bands of color marched inexorably in its wake. They waited for the Warp that heralded the night, that spoke of the power of Chaos in their world, and when it came, the rites would be conducted and the supplications made, and the balance would be maintained once more.

He had an odd affection for the grim, black Castle. It held recollections that amused him to contemplate; in the confines of its walls he had learned a great deal, suffered a great deal, and finally had regained the memory of his own true nature. He had, too, encountered the human soul for whom he had been prepared to sacrifice everything. . . .

At his side she moved, and he felt her smile. Here, in the realm beyond human understanding but which now was her own, she chose to adopt the guise of a pale-haired woman, solemn-faced, amber-eyed, only the shimmering stuff of Chaos that clothed her slim frame belying the illusion of humanity. She chose the image because she knew it pleased him; he turned towards her and adopted a form that complemented hers, black hair tangling with her white-gold, green eyes regarding her affectionately as he drew her to him and held her close. Somewhere in the distance a voice sang an awful harmony; he frowned, and the sound changed to a pure, shivering note that reminded him, pleasurably, of the brindle-furred sea creatures he had once known, and who had served Chaos well.

The blood-red sun was slipping into the sea far beyond the Castle stack, and he felt in his veins the first pre-echoes of the coming Warp. The storm was his blood, his sinew; he exerted a little of his will and felt the power rise, sweeping and screaming over the sea towards the land. And as it came roiling towards the Castle he saw, as he had seen before, a solitary figure at a high window facing out to the darkening north. A man who once had been his friend.

He called himself High Initiate because the title was an old and noble one; and, more than any of his peers, Tarod believed he was deserving of it. He no longer wore a badge of rank because the old sigil of Order had lost its significance and he could not bring himself to wear the emblem of Chaos. Perhaps one day that would change; but it didn't truly matter. The balance was restored, and Keridil was free to choose his loyalties as he pleased.

The memories that had drawn Tarod to the Castle

caused his thoughts to dwell on the figure at the
window. He remembered what it was to be mortal,
and a stirring of pity for the man with his drawn face
and haunted eyes beneath the tawny hair moved
him. Keridil had learned what it was to betray and
be betrayed, and the lesson had changed and hardened him. He had looked on the faces of the gods of
Order and the gods of Chaos, and knew that neither
could prosper without the other. He had lost the
woman he loved, and in losing her his eyes had been
opened to her true nature, so that while he grieved
for her he was nonetheless painfully aware of how
she had duped and almost corrupted him. He had
seen the death of the old Matriarch, whose frailty
had succumbed during that last monstrous encounter with Chaos on the White Isle, and with her had
gone the last bastion of the old, rigid ways. The Lady
Fayalana Impridor, who had in surprise and trepidation put on the mantle of Matriarch when the ailing
Kael Amion declared herself unequal to the task, was
young enough not to be touched by her predecessor's
inflexibility. And Fenar Alacar, nineteen now and
deeply sobered by his recent experiences, deferred to
the High Initiate and was striving to learn wisdom.

The world was at peace; perhaps more at peace
than it had been in the memory of any of its inhabitants. It wouldn't last—Chaos thrived on conflict,
and even now Tarod's mind was roused by the antic-
ipation of the next confrontation with the Lords of
Order. It would come; the balance had been set and
must be maintained, but it would be constantly challenged, and he and his brethren would relish their
joy when that ancient battle was enacted yet again.
But the pivot of that conflict, the final axis about
which its outcome would revolve, lay in the hands of
the fallible mortals who for centuries had worshipped
Order, and who now found themselves released from
its strictures and free to choose their own way. How

they would choose, neither Tarod nor Yandros nor any of the entities that served them in the Chaos realm could tell; invincibility was not omniscience, and besides, uncertainty added spice to the future. But whatever his path, Tarod thought with a faint stirring of affection, Keridil had shown, at the last, that he could withstand the challenge of his new role. There would be change; for there *must* be change. And Keridil, he believed, would prove a worthy instigator.

Fingers brushed lightly against him, and colors that vibrated far beyond the visible spectrum shimmered about the figure of the woman at his side. Tarod smiled, and the tiny microcosm that was the Star Peninsula and the world it ruled quivered away into the stuff of memory. He rose, holding out a graceful hand to her; white fingers curled about his and together they moved away from the watching place. For a moment two pulsing columns of radiance took their place; then they too merged back into the swirling mists of Chaos from which they had formed. Somewhere, laughter that was almost but not quite human rang sweetly; then the two figures were gone, leaving a brief-lived but profound stillness in their wake.

THE BEST IN FANTASY

- ☐ 54973-2   FORSAKE THE SKY by Tim Powers $2.95
     54974-0   Canada $3.50
- ☐ 53392-5   THE INITIATE by Louise Cooper $2.95
- ☐ 55484-1   WINGS OF FLAME $2.95
     55485-X   by Nancy Springer   Canada $3.50
- ☐ 53671-1   THE DOOR INTO FIRE $2.95
     53672-X   by Diane Duane   Canada $3.50
- ☐ 53673-8   THE DOOR INTO SHADOW $2.95
     53674-6   by Diane Duane   Canada $3.50
- ☐ 54900-7   DARKANGEL $2.95
     54901-5   by Meredith Ann Pierce   Canada $3.50
- ☐ 54902-3   A GATHERING OF GARGOYLES $2.95
     54903-1   by Meredith Ann Pierce   Canada $3.50
- ☐ 55610-0   JINIAN FOOTSEER $2.95
     55611-9   by Sheri S. Tepper   Canada $3.50
- ☐ 55612-7   DERVISH DAUGHTER $2.95
     55613-5   by Sheri S. Tepper   Canada $3.50
- ☐ 55614-3   JINIAN STAR-EYE $2.95
     55615-1   by Sheri S. Tepper   Canada $3.75
- ☐ 54800-0   THE WORLD IN AMBER by A. Orr $2.95
     54801-9   Canada $3.75
- ☐ 55600-3   THE ISLE OF GLASS by Judith Tarr $2.95
     55601-1   Canada $3.75

Buy them at your local bookstore or use this handy coupon:
Clip and mail this page with your order

TOR BOOKS—Reader Service Dept.
49 W. 24 Street, 9th Floor, New York, NY 10010

Please send me the book(s) I have checked above. I am
enclosing $_____ (please add $1.00 to cover postage
and handling). Send check or money order only—no
cash or C.O.D.'s.

Mr./Mrs./Miss _____

Address _____

City _____ State/Zip _____

Please allow six weeks for delivery. Prices subject to
change without notice.

ANDRÉ NORTON